Nick Roddy is a commercial diving superintendent and consultant who has spent much of his career in West Africa. An obsession with Africa began with a childhood reading of Conrad's *Heart of Darkness* and despite being kidnapped by MEND in Nigeria and held hostage for three weeks it remains undiminished. Having first moved to Africa twenty years ago, he returned to Britain for a five year stint as a police officer after which he again relocated, to live and work on the West African Coast. As a result of his inability to settle he is proficient in five languages, he has been shot at and arrested in a variety of countries. He writes to combat his paranoia that no one is listening.

He has never lived in Surrey and the last dog he had was for supper.

OUT OF JERICHO

BROKEN WALLS CAST JAGGED SHADOWS

NICK RODDY

Matador
9 Priory Business Park,
Wistow Road, Kibworth Beauchamp,
Leicestershire. LE8 0RX
Tel: (+44) 116 279 2299
Fax: (+44) 116 279 2277
Email: books@troubador.co.uk
Web: www.troubador.co.uk/matador

ISBN 978 1780883 915

British Library Cataloguing in Publication Data.
A catalogue record for this book is available from the British Library.

Printed and bound in the UK by TJ International, Padstow, Cornwall
Typeset in 11pt Galliard BT by Troubador Publishing Ltd, Leicester, UK

Matador is an imprint of Troubador Publishing Ltd

To my wife Christina for her support,
and my mother for her patience

Chapter One

Azzi stood by the roadside. Chioma, his young wife, stood beside him with Chidi, their two-year-old son, perched on her hip. Divested of all but his dignity by the futility of his situation, Azzi held himself braced, his body taught with emotion that threatened to erupt in humiliating tears as the dismal scene before him ground on, following a script that has been re-enacted across lands and cultures since man first discovered the ability to oppress his brother. Azzi's wife too was immobile, her smooth young face impassive. Only Chidi showed signs of movement. He buried the side of his head against his mother's breast. His eyes were wide, white orbs of fascination as he followed the huge, rusting, yellow bulldozers that were smashing into the side of his parents' home.

Azzi's face, at the best of times thin, was drawn, as if the flesh had been kneaded into his skull. His eyes were as dry as the *shurqui*, the wind that for an eternity had whipped off the Sahara, sucking the life-giving moisture from the once-rich African soil.

Chioma's normally rich black skin had taken on an ashen hue: it might have been a fine coating of dust from the ruins of the house she had once cleaned with such pride, or it might have been the ebbing of hope from her veins. A close observer would have noticed that her eyes, deep black fertile wells of life, were rimmed with moisture. But not one tear would she permit to leave its trail across her skin. She would not let Azzi down, not in front of these men with guns and machines. She was proud of him and she owed him his dignity. He had been brave. He had stood up to these men from the federal government, the army and the police, who had sworn to protect and serve. He had even offered up his

1

life. His courage had made her proud and she would do nothing to undermine his moment of dignified defiance. He had not always been a good husband to her, but he had been better than most. He had never been work-shy, and he had strived constantly to provide her, and their child, with a home and food. She was deeply fond of him, though she had never loved him. When he was away, out of respect for herself as much as for him, she had kept his house chaste, even though she knew full well that he never accorded her the same courtesy. When Azzi had stood in front of the government officer, with his back straight and knees trembling, offering his life in exchange for the rights of his wife and child, then for the first time she had loved him. She had, at that moment, felt for him with her whole body; tonight she would lie with him, give herself to him entirely, and in the morning she would take up her child and she would leave.

What lioness will stay where there is no food for her cub?

The house had never been a particularly beautiful affair, but it had been theirs. It had evolved over five years, sometimes slowly, sometimes in bursts, its growth mirroring their fortunes. Every time Azzi went away to sea he would come back, pay packet in hand, and they would buy meat, breeze blocks and sometimes cement. Gradually, through patience and thrift they would add to and tend their little home. They had a television and a stereo, and were generally comfortable.

These two items they had been able to rescue from the house. But the years of toil and saving were gone forever.

For some time, Azzi and Chioma had known that it would come to this. The federal government was building roads to service the rich oil fields at the base of the Niger Delta. Roads that would demonstrate to the Western oil companies that Nigeria had the infrastructure to support their continued investment. Good roads for the heavy machinery and tankers that represented the never-ending stream of money flowing from the oil fields of Nigeria into the Swiss bank accounts of its politicians.

The federal government had developed a Roman approach to road building. It was of little matter that these roads ploughed through towns, farms and villages, that these crudely macadamised arteries flattened homes and uprooted lives was of no concern to the men in power: the oil must keep flowing. Once fertile cocoa fields had been abandoned and now lay untended and overgrown. The iron ore mines were now nothing more than silent relics, for it was only the black gold pumped from beneath the sea that could fulfil their cravings. Like a heroin addict in the throes of withdrawal, unable to appreciate the fine wines and beautiful surroundings that were on offer, the government clawed its way across the fertile land, scarring, burning and destroying in a vain attempt to assuage its unquenchable thirst.

Chioma knew little of all this. All she knew was that to appease the oil company, for whom her husband had so faithfully toiled, the federal government was bulldozing her house, and that her hopes and aspirations would soon be buried forever beneath a great grey river of concrete.

The dilapidated lorries and rusty bulldozers had arrived early in the morning, then the drivers and operators had lounged around smoking and chatting amongst themselves. They had, of course, been escorted by soldiers, not that resistance was anticipated. But nor, as their presence made all too abundantly clear, would it be tolerated. There had of course been paperwork. In Nigeria there was always paperwork, not that any of it had any real value. The only indisputable paper was the dollar bill. The men from the government had arrived on the little plot of land, armed with sheaves of incomprehensible forms covered with stamps, to tell Azzi and Chioma that their house was to be demolished. Azzi had remained dignified. Everyone present had known, even at that penultimate moment, dollars would have re-routed the road by five metres and spared the family home. But they also knew – the men with guns, the men with papers and the soon-to-be-homeless family – the dollars required would be more than Azzi could earn in a lifetime.

That unspoken knowledge compounded the humiliation already heaped upon the trembling Azzi. The fat man with the sweaty armpits from the government could have saved their home. With an action as simple as the stroke of his pen, their past and their future would have been secured. There, by the roadside, they had stood, an inanimate little group on the dusty soil beneath the harsh African sun. The warm, dry wind had leafed through the papers, leafed through the family's last vestiges of hope as the fat man had stood and waited for the bribe that they all knew could not be paid. Had Azzi been a less dignified man, Chioma knew, she could have offered herself. She was pretty and young, the man from the government was old and fat – it would have been enough. Azzi's battle for his family had moved her in a way he had never managed in their seven years of marriage. But she held her peace and the last possibility of hope quietly slipped away.

Finally, the fat man, backed by the oil companies for whom her husband worked, had had enough. His patience was exhausted: these people had nothing to offer and the young woman clearly had ideas above her station. He was, he reflected, a reasonable man; if they were not prepared to sacrifice a little, why should he reach out to them? He turned away and began to walk towards the bulldozers, then stopped and pivoted his bulk back towards the family. He held out a bulbous hand in which he gripped a small, tatty piece of paper. "Dis be for you, you must put in for de bulldozer diesel."

Azzi had placed himself in front of the fat man from the federal government. Being made to watch his home being demolished was bad enough. That it was to be demolished by the people to whom he paid taxes to protect him was worse. But even after a lifetime of poverty, of constant exposure to the injustices of Nigerian civil society, being asked to pay for the privilege was too much. That he was being asked to buy petrol for the government machines that would soon destroy his own home had triggered something deep inside Azzi, something whose existence even he had been previously unaware of. He walked up to the government man and said, "My brodda, you have taken the roof from over my head, you have taken the future from the mouth of my child, please, de bullet in dat man's gun I did pay for with my taxes, it is mine, put it in my head and let me have peace, for I will not be paying your blood money."

The fat man, who was from Okrika, looked at him, "My brodda, you be from de Delta, and you did marry dis Biaffran *Jew*-girl from dem Igbo people. Maybe, if you had not betrayed your blood, we could have helped you, but you have a baby mamma from the Christ killers. I will not waste good Nigerian lead on a man like you."

Chioma had watched in silence. She knew that the curse of the blood of Abraham coursed through her young veins. She was Igbo, it was visible in her face and evident in her speech. As the descendants of Abraham, the Igbo were the lost or, some would have it, true tribe of Israel. They had been cast out from the Promised Land and estranged from the other tribes, then condemned to an existence of poverty and hardship in a forgotten corner of the Dark Continent, bearers of the blood of Cain. To be a nomad was her destiny; to be driven, a hunted thing, from place to place was her heritage. Oath-breakers they had been; centuries ago in a faraway place at the foot of a barren mountain, her ancestors had bowed down and worshipped a golden calf and broken the covenant. Now, as if nothing had ever changed, the unbelievers were driving her as one of the chosen people from her home. Now she too would, in the tradition of her people since they had left Egypt, bundle up her few possessions, place them on her head, pick up her child, and walk. That, she

5

reminded herself, was why the blood of the Israelites passed through the mother, and thus Chidi was of the chosen people, unlike his poor father.

Chioma stood naked in the moonlight, looking down upon the sleeping form of her husband. They had spent the night in the upstairs room of another soon-to-be-demolished building that had belonged to a long-departed neighbour. Not everyone was prepared to sit it out to the inevitable bitter end: some people just ran. Azzi and Chioma had not run. She did not know whether it was courage that had made them stay; perhaps it was simply that her husband had nowhere to run to. With no other options left open to him, like a captain on a sinking ship after all the life rafts have been launched, he had faced the end and gone down with his vessel. Or was it something more profound that had rooted him to the earth? This was his land, his home; his people had been here since time began; perhaps he really had no choice.

She moved quietly about the room, carefully pulled on her best silk and tied the large sash about her slender waist. She placed a small bundle on her head and, in one graceful movement without unsettling her burden, she bent down and scooped little Chidi onto her hip. For a moment she was completely still. They stood, mother and child, her back to the unglazed window, a tall black sliver of a woman silhouetted against the full, ripe moon. She looked down at Chidi, who was barely awake. "Say goodbye to Papa," she whispered, and glided silently down the stairs.

When Azzi awoke several hours later, he did not need to look, for he knew instinctively that they were gone. In a way he was grateful. He was grateful that those haunting eyes would not see the shame of his poverty. He was grateful that she had gone quietly. Chidi and Chioma were inseparable; the way Chidi rode constantly on her hip had led Azzi almost to begin to think of them as one person. Chidi was Chioma's world, Azzi knew. He had no illusions about where her affections lay and he was grateful to have had her for a while. Azzi's mother had always told him it was a marriage that would never last and that he should not have married into a tribe of troublesome people. It was true he had frequented the girls of the bush bars, that he had never been faithful, but in his way he had loved Chioma, all the time knowing that it would come to this. One day she would get up and leave. The bloodline of Abraham ran too strongly in her.

Almost anywhere in central Africa the sight of a woman with a child, possessions piled high on her head, passes virtually unnoticed, the sight is so commonplace. Africa, it is frequently said, is carried on the backs of its women. Africa's women may be taken for granted, ignored and abused, but still they walk. From village to village, from town to town, across history they walk, clothes, food, water, the necessities of life balancing atop of their heads. And still they are there, endlessly walking. Occasionally, if they are particularly attractive or striking, they will be noticed.

Chioma walked. That she was beautiful was unavoidable – the eyes of men and women were drawn towards her – but as she walked it seemed her serenity drew a cloak of dignity about her that veiled the brilliance of her beauty and shielded her from interference. And so she passed, not quite unnoticed, just casting a shadow of beauty in the minds of those who beheld her. It seemed to those she passed that a beautiful thought had entered their minds and then slipped from their grasp, and as they struggled to retrieve it she faded further into the distance.

Chioma had no clear idea of where she must go. She only knew, as millions of African women had known before her, that she must walk to find succour for her child. Her mind wandered back over her short life. She allowed herself to dwell on her husband, Azzi. It was true that he was not a bad man; those last days together had shown a side to his character that she had never before suspected was there. She felt sad for him. She knew that

7

their leaving would cause him great pain, but she also knew he would survive.

Azzi was not a man of passions, but he had cared about her, she had no doubt of that. His male pride would be hurt. He had failed as a provider for his woman and child, and the other Deltans would know and comment. Then, as time passed, they would begin to blame her, for being an Igbo. *With time*, she thought, *the community would find him a new wife, a Niger Deltan like himself; he would settle down and all the elders would nod sagely, and comment that the prodigal son had come home. He had been brave to marry her, they would say, but foolish.* Then they would advise him that it was generally best stick to your own kind. She would, as the years passed, fade from his thoughts, but she knew she would always cast a long shadow in his heart. That he would soon be living with another woman did not bother her at all; what mattered was that it would not be in her house, which was now a pile of rubble. The fact that she knew he would never quite forget her pleased her woman's pride.

But Chioma had yet again underestimated her husband.

Chapter Two

Harrison was a preacher man in his sixties. All his life he had worked on the ships that serviced Port Harcourt. Every morning he had assembled the faithful crew on the deck and preached his sermons. He knew the scriptures by heart and had a charismatic presence that motivated even the weakest of his congregations, but now, as the sun was setting over the tin roof of his house, it was also setting on his faith. Man's inhumanity to man was ever picking at the scab that life had caused to form over his faith, infecting it ever deeper with doubt. It bothered him constantly, like the pains in his back.

It was early evening and he was sitting outside his house while his wife, Sarah, pottered in the kitchen. The house was old and only a few wooden planks separated them. Harrison could hear his wife singing to herself, the inevitable gospel songs that, for four decades, had provided the soundtrack to her daily routine. Despite her age, her voice was still deep and rich, and she was still a handsome woman, immaculately clean and well presented. And she always seemed to be busy. Harrison frequently found himself wishing that she would just stop and sit down once in a while. It had recently occurred to him that, in their forty years of marriage, they had never once really had a conversation.

It was true that they spoke, though more often than not it was Sarah who spoke. She would tell him about the day, news of the children, the grandchildren, the village, what they needed and the bargains she had got at the market. Little more than gossip or 'amibo', as they called it in broken English: they never really discussed anything. If she needed to know about something important from the outside world, she would bustle about the house until she was ready, then she would come and sit next to him, smooth out her dress, fold her hands on her lap, and adopt her listening expression. She would nod knowingly throughout and when he had finished she would again nod sagely and say, "So datit den, thank you my husban'," and get up and off she would bustle. Ideas and opinions, they were his job; it was her role as a dutiful Christian wife to sit and agree with him. For Sarah, the world outside, the world of ideas – that was not her problem. Their intellectual life had not been unlike their sex life, when they had had one: something she fitted in to humour him between cooking and washing.

This particular evening Harrison had had something to tell her, but he had found, not to his great surprise, that she was far more interested in brushing the sofa. So he had taken a bottle of cold beer and sat in his old chair outside the house and watched the world go by, wondering what it would have been like to have married a woman capable of having her own ideas.

It was whilst he was thus ruminating that a tall, slender Igbo woman, bearing a child upon her hip, approached the front of the house. She was beautiful and had deep black eyes that haunted him. She asked only for food and water for her child, nothing for herself. Harrison found something disturbing about the young woman. Despite her obvious poverty, she bore herself with a quiet dignity; there was something – he searched for the word – almost *regal* about her. Not haughty or overbearing – no, not regal; *noble*, yes, that was the word: she gave off an aura of nobility.

Despite being a preacher man, with as thorough a grounding in the New Testament as any bible-thumping evangelist could wish for, Harrison harboured a secret. In the early days of his marriage to Sarah, he had tried to educate himself. He was, at heart a man who loved to read. A like-minded friend from one of the ships had given him a copy of the complete works of Shakespeare. It had been a revelation to him, but his progress was often interrupted: whenever he tried to read, Sarah would berate

10

him: "What are you wasting your time for? If you have enough time to sit down and read, you should be reading the scriptures," and so it went on. Reluctantly, he gave up on Shakespeare, but soon found the same exciting writing and intrigue in the King James version of the Old Testament. He also found his peace, for as long as Sarah saw the good book in his hand she would leave him be, and he had passed many pleasant years trawling through the blood feuds of the Israelites. It was his secret little world and he guarded it jealously from Sarah, who would have called it 'pagan nonsense'.

Now this woman stood before him, asking politely and without shame for food and water for her child. He did not catch the child's name – or maybe she had not told him. He called his wife – not that that was really necessary: despite her constant singing, Sarah's ears would have picked up the approach of the young woman. For Harrison, it was more a case of self-preservation: he did not want Sarah to find him speaking to such a beautiful woman for too long without having called her. She was, after all, the woman of the house, and even after all these years she still had a jealous streak. And yet Sarah knew her duty; she was a pastor's wife and it would not do to turn a hungry child from her door. Harrison was never quite sure whether Sarah's charity came from religious conviction, whether it was a form of superstitious self-interest (a sort of banking credit with God), or whether it was simply a question of keeping up appearances. Whatever the origins of her charity, that she gave generously was indisputable. It had not, however, escaped his attention that sometimes her comments behind closed doors – comments concerning the recipients of her generosity – were somewhat less than Christian.

Sarah bustled out, then back into the house, and in little time produced a small bundle, a bottle of milk and a bottle of water. She stood in front of their timbered house with its flaking sun-bleached paint, wiped her hands down the front of her immaculate dress and stared for a moment at the sky, almost as if she could somewhere hear the celestial cash register ringing up another good deed. She crossed herself then went inside.

Harrison found himself standing alone with the woman and child. He could hear Sarah again going about her never-ending chores and singing, perhaps just a little too loud. The young woman resettled her load upon her head and hitched the dozing child up on her hip.

"Thank you, Father," she said.

Her voice was deep and strong. She looked him square in the eyes as she spoke. There was something about those eyes that scared Harrison, the blackness, the absolute pupil-less blackness, huge wells that seemed to plunge back across time.

As the woman moved away, Harrison felt his legs weakening, his chest tightened, there was a rising sense of panic – he was, after all, not a young man. He felt himself falling, plummeting through the well thumbed pages of his treasured Old Testament into some harsh and barren land, where he saw a young woman toiling with a small boy-child. All around him lay a blasted stony desert, not rolling sand dunes but burning yellow rock. Light and heat seemed to leap from the stones; the sky felt as if it were pressing down upon the earth, as if to squeeze the last drop of life-giving water from the rock-strewn dust; the place was ringed by the most brutal looking mountains Harrison could imagine. It was clear that the woman was not far from death, for nothing could survive in this heat.

He knew immediately where he was: deep inside one of his favourite stories. He was terrified. He fell to his knees and prayed harder than he had ever prayed in his life. He knew that he was witnessing the exodus of Haga the slave girl and the infant Ishmael, who had been driven from their home into the wilderness by Sarah, the mother of the Israelites. And yet there was something different now to the way Harrison had always imagined the story. It took him a little while to identify the discrepancy. When he found it, it was like a thunderbolt hurtling through his pain: Haga was black. In a moment he knew her. Her beauty was unmistakable despite the tortured face, so parched and dehydrated. He knew her. She was the woman to whom, moments ago, his wife Sarah had handed a bundle of food and then sent on her way. She had been standing on his doorstep.

Harrison felt the pain shoot from deep inside him, tearing up through his being. His body was heavy and out of control; feeling seemed to ebb from his limbs. His last thought before his mind went dark was that at least God had sent a prophet for his soul, but why the burning desert? Why the vision of exile? Was this to be his reward for a lifetime of service? Had his life been such a failure? Had he not given himself to the service of Christ? Mercifully, consciousness slipped away before absolute panic could take root.

Sarah heard her husband fall, the grating sound as he fell against his chair and the legs were pushed across the wooden porch. It was true she had been listening. She still felt insecure; even after forty years of marriage, pretty young girls made her feel uncomfortable. She had never suspected Harrison of infidelity – he was after all a man of the cloth – but it did not do to take chances: he was a man first and last, *Even our Lord had to fight against temptation,* she thought.

The problem was, she had to admit, that she did not deserve him. When they first met he was a rising young man in the area, a pastor with a good job at the port; many girls had their eye on him, girls who were pretty, educated and bright. Sarah had been the first, but she knew all too well that she was neither educated nor bright. Being pretty and having little prospect of employment, she had discovered quite early on that she could pick up a little money now and then behind the bush bars, enough to buy nice dresses, and then men in the bush bars would buy her drinks and entertain her.

Every Sunday, however, her mamma would dress her up and

take her to church. The one true talent Sarah had was that she could sing, and in the evenings her renderings of Ella Fitzgerald, Aretha Franklin and Etta James earned her drinks, a few pennies and plenty of attention. On Sunday mornings her gospel voice earned her attention of another kind, that of young Pastor Harrison. And one fine morning Pastor Harrison had asked her mamma if he might walk out with her daughter. It had been a rope to a drowning woman, and she had grasped it with both hands.

There had, however, been one small problem, and it had been growing in her womb for nearly two months. Harrison's interest in her was clearly honourable, and this was her chance to make good. For another month she continued to bind her stomach, but knew that that solution had a limited time span. Eventually, in desperation, she had gone to her mamma.

Now, Sarah's mamma had been a widow for more years than she cared to mention, or so she claimed, and she was a practical woman who loved her only child. From experience, she had had no illusions about the life of an uneducated single mother. She sucked her teeth, looked long and hard at her tearful daughter, and decided to take the situation by the horns. Like any mother, she wanted to be sure that her wayward child would be well cared for after her death. So she set about scheming in the way that only a woman with a cause can.

The first thing was to find out when Pastor Harrison was next likely to go to sea. It so happened that the good man was due a two-month trip in about a month's time. Her first instinct, that her daughter should seduce the young man and blame the child on him, was clearly impractical: Pastor Harrison was known for his integrity, and the timing was too far out. So Mamma devised another plan.

They were lucky Harrison was no hypocrite. He did not touch. Mamma had figured that for another six weeks they could keep their secret with some baggy clothing and tight bandages;

Sarah was a big girl any way and that would help. Her mamma had started to spread a story about her own sister in Lagos being ill. As soon as the good pastor went to sea, the pair of them rushed off to Lagos, and there they stayed until the baby was born.

There were two final stages to be accomplished; the first was a trip to a doctor who, with needle and thread, re-established Sarah's virginity. The result was painful and would not have fooled a gynaecologist, but it would, or certainly should, have fooled a naive young pastor. For the second part of the plan, fortune played into their hands. A woman in another village, who was a friend of her mamma's and whose husband was serving on the same vessel as Pastor Harrison, gave birth to a stillborn daughter. All it took was some female conspiracy and some luck, and Sarah's baby was placed in its new home. Other than the new mother and Sarah's mamma, no one else knew. Not even Sarah knew the home where her baby had been placed: her mamma was not taking any chances; the maternal instinct was a powerful force, as she well knew. The good pastor and Sarah were reunited and Mamma saw married at last the little girl about whom she had worried so much. The marriage appeared to be consummated without any scandal and her mother breathed a sigh of relief; her happiness was complete when Sarah proved to be still fertile and, nine months later, another baby was born.

Sarah's initial feeling when she married had simply been one of relief: she was married to a respectable man and there was food on the table. What more could she want? She had had a lucky escape. Harrison, though, had been a revelation to her: his religious convictions, his genuine caring kindness – he was not like other men she had known. Sarah began to think that Harrison might actually prove not merely her saviour in this world but also the next, and slowly church began to change for her. It was no longer somewhere you went to put on a pretty dress, have a good sing and a look at the boys all dressed up in their suits; it started to matter to her. She did her best to be a good pastor's wife, and she took good care of him the only way she knew how. She cooked and cleaned and kept his house nice; his Bible was always ready for him when he came home.

In the early days of their marriage, he had started to bring home other strange books, books full of pagan stories, and Sarah had begun to panic. What if her saviour fell from the path? Would he bring her down with him? Would God punish her for not keeping him on the straight and narrow? Also, and more credibly, she loved him in her way: he had given her everything; respectability, dignity, a future and salvation. She desperately did not want any harm to come to him, in this life or the next, so whenever she saw him reach for that pagan nonsense she would remind him of the word of God. It was for his own good.

For forty years all had been well, she had done her best, the Lord knows: she had kept his house, borne his six children (two of whom had died before adolescence) and hidden from him the fact that she could barely read. Whenever he asked her to read something or posed a question that would expose her ignorance, she would bustle, finding some chore that could not wait. Then, in the dead of night, when her preacher man was sleeping, by candlelight she would pick her way through the relevant verses of the New Testament, that she might not be found out.

Only once did her past come close to her. Pastor Harrison was in his little chapel, one Sunday morning, when a baby was brought for him to baptise. Only two people in the congregation knew who the true mother of the child was: the woman carrying the baby and Sarah's Mamma. Sarah sat in the front row gazing at her wonderful husband, her hand resting on her stomach, knowing that another little life was beginning inside her and that this time it would be coming to a happy home. So intent was she on her daydream that little of the service made an impression on her; she did not notice the knowing look and smile that passed between her mamma and the beaming mother of the newly baptised baby, nor did she recall the name they gave the child. After all, it was nothing to do with her.

The child's name was Azzi.

Now Harrison was on the floor in front of her, and this strange Igbo woman was standing over him. Sarah was filled with panic; she did not want to lose Harrison, he was her everything. As she saw him lying there gasping for breath like a fish out of water, she had a vision of life without him. She did not recall ever having told him that she loved him.

Chioma looked at the trembling woman before her. Moments ago this woman had been looking down on her, she knew, but the sight of her pain touched her. She placed her precious Chidi on Harrison's vacated chair. "Mamma com help me send Papa inside de house." Together they lifted Harrison through the door. "Where de doctor?"

They helped Harrison onto the freshly brushed sofa. Chioma took control. She opened windows, sent Sarah for water and then for the doctor. She would have gone herself and allowed Sarah to stay with her husband but, as she pointed out, they would respond much quicker to the pastor's wife than to an unknown stranger.

Whilst Sarah was gone for the doctor, Chioma sat with Harrison. She talked quietly to him, even so her voice seemed to fill the room. Harrison knew he needed to talk to her, needed to tell her that he knew who she was. It was desperately important, and he cursed himself for his failing faith. Maybe this was his punishment; salvation was so close yet so far. God was showing him paradise, punishing him with the knowledge of what he could not have, a fading vision of a paradise lost. Inside his paralysed body, Harrison struggled; there was a tingling sensation all over his body, breathing was an effort. He tried to talk, the words formed themselves in his mind but his lips no longer held dialogue with his brain. He knew that saliva was running from the corners of his mouth because the young woman would frequently lean forwards and wipe the traces from his skin with a cloth. The dribble he could not feel, but when she wiped his face, he had a vague sensation of the cloth passing over his skin, which felt like rubber. His whole body seemed far away, almost as if it belonged to someone else; he had a sensation of weight, that he was still inside it; it was just no longer his. His eyes alone seemed fully under his control. He desperately searched, though he was limited by the mobility of his head. He looked pleadingly at the young woman. He had often heard people say that the eyes were the windows of the soul, that the eyes could 'talk'. He tried to express to Chioma his need to communicate. She looked at him, and it was true, *her* eyes talked, and they spoke eloquently and with compassion. As is so often the case, compassion is barbed with cruelty, and Chioma's flawless black eyes told Harrison that all she could see in his was an old and dying man. Her face was kindly as she sat and talked to him. But her quiet voice, which under other circumstances would have filled Harrison with so much pleasure, was almost an irritation. The more she talked, the more he was made conscious of his own inability to communicate. Sometimes there was a pause in her monologue, and Harrison hoped for a brief moment that maybe she had picked up some message from his face; but then she would continue and his hopes would again be dashed.

With a sudden movement her eyes left his face. Her whole posture changed, and the face that had appeared so tranquil was illuminated. Harrison did not need to be able to move to know what had happened. Her whole body told him: little Chidi had toddled into the room.

At that moment Harrison knew that he had ceased to exist for her.

As Chidi came into Harrison's now limited field of view, the old man felt a surge of emotion. Harrison was sure that this child held his salvation – this child, this throwback to the house of Abraham, this small toddling child in whom the blood seemed to run so pure that Harrison felt he might even be looking on the face of Abraham himself. The thought started a process in Harrison that, had a blood clot not lodged in part of his brain half an hour earlier and paralysed him, would have caused a shiver to run through his entire body.

Chidi had been perched in his favourite place on his mamma's right hip when the big tall man with white bits in his hair had suddenly fallen over and made strange noises. He had seen the fat lady, who had given his mamma food but been cold with her, come running out of the house. She had looked upset when she had seen the big man on the floor. At first he had thought she might be angry with the man for lying there, because he would get his clothes dirty. Then, when he looked up at his mummy's face, he grasped that something was not quite right, and she had placed him on the man's chair.

Chidi was not worried. He knew his mamma always came back for him. He had watched with interest as the fat lady and Mamma had helped the big man into the house. Then, as nobody seemed to be interested in him for the moment and he wasn't particularly hungry, he had nodded off.

When he awoke, Mamma was not in sight but again he did not worry, she always came back, and anyway he could hear her voice not far off. He sat for a while, blinking in the afternoon sun. Then he decided that he was hungry after all, so he twisted round on to his tummy, slid off the chair and on to the ground, and walked into the house. It was a bit dark inside and it took his eyes a few moments to adjust to the gloom. Again he was not scared: her voice, deep and soft, told him where she was. He made his way towards it. Not long ago when he had been hungry, she had put him to her breast. She didn't do that any more; now when he was hungry he had to wait, but Mamma always found food for him. He liked it too when she picked him up and held him close to her. She was all warm and he would usually fall asleep again.

As he came closer to Mamma's voice, he saw that the big man was still lying down but now he was lying on a sofa. *He must be very tired*, Chidi thought. Chidi could see that Mamma was talking to the man. He listened to her, he liked listening to her: she was using the voice she used to sing to him when he was sleepy. But she wasn't singing now, just talking. Maybe the man didn't like singing.

Chidi thought he would go and look at the man who did not like to listen to Mamma singing. As he came round the side of the sofa, Mamma looked up and smiled at him. It was as if the lights had been turned on, and he forgot all about the big tired man who did not like singing. He ran to Mamma and she scooped him on to her lap and squeezed him. It was not long before he fell asleep again.

Harrison watched in despair. He knew that his body was beyond salvation, but his soul? If only the child would turn to him, if only he could look into those eyes and find truth, confirmation to bolster his floundering faith. The salvation of his soul was so close but his body had been transformed into a prison, and paradise was only to be glimpsed between its bars. He tried to scream. In his heart he knew that he was in the presence of a prophet. But his brain was still reeling from the shock of being temporarily deprived of oxygen. It clung to the vision that it had been granted before the gift of communication had been so cruelly removed: the vision of Haga and her child. He knew absolutely that Chioma and Chidi were there for a reason: something needed to be done, some prophecy fulfilled, some debt paid. His damaged brain grappled with his beloved scriptures, desperately seeking meaning in the chaos. If only he could hold the good book; perhaps that would give him strength, perhaps that would give him the answers he needed. *Oh Lord,* he thought, *why hast thou forsaken me?* Harrison's despair was absolute.

20

Sarah came rushing back into the house, the doctor in tow. As she entered the gloomy front room, she saw her Harrison lying as she had left him on the sofa. The strange Igbo girl was sitting by her husband's head; the quiet child had fallen asleep in the woman's arms. Her headdress she had loosened and allowed to fall about her shoulders; the room had an air of peace about it. Just behind the girl's left shoulder was the shuttered window that opened on to the yard behind the house; the occasional ray of sunlight crept through the uneven wooden slats, casting a gentle pall of light about the group. Sarah stopped still as if jolted: for a moment it appeared to her as if she were looking at a black Madonna, seated at the head of her own dying husband.

Sarah felt that her own inadequacy was being thrust upon her. Deep down she had always known that she had never deserved this man. Now it was being confirmed: all these years she had been living with a saint, and the Lord had sent the Madonna herself to claim his soul.

The revelation was too much. She was going too lose her Harrison, that was clear; that was the only reason the Madonna would appear at the good man's head. She was going to be alone, and she suddenly realised how much she loved this man who was leaving her. She fell to the floor, sobbing and pleading with the Lord to have mercy on her. She prayed in the name of the Holy Virgin that, should her Harrison go, she be taken with him.

The doctor, standing behind her, saw Sarah fall to the ground. He was a local man and used to these demonstrative displays of grief. Unshaken, he stepped forward and helped Sarah to her feet. As he did, he noticed a pretty young woman, who had been sitting by the old man's bedside, gently place a sleeping child next to him and then hurry towards them. The doctor's only thought was that she was uncomfortably beautiful; then his brain switched into work mode and he saw her simply as another set of hands that could help him with his patient.

Together they helped Sarah to a seat beside her husband. The doctor dispatched the young woman to bring Sarah some water then turned his attention to Harrison. As two local professional men, they knew each other, and he was saddened to see his old friend in such a condition. It was clear that Harrison had had a stroke.

Chioma stepped back into the room and handed Sarah a pot of cool water. Sarah took it with both hands and drank. She gulped it down, feeling the cool, refreshing liquid bring stability to her mind and body. She looked up to thank the young woman, and saw not a saint, not the Madonna, but only a simple Igbo girl, who less than an hour ago had come to her door asking for water for her child. Sarah felt foolish at having taken this woman for the Madonna. Then, as if venom were seeping through her body, she felt a vicious surge of jealousy. This beautiful young woman had been alone with her husband, and now he was dying.

The doctor explained to Sarah that he did expect some improvement in Harrison's condition, but it would be slow and limited. Round the clock care would be needed, and Sarah was not a young woman either, so she would need help. Was there not a woman she could engage to help her with the care of her crippled husband?

Though she was loath to admit it, the answer was obvious: the Igbo girl. She was young, strong and seemed to be in need of employment and apart from Sarah's irrational jealousy of her beauty, she had to admit that she seemed a quiet, kind, capable woman. So it was settled: Chioma had a new home.

When Azzi finally woke to his solitude, he bundled up his few remaining possessions and took the road to the port. There was no point following Chioma, he had nothing to offer her and he was not going to beg. So he made his way down to the port and, through his remaining contacts, he managed to secure himself a post on one of the offshore supply vessels as a deck hand. The vessel was sailing in two days' time, so he took what little money he had and went to the first bush bar he found, where he made himself a promise. From the time he set foot on the deck of his new vessel, to the time he reclaimed his wife and child, no strong liquor would ever pass his lips. But that was tomorrow and today was today, and he proceeded to drink himself into oblivion.

Chapter Three

Shimon Daniel Ashkenaza enjoyed his job, almost as much as he hated Palestinians. He sat atop the enormous green bulldozer, the heat from the engine vying with the heat reflected from the metal. The sun in the Holy Land is a strong sun, a sun of righteousness, of scourging fire, of nemesis, and today he, Shimon, would be another such agent, a righteous visitation of the wrath of God upon these insects. All around him his compatriots, dressed in olive drab and Kevlar, bore automatic weapons to defend themselves against the 'Atfal Higara', the children of the stones.

From his seat high above the caterpillar tracks, Shimon looked around at the misery he knew as Gaza. Palestinian youths, their faces sullen in defiance, were standing in huddles; then there were those ridiculous women in their black robes and white headscarves, who were always wailing and beating their breasts. Now those awful women were gathered on the debris-strewn roadside, howling in that harsh tongue of theirs. *Even their language*, he thought to himself, *was a debasement of Hebrew*. Everything about them was a perversion of Semitism. Now God was at last keeping his side of the Covenant and coming good once and for all. God was showing the world whom the chosen people really were, and making it quite clear that it was them to whom the Promised Land belonged. Not since the time of Joshua had the hand of the Almighty been so clearly evident in the obliteration of the gentiles. *Many lifetimes ago on this very land*, he thought, *a small Jewish boy had faced the Palestinian giant of war armed only with a single stone, and the Lord had granted him victory. Now that history had come full circle and*

Palestinian children, like a plague of locusts armed with stones picked
from the rubble of their homes, faced the might of the Israeli army,
God was showing that such victories were granted only to the chosen.
These descendents of a slave girl, who were little better than the black
apes of Africa, were just an infestation, a plague to be cured once and
for all.

Shimon revved the bulldozer's engine, savouring the power
that throbbed beneath him. But he was growing frustrated. To
Shimon it was clear that, even in talking to these people, the
lieutenant was a disgrace to his uniform. Now he was out there
talking to these squatters of God's land in Arabic. How could he
call himself a Jew?

In fact, Lieutenant Samuel Ashraf had no problem what so
ever in calling himself a Jew; it was the Israeli bit he was
struggling with. Ashraf was an intellectual who, in Shimon's eyes,
should have stayed where he belonged, in the university, and let
the real men get on with the soldiering. An intellectual and
Sephardic, it was no wonder the man was an Arab-lover. It was
men like Ashraf who let these people prosper. It was men like
him, with their liberal values, who let these Arabs breed more
little bombers to stream through the border crossings wrapped
in Semtex.

Lieutenant Ashraf would not have been surprised by what was
passing through the mind of his subordinate. These were
sentiments he heard on a daily basis in the canteens, and he had
long ago given up trying to reason with the men who espoused
them. Now, however, he had more pressing things on his mind:
a house needed to be demolished. It was not the solution, he
knew that. One look at the sullen young faces that surrounded
him was enough to tell anyone with even half a mind that the
moment the blade of the bulldozer impacted the side of the
house, another suicide bomber would be created and every house
that was crushed wrote the death sentence of another randomly

25

selected Israeli life. These, however, were not his decisions to make. He was a soldier and he had his orders. It was a sentiment that had a horrible taste. There was an echo of a not too distant past that he preferred, for the sake of his sanity, not to consider too deeply. The man battled with the soldier, a daily struggle that was carving ravines into his once handsome face. He hated his job but, he reasoned, it was better that people like him remained in command than to step aside and let Shimon and his ilk off their all too slender leashes.

The woman howling and pleading before him was pretty. She was a mother. She looked disturbingly like Hannah, his wife. Hannah was an ultra left wing lecturer at the university in Tel Aviv; she hated his job more than he did. She did not buy into his logic; the blood of children was on his hands, she said. Hannah's mother had been an Auschwitz survivor, which gave her a right to talk. Sam, though, was Sephardic: his people had not suffered in the camps. For centuries his people had farmed these lands alongside their Christian and Muslim neighbours, and nobody had bothered them. The lieutenant's grandfather spoke Arabic and Aramaic better than he spoke Hebrew.

It was in Arabic that Lieutenant Samuel Ashraf now spoke to the woman who reminded him of his wife and whose house he was about to destroy. Sam knew that he could not justify to her why it must happen but he knew as a man, as a human being, as a believer in the word of God, that he must at all costs avoid the loss of human life. 'Thou shall not commit murder' was not a difficult concept to grasp. As an officer in the IDF he also knew that he must avoid the loss of life: dead Palestinian women and children were fuel to the Al Jazera news programmes, to Amnesty International and to his militant wife. He was deep inside enemy territory and he could not rely on the idiots under his command not to panic and cause a massacre that could lead to them being overrun. He offered up a silent prayer: that it would be the conscience of the *man* that would guide and inform his actions,

26

and not the uniform of the IDF. His wife, he knew, would have called him a hypocrite.

A sudden movement caught his eye. He turned to his right and saw a little girl of five, maybe six, years old. She had climbed on top of a pile of rubble and now stood directly in the path of Shimon's bulldozer. She was holding the remains of a soft toy. She looked at him. Her eyes bored through his skull. She was about the same age as his daughter, Debby. She just looked. And her indifference to the carnage around her was shocking.

Now the girl stepped forwards. She smiled at him and held out her tattered toy. "They killed my teddy," she said.

It is in the eyes of the children that we see ourselves, he thought. He looked at her and what he saw harrowed him for the rest of his life.

Sadly for humanity, the rest of Lieutenant Ashraf's life was destined only to be a few seconds long. Just as he bent forwards to speak to the little girl, a bullet, fired by a twelve-year-old Arab sniper, ended the days of the one man who could have stopped the carnage. The firefight that followed, if that term can be applied to children with stones against men with automatic weapons, left fifteen dead and countless more wounded, orphaned and embittered. The tragedy was to be played out continuously across the Arab news networks for days. In America, Fox News reported only that an Israeli officer had been assassinated by Islamic militants.

Said had never shot a man before. In most other parts of the world this would not in itself have been unusual. Twelve-year-olds did not generally shoot people, American high schools aside. The Gaza Strip, however, is like nowhere else, and Said's education, whilst not typical of every child's in Gaza, was certainly not exceptional. Said could shoot, run errands after curfew, identify different types of Israeli armoured vehicles and throw stones with an uncanny accuracy; he could also recognise incoming munitions by sound. The bullet, and the gun he had used to send it on its journey through the brain of Lieutenant Samuel Ashraf, had been manufactured in America, an irony that was lost on Said but had given great pleasure to Khallid, his older brother. It was Khallid who had taken him to the third floor of the bombed-out apartment block, overlooking the soon-to-be demolished house. Khallid had helped his little brother set up the gun and arrange its tripod. Khallid had taught his younger sibling everything: how to breathe, how to squeeze gently on the trigger. Said was his protégé. They had lain together side by side for hours waiting for the Israelis to come. Everyone knew that the army would arrive and one of the houses would be demolished. There had been a suicide bombing a few days earlier, on a crowded school bus in Haifa. The bomber had come from this street.

The army had arrived and, as they had anticipated, there had been some spasmodic stone throwing by the youths of the area. It was almost a ritual, but there had been little real resistance. The men with the masks and the guns were long gone: there was no one there to goad the children into throwing stones at the armoured vehicles. The only people left were the women, children and old men, who went about their daily business trying as best they could to fabricate some semblance of normality out of the tatters of their occupied country. Khallid and Said looked on. Khallid was not yet really one of the men; it was true he was armed, and he was eager and talented, but the masked men of Hamas and Islamic Jihad humoured him and kept him at arm's length. He was too eager. He was not a religious believer, an abstainer from things declared Haram nor an observer of his five daily prayers. This was a failing that alienated him from many of the more disciplined groups. Nor was he politically mature. He had no hankering after the socialist state, nor did he really understand all the issues. Anyone could understand that they were occupied, that they came from a people who had been submitted to one of the great injustices of history, but Khallid was one of those people who thrived on conflict and tension. An imagined righteous indignation gave fuel to his ardour, his desire to kill. He was uncontrollable, and the masked men with guns knew this; they used him when he was useful to them but even then his uses were limited. Had he been less intelligent or more religious he would have been a suicide bomber, but Khallid liked to gloat, and suicide bombers never get the chance to gloat. Khallid wanted to kill, and he was a racist. Neither man would have appreciated the comparison, but Khallid and Shimon Daniel Ashkenaza actually had quite a lot in common.

The convoy had pulled in to The Square, a large open space at the end of the street that had been created by the combination of home demolitions, artillery shelling and an air strike. A local wag had named it Time Square: if you stood there long enough it was only a matter of 'time' before you got shot. The name had stuck, and all the locals now referred to it as simply The Square. The bulldozer had arrived on an army low-loader, and the whole procession had been escorted by armoured cars. Khallid had watched intently as the proceedings unfurled. He had known the suicide bomber – not as well as he liked to boast, but they had frequented what passed for a school together (though 'infrequented' would have better described Khallid's educational career). As a result of Khallid's tenuous acquaintance with the suicide bomber, he knew that the Israelis were indeed demolishing the house of the dead boy's family. He also knew that Abdul-Ghafor had not in fact lived in the house for over five years: his family had disowned him as a result of his association with the armed groups. To Khallid's immature mind, the fact that Abdul-Ghafor no longer lived there and that the family would have in no way approved of his actions was entertaining; he saw it as evidence of the occupiers' stupidity, that they were knocking down the wrong house. The travesty of justice being inflicted on the family was invisible to him, so focused was his mind by his hatred of the Al Yahood (Jews). This was another trait he shared with the man on the bulldozer: an inability to put himself in the shoes of another and an absolute inability to foresee consequence.

It was Khallid who had instructed his little brother to shoot the officer. His main motivation was the kudos: an officer would gain him more respect with the armed men of the paramilitaries. That, though, was not how he explained it to little Said. "It is simple," he had said, "It is like when you chop the head off a chicken. The chicken flaps around aimlessly, then dies. The officer is the head and his unit is the body, so we chop off the head."

What Khallid had forgotten was that, even in the Gaza Strip, chickens do not carry the fire-power of the IDF. The massacre that they were to witness was entirely foreseeable, even using his logic: once the restraint of the balanced conscience of Lieutenant Samuel Ashraf had been removed, the body (which consisted of Shimon and a number of frightened conscripts) did indeed career out of control.

One of the first people to die was the woman who had so much resembled the lieutenant's wife.

Little Said could not believe the chaos he had unleashed. His shoulder hurt from the gun's recoil. He had heard gunfire before, and seen levels of violence and devastation no adult should be exposed to, let alone a young child, but this was the first time he had been directly involved in anything more than a bit of orchestrated stone throwing.

It was horrible. He saw the body of the pretty lady, who had been talking to the man he had shot, picked up by the force of the bullets that smashed into her. He knew, even at his tender age, that when it was all over, the occupying soldiers would say that they had thought she was reaching to detonate an explosive device concealed on her body. That's what they always said. That a body so slender could not possibly have concealed anything of the sort would not, of course, be mentioned. Said, despite his youth, was not like his brother. He understood that in a way he had been responsible for the death of the pretty lady, and he did not want to do it anymore. He would tell Khallid that it was over – never again would he pick up a gun – then he would go to see the Imam.

His shoulder was starting to hurt more and more – perhaps he had fractured his collarbone. He turned to tell Khallid that he wanted to go home. He was trying not to cry, but between the pain in his shoulder and the knowledge of what he had done, he was fighting a losing battle. He would tell Khallid now. As the courage to speak the words came, so did the tears, and with the falling of the first tears he lost control of his voice, and the tears came and came in torrents, shaking his underfed body. His tears were not the tears of a soldier but those of a child, lost and frightened.

But Said had no need to be ashamed: Khallid was too busy choking to death on his own blood to notice.

Three storeys below the two brothers, the bullets flew and the bulldozer advanced towards the house of the dead mother of the suicide bomber.

For all his faults, Khallid had been a good teacher. It was a strange gift to be bestowed on such an egocentric individual, but he had had an ability to communicate, patience and a love of his subject, ideal qualities in a teacher. Friends of their parents (before they were blown to bits by a missile launched into a residential area of The Strip from an American-built F16 fighter plane) had often speculated that, had Khallid been born into a more stable society, he might have been a lecturer, or an educator of note. They lamented the fate that had brought such a gifted youngster into such a violent world. Their speculations were, though, at best naive, but more likely wilfully ignorant of the all too evident truth: Khallid was totally amoral. The best he would ever have achieved would have been pimp or drug dealer, or perhaps politician, since his personality hinged on a need for self-gratification at the expense of everyone else. The fact remained, however, that he had taught his little brother well.

As the lieutenant leant forwards, Said breathed out and held the breath, his whole body calm and steady. He anticipated the arc the lieutenant's head would follow and where it would stop. Khallid had made him watch the assassination scene in *The Day of the Jackal* so often that that was hardly a mistake he would make. He had allowed for the elevation of the shot. At the correct moment he squeezed the trigger. The bullet pierced the lieutenant's helmet just above his right eye. The first impact with the helmet and then with the lieutenant's thirty-two-year-old skull absorbed some of the energy of the shot. In doing so, the nose of the bullet compressed slightly and expanded. The bullet, with its wider flatter end, continued at incredible velocity through the lieutenant's upper right cerebellum, forcing part of his frontal lobe into the left side of his brain.

As the bullet passed through, thirty-two years of accumulated education, a master's degree in liberal humanities, acquired wisdom and a wealth of knowledge of both Arabic and Hebrew culture, were scrambled by a huge compression wave passing through his cerebral tissue. When it arrived at the base of Lieutenant Samuel Ashraf's skull just to the left hand side of his pituitary gland, it had nowhere left to go. The residual energy caused the whole of the lower part of the lieutenant's head to spray itself over the young mother to whom he had been speaking in her own tongue.

Halima, as she was called, had just enough time to register the fact that she was looking down at morsels of skull, hair, and brain tissue that were stuck all over her starched white blouse. Only minutes before she had wondered how such a nice-looking young man who spoke such good Arabic could be about to do such an evil thing to her family; and now his brain was splattered all over her. She had just enough time to draw the breath that would form the scream that would have been the normal human reaction to such an occurrence, before the bullets from the heavy machine-gun mounted on the armoured car penetrated her chest and ripped her lungs through her back. The air that had been destined to form the scream exited almost silently through what was left of her torso and she died without a sound.

It was at about this moment that a single round punched through the wall of the abandoned third-storey flat towards the perceived source of the sniper's shot. It ripped off Khallid's aorta, causing his chest cavity to flood with blood. Of the 800-odd rounds fired, only two were not fired by the IDF: the shot that killed Lieutenant Samuel Ashraf and the shot that killed Khallid. The masked men with the guns had had enough of Khallid: he had served his purpose and was more valuable dead as a heroic martyr than alive as a dangerous lunatic with a silver tongue.

The great irony of the situation was that the faults that Khallid and Shimon shared perfectly mirrored the qualities shared by the late Lieutenant Ashraf and Said. Had they been fortunate enough to meet under different circumstances, they would almost certainly have appreciated each other. Such, however, is the curse of the children of Abraham: Sarah's jealousy weighs heavily on their shoulders.

Mohammed Mustapha Al Qader was an engineer. He was by birth Palestinian, but a combination of hard work, good luck and intelligence meant that he spent as little time in his homeland as possible. It was only an aging mother and a sense of guilt, engendered by his own good fortune, which kept him coming back. And the more he came back, the better he learnt to deal with the guilt. He felt confident that one day it would wear off completely and he would be free of the place.

When his father died, he had tried to persuade his mother to leave with him. "There is nothing left of the homeland," he had argued, "why stay and torture yourself?" He had enough money so that, if she wished, she could go and live out her days with him, pretty much in luxury.

Alas for Mohammed, his mother would not go. She had spent most of her life in Canada Camp, where she could look through the barbed wire fences and see what was left of the olive groves her family had farmed for centuries, now submerged beneath an illegal Jewish settlement. Every day she would make the pilgrimage to the wire. Mohammed, or 'Mo', as he was more commonly known by work colleagues and left-wing university friends, would become increasingly frustrated with her stubbornness every time he stayed with her. Eventually he would make a break for his old college friends in The Strip, swearing never to return to that accursed piece of land again. He knew, though, that as long as his mother was still alive he would be back: like all good Arab boys he loved his mother. He had been brought up on the words of the Prophet after whom he had been named twice. Such was his father's enthusiasm for the faith, he had been called Mohammed Mustapha, both names of the Prophet (however, much as the names might have carried a benediction in the eyes of God, Mo had found that they frequently had the opposite effect on Western immigration officials). He had been brought up in a relaxed but traditional household, and whenever their late father had detected a lack of respect for his wife in the children's tones he would trot out, "The Prophet of God (peace be upon him) said, 'Paradise is beneath a mother's feet'." He would then lie back and draw deeply on his curled hookah pipe in the knowledge that he had imparted the word of God to his miscreant offspring – the Prophet had also said, had he not, that the reciting of a *hadith* was a form of charity? Mo's father was in this respect a very charitable man. So Mo had grown up in a typically matriarchal household, and loved his mother dearly – after all, she had brought him into this world and cared for him – but now there were days he could have wrung her neck, she was so stubborn.

It was, however, entirely thanks to his mother's stubbornness that he was who he was today and that he, unlike the majority of Palestinians, had a choice about where he lived.

As a child, Mo had been pushed at school. When the schools were closed due to curfews or bombings, his mother had arranged that he be taught at home. She had pushed and eventually he had achieved a place at that much-abused place of learning, the Bir Ziet University. Mo had participated somewhat half-heartedly in the various student demonstrations – politics did not interest him. He had decided long ago that, yes, an enormous injustice had been committed against his people, but life must go on, and he was not going to fritter his life away hurting about something the world community showed no inclination to change. What difference would the activities of a bunch of dispossessed students make? So he studied.

From Bir Ziet University he had progressed to AUB (the American University of Beirut). It was at AUB that he had a stroke of luck. Until that point he had been travelling on a UN travel document, issued to the stateless people of Palestine. Earlier, during the Lebanese civil war, the Nigerian government had granted asylum to a large number of Lebanese nationals, and given them passports. Mo was noticed by a visiting engineer who was looking for talent. Money changed hands and Mo acquired first a Lebanese passport and then a Nigerian residence document. Two months later he was laying pipelines in the Niger Delta. He never looked back.

When Said's bullet ripped out the back of the Lieutenant's head, Mo was standing not far off from Shimon's bulldozer. He was in The Square, trying to track down a girl he had been with at Bir Zeit who was rather pretty and quite left-wing. Mo, being bored, had figured that she would be pleased to see him and that either her liberated views would lead her into bed with him or they would end up in a heated debate over the role of women in a neo-Marxist state. Mo knew that the first scenario was probably wishful thinking, but in either case he would spend the afternoon with a pretty girl with a brain and the time would pass more quickly whilst he waited for the last transport out of The Strip, back into Israel.

Salima had been out, and her harassed-looking mother had informed him that Sally, as she preferred to be called now that she was a reconstructed post-Islamic liberated woman, would be back after lunch: she had gone to the market to buy *Za Ta*. Her feminist views had obviously made little impression on her two brothers, who were sitting inside drinking tea whilst their little sister went to market and dodged the checkpoints. In fact, this was not quite as chauvinistic as it appeared; young men of fighting age were far more likely to be given a hard time by the IDF patrols than a woman with a Westernised appearance. Mo had been invited in for tea and had accepted, but it was uncomfortable: he was too Westernised to feel at home in that environment any more. Generally, any male visiting an Arab household asking to see a woman was asking for marriage or a beating from her brothers. Salima's family had been worn into submission on this point and, as she was the only family member who earned a decent salary, she held the whip-hand. However, as he sat and sipped his mint tea with the two brothers, Mo knew they were regarding him with a mixture of envy and hope. Envy for the free life he so obviously led, and hope that he might actually marry their sister and improve the family's lot. At the same time, he knew that they were also wondering what sort of respectable Muslim would marry a liberated tearaway like Salima. He finished his tea, made his excuses and left.

It was whilst he was loitering around The Square that the Israeli convoy arrived. Mo stepped back to watch. Of course he knew what was going to happen, he had grown up here and still watched Al Jazeera TV on his satellite dish in Lagos. He had half a mind to try and get some photographs with the camera on his mobile phone; he had a friend in one of the news agencies so he might even be able to sell them.

Not far from Mo stood a young Israeli conscript, on his first tour of duty in The Strip. He was not enjoying himself. Danny Ben Attar had grown up in Morocco, as part of the large Sephardic community in Casablanca, and at the age of eighteen he had moved with his parents to Israel. Danny had spent the best part of his teen years surfing the beaches around Casablanca and Rabat with his school friends, most of whom had been Arab. Morocco had instilled in him a different culture, one of integration; even the government assembly in Morocco had Moroccan Jews as ministers. Morocco had been the first Arab country to recognise the existence of the State of Israel, and now he was about to participate in the destruction of exactly the type of house in which he had grown up. He felt decidedly uncomfortable.

When his family first came to Israel, Danny felt that they were more in Europe or America than the Middle East. The American-style suburban homes seemed to him cold and indifferent. He missed the frantic, claustrophobic huddle of life in a North African city. Whenever Danny got the chance he would use his illegally retained Moroccan passport to slip into Syria or Lebanon and spend an afternoon relaxing in one of the cafes, listening to the hubbub of colloquial Arabic and inhaling the rich aromas of the ever present *shisha* pipes.

Danny had liked the lieutenant; the older man had made him feel welcome in the unit, and Danny had always appreciated the man's intelligence. Now Danny had seen his mentor die, and heard the heavy machine gun open up. The death of the pretty Arab woman had almost paralysed him with revulsion. He had pivoted towards the armoured car, the source of the deathly fire, an anger bordering on rage surging inside him. This was murder, exactly the sort of thing his more militant Arab friends in Morocco had accused the Israelis of, exactly the sort of thing he had believed he would never be part of. The fact that he held an automatic weapon in his hands offered a dangerous temptation. His rage was pushing him to use it to silence that infernal chugging from the vehicle-mounted machine gun.

As his body swung round, his emotions battling with his training, he caught sight of a young Arab man. He had noticed the man before, standing apart from the others men in The Square, and in other subtle ways, too, he stood out from them. Clearly, his clothes were not bought locally, they were too expensive, and his body language did not radiate that sullen hopelessness so common in men of his age in The Strip.

Their eyes met, Arab and Jew, dysfunctional children of Abraham, and something passed between them that neither man would ever be able to explain. The Arab turned his head and Danny instinctively followed his eyes. They led him back to a small girl standing directly in the path of Shimon's advancing bulldozer, a battered teddy bear extended in one hand.

Mo met the young soldier's eyes and read there a compassion and anger that mirrored his own. It was a moment of shared humanity that pushed him to execute what was perhaps at the same time the bravest and most foolish act of his life. He never did decide what it was that finally made him act; even years later it remained a source of wonder to him – a basic human instinct, or perhaps a deep-seated, long-buried sense of being Palestinian? Whatever the cause, the emotion had been building up inside him as the drama had unfolded. He had felt chained to the spot; the nerves in the backs of his legs shaking as adrenalin pumped through his body. Yet something in the look of the young Israeli, some mutual understanding had now broken the bonds that had held him fast to the soil of that bloodstained land. The horror in the eyes of the young man in the uniform of the occupiers of his homeland had freed him, and he, Mohammed Mustapha Al Qader, a Palestinian engineer, started to run, to run as he had never run before, in the same direction as the bullets that were filling the hot, dry air. He ran; right into the killing zone.

The little girl had been looking at the nice soldier who had been talking to her mummy in Arabic when his head exploded. Then, before her young mind could find something to latch onto, she had seen her mummy die. No child should see such things, but then this was the Gaza Strip, and the Promised Land had claimed the lives and minds of many children of Abraham. The little girl stood transfixed, her battered toy still in her outstretched hand, the lieutenant's blood on her face. A big machine was coming towards her. She could not move.

She felt an enormous impact lift her off the ground.

Danny Ben Attar saw the young Arab start his run. He knew that the man's chances of reaching the little girl were slim; he also knew that this would be the defining moment of his own life. His next action, he knew with absolute clarity, would be the moment that would be held up before him at Judgement Day.

The vehicle-mounted machine gun was traversing, pumping its messengers of hate into the path the running man was taking to get to the little girl. Danny stepped forward, almost into the line of fire, and took up a position, as if he were about to shoot the Arab in the back. Now the gun would be unable to continue its traverse without cutting him in half. He opened fire, aiming just over the head of the running Arab.

Danny prayed. As the rounds left the barrel of his weapon, he felt they were messengers of hope shielding the young Arab from being cut in two. He felt more alive than at any moment in his life. He was, in this instant of defiance, in absolute control of his identity.

Mo ran. He passed just metres in front of the blade of the advancing bulldozer, so close that he felt the heat reflected off it.

Shimon saw the running Arab and accelerated: the machine would crush him like an insect. But bulldozers are not designed for speed and, despite the swathe of red mist engulfing his brain, Shimon was aware that he was pushing his machine into the line of friendly fire. Crushing the young Arab was just wishful thinking.

As Mo cleared the blades of the advancing machine, he threw himself over the mound of rubble. His body connected with the little girl whilst he was still in mid air; he wrapped his arms about her and held the little body close to him. He hit the ground hard, back first, protecting her from the impact. Together they rolled down the pile of rubble into a trench that had once been a sewage system, and there they lay.

Mo was in pain. He knew he had injured his shoulder, he could feel it starting to sting, and there was blood in his mouth. Where they were was not somewhere he would have ordinarily described as safe, but they were out of the line of fire.

Salima had been returning home when the firing started. She had not been far off The Square when Said's shot sounded a dull crack in the oppressive heat. Salima had run towards the sound, it was part of her nature, she was an idealist. In her mind it was a battle between two ancient oppressive chauvinistic cultures; concepts such as 'occupation' and 'nationalism' did not interest her.

She had been on the edge of The Square when Mo had started his long run. She had only half recognised him, but she saw what he had done: selflessly saved a child's life. She knew the *atfal higara* would be gathering to commence their stone throwing, so she skirted round the back of The Square. She arrived behind the abandoned block of flats, which gave her a direct line of sight on to the trench where Mo was lying. She put two fingers in her mouth and gave a piercing whistle of which any football hooligan would have been proud.

By the time the IDF had collected the remains of Lieutenant Ashraf and withdrawn, The Square was returning to its bloody normality and Mo, Salima and the little girl were back at Salima's house. The younger of her two brothers was despatched, without much hope, to research the whereabouts of the girl's surviving relatives. Salima's mother had been fairly adamant that the child, after her mother, had few close living relatives. Her father had been interned by the Israelis years ago, and little had been heard of him since. Word had got back to The Strip from a released prisoner that, after years of torture, little remained of his mind that would have been recognisable to anyone who had known him before. Salima's mother fussed and the little girl sat still with her battered toy. All she would say was, "They killed my teddy." The enormity of what she had seen was far too much for her young mind, and she had retreated into the simplest reality she could find.

Mo found himself exactly where he did not want to be, involved in this country's interminable pain. The easiest thing to do would be to hand the little girl over to Salima – she was a competent, practical sort of woman – then get on the last bus out and go. But the child looked at him with wide, uncomprehending eyes. "They killed my teddy," she said. And at that moment Mo knew his life had changed forever. He was no longer a cynical observer.

Oh, he couldn't stay. He had prayed so hard to get out of this godforsaken land and it would not suck him back in to its misery. So there was only one solution, however irrational: he would take the girl with him.

Salima had changed somewhat from when Mo had known her at college. She had matured and her fiery temper was more under control; she had with some difficulty learnt that not every battle was worth fighting, however noble the cause – it was the war that counted. She was still a pretty girl, with the large, dark eyes so typical of Palestinians, and very pale skin. Had she been born in northern Europe then her frame, which was just a little too broad to be beautiful, would have made her look at home on a large farm. Her hair she still wore short, a vestige of her defiant student days. Mo well remembered the day at Bir Zit when she cut off her luxuriant black locks and announced to the student body that she was, for political reasons, going to become a lesbian. It was, she said, "A statement against the phallocentric misogyny of monotheistic theocracies."

She had almost got herself killed. Once they had picked their way through the words, which were rather unfamiliar in colloquial Arabic, the conservative Palestinian middle-class decided that they were definitely not ready for that sort of thing. It was only the intervention of a genuine, though closet, lesbian senior lecturer in contemporary politics that the scandal died down and she retained her place in the faculty. For her dissertation she had translated *The Female Eunuch* into Arabic and somehow, whether by grace of God, force of personality or simply an uncommon amount of good luck, she survived university without having acid thrown in her face, being expelled or picked up by the occupying troops. Now she wore her hair shoulder length, held back in an Alice band. She still wore no obvious make-up, but her jeans drove her father up the wall. She would have looked more at home at an English gymkhana than on the streets of Gaza.

Mo broached his plan to her and she became immediately businesslike. He had half expected – and if he were really honest, half hoped – that she would try and talk him out of it. To his even greater surprise she announced that she would come with him. Salima still had contacts in what was left of the Marxist old guard of the PLO, and she demonstrated an organisational ability that Mo, having become used to West African chaos, found quite unnerving. Their exit plan was entirely of her devising.

She disappeared from the house for three days, taking his passport with her. When she returned she had another Lebanese passport and a stack of official-looking documents. The plan was simple: she and Mo would cross the border as Lebanese husband and wife. They had come to The Strip to collect Mo's autistic niece and take her for treatment in Cairo. Once they arrived in Israel, another contact would provide a Lebanese passport for the child as Salima's daughter. Salima's passport gave her name as Sally, and was complete with stamps and visas to show that she had right of residence in the United States. Mo's passport had been similarly doctored. Salima explained that, as a Lebanese Christian, she would attract much less attention than a Muslim, and a mixed marriage was less likely to arouse the interest of the security services. All their dealings with the Israelis would be in English (they both spoke excellent English) so that their accents would not possibly betray them as Palestinians.

The child's name was Houda. Salima's mother fussed and flapped over her continuously, as would any Mediterranean matriarch. For the most part the child just sat with her damaged teddy, in front of the flickering images on the TV screen. Mo found an irresistible fascination in the child; he would sit for hours talking gently to her, telling her stories of Africa, of the animals he had seen, and reciting half-remembered stories from his childhood. Barely a response did he elicit; it was only when she was tired that he knew that somewhere in her poor, damaged mind he was making progress, for when she wanted to sleep she would crawl up close to him, still hugging her teddy, put her head on his lap, and sink into troubled dreams Mo did not even dare to imagine.

When the day came, the little family crossed the checkpoints virtually unhindered. Sally's brash American accent and the forged UN documentation worked wonders: the Israelis were used to Lebanese Americans – not much different to Jewish Americans. It was an identity they could relate to and few questions were asked. That evening, they checked into a hotel in Tel Aviv. They fussed over Houda until she and her teddy were fast asleep and then, finally, six days after he had planned it, Mo ended up in bed with Salima. Once the stress and emotion of the day had been expended, Salima propped herself up on one elbow, looked him right in the eye, and said, "I hope you don't think this means that there is anything between us."

She then pecked him on the cheek, rolled over and went to sleep. Mo lay for a while, staring at the ceiling and listening to the gentle sound of her breathing, wondering what he had gotten himself into. He had been absolutely terrified crossing the checkpoints; he was not a natural revolutionary and he knew it. Salima, though – he must stop calling her that – *Sally*, then, had appeared to thoroughly enjoy the whole thing. Indeed, judging by what had just passed between them, it appeared to have excited her.

Mo had never really considered what would happen next; he had never entirely believed that they would make it through the checkpoints.

The next day the three of them boarded a series of flights that would eventually take them to Lagos. There, Mo was already resident and, as he well knew, forged papers were not required to acquire visas: dollars would do nicely, thank you.

Some twelve hours after Mo, Sally and the child checked out of the hotel in Tel Aviv, two Polish Jewish families were celebrating the matrimonial union of their offspring. The banqueting hall and the ballroom had been hired for the occasion, there were two live bands and an abundant supply of food, alcohol and distant relatives. The ceremony and festivities represented a cultural confusion that could only be found in Israel: Western pop music vied with mournful Polish ballads extolling the misery of the diaspora; the accents ranged from Warsaw to Brooklyn.

At midnight the music stopped and the father of the bride presented the young couple with the traditional double cup from which they should both drink simultaneously, not shedding a drop so as to ensure a happy union. As she received the cup, Ruth looked at David: soon they would be out of this place and in a small flat in New York not far from his practice, and all these tiresome old people and their politics of hate would soon be a thing of the past. David looked back at her: she was pretty, it was true, and bright, exactly the sort of girl his mother would have chosen.

In fact, had he but known it, his mother *had* chosen her. She had not only arranged the meeting but had also invited the family over for a long weekend, and arranged the sleeping quarters with easy access for her son. She was a smart woman and had calculated on her over-hormonal offspring behaving according to his nature. She had been right, and now Ruth was pregnant. Now she could let her son go back to New York without having to worry that he would embarrass her by bringing home some filthy goy.

The happy couple raised the twin-armed goblet to their lips and drank. Ruth noticed to her dismay – not that she was superstitious, of course, she was far too modern for that – that a tiny droplet of red wine had stained David's shirt. She prayed that her mother had not noticed; she would never hear the end of it.

Ruth should not have worried, however, because at exactly one minute past midnight a suicide bomber drove a van packed with explosives into the hotel lobby and brought the entire building to the ground.

Chapter Four

When Azzi awoke, he wished he hadn't. He was curled up on the hard floor, a ragged splash of concrete, in front of the bush bar that had taken his last pennies. He lay still for a while, dreading the pain that he knew would soon start to grind away at the base of his skull. His mouth was dry but he could taste the beer he had drunk the night before. His nostrils were saturated with the acid stench of cigarettes and chemically fermented hops that seemed to have infested his clothes.

A compact young woman was sweeping around him in a businesslike manner with a broom made out of palm ferns. She noticed that his eyes were open. "Waiting ye do for dere, why ye need sleeping again oh?" She laid her makeshift broom against a breezeblock wall that carried sun-faded adverts for unavailable drinks and local pop stars. Then, drawing herself up to her full but not remarkable height, she placed her fists upon her hips and looked down at him sternly. "Get op. Ye savy is ten o'clock gon by oh? Get op or I will beat you very well oh!"

The young woman was joined by another, older woman who was clearly the younger woman's mother. "Dis lazymon no wan get op Mamma!" the daughter announced. The older woman looked down at Azzi curled helplessly on the floor. She said something to her daughter in Yuroba, a language that Azzi could identify but not understand. It must have been in his favour, however, because the younger woman arched her eyebrow, thrust out her hip, huffed, picked up her broom and strode off, still muttering to herself in her own tribal language. The mother bent down to Azzi and said in English, "Ogga, I do savey you very well, now you be dat man dey broke da house yesterday. You be Azzi, I knew your mamma, when I was still small I did clean for her. Cum inside de house you, I make coffee for you. I hope say you never forget for go new work to day oh?"

This was the first day of Azzi's new life, and it had been born in searing pain with contempt following hard upon its heels. But succour had been offered; he had found himself rescued by unexpected kindness wrapped in the memory of his late mamma. He hoped, through the pounding inside his head, that this was a good omen for his new career. He also remembered with a jolt that he had forever forsworn strong drink.

The coffee was rich, sweet and instant. The woman who had cleaned for his mamma showed him to a standpipe behind the bar. Azzi stripped down and washed himself in cold, fresh water. For a moment he wondered what Chidi and Chioma were having for breakfast, and then tried to put the thought out of his mind, as if it were a photograph that could easily be slipped into a wallet and left there until needed.

Freshly washed, he returned to the front of the bar where the mamma who had surprised him in his misery with such kindness was sitting. The morning sun fell across her features and suddenly Azzi knew her. "Jesus be praised! You be Amanda, no? You be the small girl came wash Mamma clothes and be that girl who shoot me stone awhen I did go for school when Mamma nay be see?"

"Shine your eyes, Mr Azzi! Remember say when I was still small girl I be love wid you? Com o't for my house now go back for your new boat for de blessed memory of your late mamma God bless her soul."

She smiled and the years fell away from her, and for a brief moment he was standing again before the pretty, bossy little girl who had tormented his childhood, and in an instant he understood. *Why*, he asked himself, *do we always understand when it is too late? Why does life need to be so complicated?*

"How you do look me so! Com o't for my house now!" Her face was stern but there was laughter bubbling somewhere in her voice. "Com o't for ma house od'er wise I will give you more wahalla than shoot you stones, young master Azzi!"

He tried desperately to thank her for her kindness, but he was grasping for words as a man who crawls up a steep bank grasps at shrubs and roots to prevent himself from slipping backwards into the abyss whence he hauled himself. The woman just laughed, she was having nothing of it and kept shooing him away.

Her words were still bouncing off his head, as the stones had done so many years ago, as he made his way to the port.

After Azzi was gone, Amanda sat for a moment in the chair outside the bar. She fanned herself and smiled at long-forgotten childhood memories, of how her little heart had fluttered when Azzi came home from school. She fanned herself again, then remembered she had things to do and could not be sitting around all day, daydreaming like this. With more focus than was strictly required for the task, she cleared a few empty bottles from the rickety, plastic-covered tables in front of the bar, and then, humming to herself, walked into the shade of the bush bar. As she walked towards the area that served as a storeroom, she caught sight of herself in the scratched mirror that hung outside the washroom doors. She paused for a moment and looked at the middle-aged woman staring back at her, distorted slightly by the mirror's imperfections – or were they her own? She held the eyes for a moment, as if seeking some hidden truth, then slowly she smoothed back her hair and sucked in her cheeks.

What if things had been different? she silently asked her reflection. She turned her head slightly to one side, in what she imagined her reflection would have considered a coquettish manner. "Silly old woman!" she chided herself.

Azzi's childhood admirer's daughter noticed that her mother

was decidedly odd for the rest of the day, but she never gave the sad, drunk old man another thought.

The *MV Rawanda* was an offshore supply vessel and, like the unhappy country whose name she bore, the years of abuse had taken their toll on her once proud frame. She was captained by an elderly, bearded Welshman, whom a history of alcoholism and a messy divorce had denied the financial possibility of retirement. He was working out his twilight years in Africa, where no one looked too closely at your tickets.

Hugh Evans had taken 'The Pledge' at fifty, and since that day not a drop of liquor had passed his lips, but it had been too late to save his career. The enquiry into the accident that had paralysed his first mate had failed to prove beyond reasonable doubt the he had been drunk at the time. However, the subsequent civil action brought by the unfortunate man's family, where the burden of proof was considerably lower, had found against him.

That and the divorce had ruined him. He was unemployable in the UK, so he had taken the first plane out to the first oil-producing country he could find, and ended up in Gabon. There he became what he always should have been, a sober, hard-working skipper, and worked his way around West Africa. After a few years he remarried – a much younger local girl – and now lived quietly ashore in Freetown.

Life had never been better.

Azzi's first contract was for three months. He started off life as a simple deck hand; he was not lazy and was a quick learner. Having nowhere to go at the end of his three months, he signed on again for another three. *There was*, he thought, *no point in going ashore: at sea he had bed and board, and was paid (by the standards of his previous employment), handsomely.* In all, Azzi spent a year at sea. Offshore supply vessels are culturally not like other boats: the small crew live cheek by jowl for months on end, and tend to know each other better than they know their own families. Due to his permanence aboard, Azzi became a trusted hand to the captain, who, in learning his life story, felt they had much in common. Having been sued for negligence, Hugh Evans was probably the first bit of really good luck in Azzi's life.

Living in Africa, and marrying an African woman, had changed Captain Evans's world view considerably; he now understood how disadvantaged many people were, and how bleak their futures must look. He had frequently listened to the stories about the Niger Delta militants who kidnapped white oil workers to draw attention to the pitiful neglect of their region by the federal government – a government who seemed all too happy to tax the oil companies to the point of non-profitability, but seemed totally disinclined to reinvest it anywhere other than in numbered Swiss bank accounts and the casinos of Las Vegas. Evans had frequently thought that, had he been born a Deltan, he too would have been out there with an AK47, kidnapping rich foreigners. And so, as he got to know the quiet, affable Azzi better, he felt for him.

Evans spoke to his employers. The situation at the time was that the Council of Chiefs guaranteed the safety of the vessels working in the area as long as the companies employed a certain number of local hands. The reality of the situation, though, was that many of the hands were on the books only: they were paid their salaries, the chiefs were happy and the jobs were done by Filipino seamen. But a true Niger Deltan who seemed happy to spend ridiculous periods of time at sea and was competent, teetotal and enthusiastic, Evans argued, was worth investing in; it would be good public relations as well. After four months of deliberation, the company decided in Azzi's favour and sent him back to school.

Azzi was happy. He was learning, he was being well paid and spent nothing. It was true that the company benefited massively from his presence: he appeared in company manuals, and whenever there was a newsworthy story about the company, the invisible men in the marketing department (which was in Aberdeen) always managed to contrive Azzi's presence when the men from the press corps arrived. The UK version of the company's annual report even mentioned Azzi by name as a rising local talent, thus demonstrating the company's commitment to local employment, equal opportunities, diversity and all the other politically correct buzzwords that could be stretched to cover a single black African fast-track employee. The fact that he was paid less per month than the price of the average executive lunch in the UK was, for some reason, never mentioned.

Azzi, too, was proving to be an impeccable employee. His readiness to stay aboard and his aptitude for learning quickly convinced his employers that he had been a good investment. The change in environment was also producing noticeable changes in him: he had lost the gaunt, almost skeletal appearance; good food, fresh air and a less stressful life had seen the years fall away. He became more photogenic and more valuable to the company.

During his rare visits ashore Azzi would invariably visit Amanda's little bush bar. Not only was she a contact with his old self, providing a stabilising continuity, but she also seemed to provide a safe and nourishing environment where the newly emerging Azzi could relax without feeling that he needed to prove anything. Amanda's bar began to function as an emotional home for him; he had no other ties ashore and Amanda herself became his sole point of contact with the world beyond the freeboard of his vessel.

Azzi was indeed a new man: his features were fuller, his speech more assured and he had found in himself a peace that he had never imagined possible. He had kept his vow: since that painful awakening on the harsh concrete in front of the bar, no strong liquor had passed his lips. When he planned to visit Amanda, he would be sure to arrive in his new smart clothes, which felt strange on his body after months in overalls and rigger boots. Sometimes he would go to the bar carrying a small leather briefcase, which he felt befitted his new position in the company, and drink Malta (alcohol-free Guinness) with Amanda.

Amanda's daughter Theresa (or 'Terry', as she was more commonly known) began to notice that she could predict the arrival of the smartly dressed stranger, because her mamma would take a little more care with her appearance on those days, and his 'surprise' appearance would invariably be heralded by an excessive amount of largely unnecessary bustling and cleaning. Every time the smartly dressed man visited, Amanda would sit with him and nod intelligently. Much to her daughter's mirth, Amanda, who, when dealing with the majority of her clientele would blaspheme like a drunken deckhand, would develop a vocabulary befitting a mother superior. In her daughter's humble but informed opinion, she was one of, if not the most, argumentative and generally stubborn women in Africa, yet she would sit for two hours patiently agreeing, smoothing back her well-groomed weave and looking as docile as the Virgin Mary.

Theresa did not begrudge her mamma her little liaison. She barely remembered her father – in fact her last memory of him was a drunken fight when he had smashed up the kitchen whilst she had hidden, terrified, beneath the table. She had been five years old at the time. Since then, Mamma had taken up with no man. Theresa was well aware Mamma had had her 'friends' over the years, but they had never amounted to much and they had never been invited back to the house.

This pattern of visits continued on a regular basis for five years, and it was the day that Azzi was formally confirmed as first mate on one of the company's smarter vessels that Amanda finally ran out of patience.

Chapter Five

Azzi was positively beaming when he walked into Amanda's bar. He was still on a high from the events of the past week: his rank had been confirmed and, for the first time in his life, he felt that he was somebody. He sat down on his regular chair and Amanda brought out his glass full of ice cubes and a cold bottle of Malta Guinness. She opened the bottle and poured it carefully down the inside of the glass, ensuring that a perfect head formed on top of the dark liquid. She then cracked open a bottle of Guinness for herself, clinked it against his glass and took a long pull.

For Azzi it was a special day, but he was not so self-focused that he failed to notice that the ever-vibrant Amanda seemed somehow super-energised. *It was good,* he thought, realising that for the first time in his life he was happy and could recognise it.

Amanda took another long swig from her bottle and stared at him over the curve of the glass, her dark eyes framed between the raised bottle and her strong brow. She placed the bottle deliberately on the table and thoughtfully sucked the last of the Guinness from her lips. She was wearing traditional silk with an enormous green headdress piled high on her head. She wiped an imaginary speck of foam from her lips, then slowly and deliberately smoothed her dress. She breathed in audibly.

Azzi knew something was coming. The carefree moment had passed and he felt as if he were being held by the pure force of a moment that seemed to have suspended time. Even the gentle breeze that had been softly ruffling Amanda's headdress appeared to have been put on notice. Amanda straightened her shoulders, then leant forward and looked Azzi square in the eye. "I know you for long time we not still young again, for five year you did com for my bar, an now you a big man na so, Mr First Officer Azzi. Well, is you going to finally get dat fat ass of yours into dat house and jig me like you should have been doing for all dese years or are you going to leave me till I is just a shrivelled up old prune and no good to man nor beast, so what is it to be Mr Azzi? You take me in dere an make me scream or ah give you a whippin' like your mamma should ha' done years ago for not respectin' a lady an given her her needs."

For the ability to instil pure terror in Azzi, the sea had nothing on Amanda.

And much to Terry's relief, Azzi gave in. *Now Mamma would be a damn sight less moody,* she thought to herself.

Chapter Six

Sarah found Chioma irreproachable. She was a quiet girl, polite and respectful, and Sarah had to admit, she would have struggled without her. She had agreed that Chioma would work for food and lodgings and also a minimal salary, so that she could buy clothes and necessities for her child. Sarah was not a rich woman and there was little income in the house. It was true her children sent money, but she knew she must practice careful husbandry for Harrison's sake: there would surely be expensive medication to come.

There remained, however, something that irked her. Sarah knew herself well enough to recognise it for what it was: jealousy, a feeling she had not felt for years, not since those early days with Harrison, when every pretty girl seemed to be a threat. It was, she knew, an unworthy emotion. For one thing, Harrison was hardly in a position to get up and leave her, and she had never suspected him of having designs on younger women. Furthermore, she did not think that Chioma was the sort of girl one could describe as easy and she, Sarah, should know. But still there was this deep unease that Harrison had been affected by this woman, and something, some feeling in the house, changed when Chioma was near him.

Sarah tried to convince herself that Chioma was some sort of untrustworthy destitute – perhaps she was a thief. She started to spy on her helper, while pretending to herself that she was not spying. *Just checking,* she told herself, but deep down she knew she was desperate to find a chink in the innocuous exterior through which she could insert her spite.

The more she felt this, the more she hated herself; she knew her feelings and actions were unjustified and un-Christian, and that she was destroying her forty years of hard-earned salvation by her actions. But still she persisted, hating herself, and disliking Chioma even more for making her behave in such a manner.

In reality Chioma's presence placed very little strain on the household; indeed, Sarah began to remark that she actually seemed to be better off. Sarah had always been careful with food and money, but Chioma seemed to be able to feed all of them for less than Sarah had been able to feed herself and Harrison alone. Sarah noticed too that Chioma was a good nurse; she showed the same tender patience whilst ministering to Harrison as she did with her own child. She would sit and gently feed him as she would feed Chidi, talking gently to him all the time, frequently reciting favourite chapters of scripture or reading from the Bible.

Chioma noticed that some sections of the book were more well thumbed than others. Those, she assumed, were Harrison's favoured chapters, so it was from those that she read to him. She noticed they came predominantly from the first part of the book. It did not bother her: for some reason that she had never been able to explain to herself, she too had always taken much greater enjoyment in the stories of the Old Testament than the New.

Harrison showed a degree of recovery that pleasantly surprised his old friend the doctor, who, on his daily visits, would frequently remark to Sarah on how lucky she was to have Chioma in the house. The presence of small children often had a very therapeutic effect on the infirm, he pointed out to her. Indeed, when Chidi was in Harrison's line of sight there was a discernible change in him, despite his inability to communicate. When Chidi was close, any visitor to the house would remark that there was a more contented air about him; it was nothing they could identify, just a feeling.

Sarah had noticed this too. She knew her Harrison, and knew that deep down somewhere inside this immobilised carcass there was still her husband of forty years. Knowing the effect Chidi had on him, the jealousy tormented her, but her love for her husband would not let her take from him something that so clearly comforted him.

The conflict inside her was agonising. Chioma seemed immune to what was going on; she had no inkling of the war being waged in Sarah's soul. Chioma would go about her chores without complaint, sometimes singing softly to herself. When Sarah spoke to her she was polite, those impenetrable black eyes revealing nothing. When she had no chores she retreated into the world of her child; they would sit together for hours and she would talk to him, play with him, totally involved in his world but never inattentive to the ever-present needs of her employer's invalid husband. There was nothing for which she could be reproached and it drove Sarah insane.

When she was not busy, Chioma frequently found herself wondering what had become of Azzi. She wished him no ill, and as she watched Chidi grow she often thought back. She remembered affectionately what she considered to be Azzi's finest hour; now, when Chidi asked, she could tell him that his father had been a brave man of whom he could be proud.

For the first year in the house, Chioma's relationship with Sarah had remained slightly strained, though it affected Chioma little. She remained wrapped in the world of Chidi, and as Harrison began to make progress she became more attached to her charge. During the second year, there were significant improvements in Harrison's condition: he regained use of his right arm and partial control over his facial muscles, though coherent speech still eluded him.

It was Harrison who had broken the ice between the two women who were caring for him. It had been early evening and Sarah had been in the kitchen whilst Chioma sat with Harrison and read him extracts from the Bible. Harrison had been propped up on the sofa and Chidi had been sitting next to him, soothed by the sound of his mother's melodious voice. Chioma, as so often, had been reading from the Old Testament and, as she read of Abraham's trial, of his torment as he had been asked to offer up his son to the Lord of Israel, Harrison's hand had come up and laid itself gently on Chidi's head. Chioma had almost shrieked, as the movement caught her eye. She leapt up and ran to the kitchen. "Misses Sarah. Misses Sarah, do cum sharp."

Sarah, fearing some terror had befallen Harrison, pushed brusquely past Chioma and rushed out. What she saw stopped her dead. Harrison's hand, which for so long had barely twitched, was resting on Chidi's shoulder. Chidi was looking up, wide-eyed and smiling, at the man who slept a lot. A tear formed slowly at the corner of Harrison's eye. Sarah's hand still tightly gripped Chioma's arm as both women watched the tear swell and roll down Harrison's cheek. As the drop hit the floor it was as if a sluice gate had been drawn and the emotion that had been straining against the rough lock gates gushed into the room. Sarah threw her arms about Chioma and burst into tears.

As Harrison's condition improved, the atmosphere in the house changed considerably. The improved relations between the two women seemed to affect the very structure of the building. The dull brooding air that had settled over them lifted, and Sarah felt herself more and more drawn to this strange, quiet young woman and her child. Sarah recognised the injustice of her suspicion of Chioma, and she did her best to make up for it. The fact that Harrison's first action had been to touch the head of the child was to Sarah deeply significant. She instinctively and graciously understood that the doctor had been right, the presence of children could have a very beneficial effect on the ill.

For her part, whilst Chioma relished the change, and was happy for the old lady that her husband was getting better, deep inside she was worried. Chidi was growing up, and this was not the life she wanted for him. She would not be able to afford schooling nor was this the Ijaw community where he belonged. When they were alone she always spoke to him in Igbo, but he was, she felt, not truly learning or living his heritage.

She was torn: she wanted the best for her son, had been brought up to believe that to be Igbo was special. It was that same culture, however, one that so little valued women, that had deprived her of a future. When her marriage took her outside the Igbo community, she was astonished to see that other Nigerian tribes appeared to value education in their women far more than did the Igbos. In the village where she had grown up, only the boys' education was given any importance. An educated woman was frequently seen not only as a waste of money but even as undesirable.

Events from her own childhood had made this abundantly clear to her. When she was still a young girl, but old enough to understand the implications of what she was witnessing, her senior brother had been in love with an extraordinarily beautiful girl. The girl's family was originally from their village, but they had moved to Lagos when the girl was a child. A couple of times a year she would return to the village with her family, and the village had high expectations that the couple would soon wed. One day, Chima, her brother, had been in Lagos and had decided to visit his beloved at the engineering company where she worked. He had arrived and been astonished to find that she was not, as he had always assumed, a cleaner, but in fact the head of the personnel department. He left in a fury at her perceived duplicity and she was never mentioned again. It was not lost on the young Chioma that whenever the poor woman visited the village after that, not a young man was to be seen. Eventually Chioma learnt that she had married a French engineer and moved to Paris. "Best thing for her," she once heard an elderly village papa contemptuously remark.

And even at her tender age Chioma had thought exactly the same thing, though for entirely different reasons.

Chioma had been the youngest bar one in her family. She had been born in a village not far from Onitsha in Anambra state. An old man who had been a friend of her father had once remarked that whatever happened to the Igbos still happened in biblical proportions and, whilst it was not imposed by God but by the federal government, Onitsha was home to a leper colony. In a moment of apparent enlightenment, a teacher training college for women had been constructed in the city, but Chioma could still remember her senior sister remarking bitterly that it was just another leper colony: the educated women were segregated and kept behind walls lest they should contaminate anyone with their literacy.

Chioma's father had been a trader and her mother ran a shop. They had been, by the standards of the village, comfortably off, until her father was knocked off an *okada* (motorcycle taxi) and the crippling hospital bills, which ultimately proved futile, ruined the family. The stress of the experience and the loss of her husband had made her mother ill and more expenses were incurred. As so frequently happens in times of crisis, cracks that might otherwise have remained invisible are subjected to too much tension and at the weakest point they fail. In Chioma's family, the weakest point had proved to be Chima.

As the family's finances dwindled, so did Chima's patience. Economies needed to be made (but not, of course, ones that would affect his own standard of living). Chioma's education was the first thing to go. She was twelve years old and a promising primary school student.

There had been a young man who had been a business associate of her father's before the accident, who had always been fond of the quiet girl with the impenetrable eyes. He himself was little more than a child – eighteen years old – but he had left school at fifteen and shown natural business acumen; within two years he had built himself a little business that had brought him a house and a car. Immediately after her father's accident, he had told Chioma that if she ever needed anything she should ask, and so, driven by a combination of desperation and the trusting naivety of the pubescent, she had packed her bags and walked out of the house to look for him. Ike had been surprised to see her but, touched by her faith, had taken her in. She reminded him of his own sister, who had died of tuberculosis as a child. Ike was as good as his word and sent her to the local secondary school. She lived in the dormitory during term time and stayed in the house during the holidays. For him the expense was minimal; when she was at home she kept the house cleaner than he ever did and she provided company. Any girlfriends he had invariably assumed that she was his sister, as did the neighbours.

Chioma loved boarding school. She was in paradise: girls her own age to talk to from other communities opened her eyes to endless possibilities, and books – she loved books.

All went well for three years. One day she came home from school. She got off the school bus and to her delight she saw Ike's car parked outside the house. She ran to the house; she had not seen him for four months and she was full of stories of school and things she had read that she wanted to share with him. As she came through the compound gates, Ike was standing at the door with his key in the lock. She could not have been happier. He turned to look at her as she called his name, and smiled as she walked up to him. As ever, they hugged, and then he held her at arm's length and looked her up and down. "How you change so!" he said. "You no small girl again you big girl you don't reach for married! You be a woman na!"

They went inside. Chioma prepared him food, talking endlessly about netball, and who had said what in the dormitories, and her exams, and the teachers she liked and those she didn't, and the scandal that had occurred between the headmistress and one of the female teachers. Ike ate his food and listened, and all the time he watched her.

That night, when he came to her, she offered no resistance.

61

Rape is seen and interpreted differently by different cultures around the world. In that Chioma was not a willing participant – in that, had she been asked, she would certainly not have consented – it would be clear to many people that it was rape. But she acquiesced and, when he climbed into her bed, her world had collapsed. Resistance would have been futile, and so the beliefs and hopes cherished by the happy schoolchild crumbled away into little piles of dust, disturbed only by the gusting winds of despair and Ike's laboured breath as he forced the pain into her arid resignation.

That night, the bubbly, netball-playing schoolgirl died in the arms of her adoptive brother, and the haunted woman was born.

Throughout nature there is a marked difference between the male and the female. Males of all species will fight each other, sometimes to the death, be it over females, territory, status, sacred land, oil fields or ideals. As long as one survives, the species continues. Some people see it as part of the process of natural selection. The female, however, must survive at all costs, for without her there is nothing. Throughout the history of creation, different females have developed different survival strategies, from the praying mantis' cannibalistic copulation to the submissive, circumcised women of the Nile.

What happened to Chioma was no more and no less the instinct to survive: the Divine Matriarch made her adapt and survive. It is easy to give such phenomena defining classifications, such as Stockholm syndrome, from the abstract security of a research department, but for Chioma it had no such name, nor did she understand what was happening herself; it was simply her need to survive. So gradually she convinced herself that she loved Ike as a woman. In her quiet moments she knew that this was not true, but what choice was there? 'Man shall not live by bread alone,' she had heard so often from the priests, although usually as a justification of God's bountiful distribution of poverty. It is not only the body that must survive; the spirit too must live, and Chioma's spirit built her a fantasy in which she could live in relative safety. It is a phenomenon that frustrates police officers and social workers the world over: the battered wife and abused child that refuse to give evidence against their tormentors, and even lie to protect them.

Three weeks later she returned to school. Her concentration was gone, and her teachers noticed the change in her and were saddened. She had been a promising child, and without needing to go into details they speculated that there was probably a man involved somewhere. They guessed that, as she was Igbo, it might be that she was being pressurised into a marriage against her will. They knew better than to get involved: this socially accepted form of legalised rape is so prevalent throughout a world where women are dying daily on the cutting edges of machetes, being stoned to death by religious fanatics and burnt alive over unpaid dowries, that one more lost soul would make little difference. They also knew instinctively that if a woman was being pressurised into a marriage it was because the parents perceived that the marriage would be advantageous, that there would be food on the table, and in the end it was survival that counted: happiness is an abstract luxury afforded to those whose time is not taken up by the simple exigencies of daily subsistence. So they looked on in pity, knowing but not knowing, unable to stem the lava flow of human history as it ploughed relentlessly on, scorching hope and fossilising desire. Chioma was just another casualty of life; the spirit might have been crushed but the woman would live. The species would survive. As a lost cause they paid her less attention in class, and she slowly drifted away, retreating ever further into herself.

After school she would return to the dormitory, a long bungalow with beds pushed up against the faded yellow walls. With barely a metre between the beds there was just enough room for the dented old lockers between them, into which the girls crammed all their possessions. She would lie on her bed still in her uniform, staring up at the single functioning fan that rotated half-heartedly in a vain attempt to move the dense air. She would lie silently chewing her bottom lip whilst the other girls giggled, shrieked and squabbled, where a month ago she would have been one of them. It seemed like a lifetime ago. She watched the limp movement of the fan, rotating so slowly that a fly actually settled on the blade. She wondered why the fan bothered to keep going. And yet she knew the answer, which did not lie in electrical current or the machine's mechanical interior. It simply had no choice.

Ike was not a bad man at heart. He was bright and ambitious, but his education had been limited. His own parents' marriage had been one of habit, and he did genuinely care for Chioma. He was not, however, sufficiently mature or experienced to understand that that might not be enough. In his mind they were close: they got on well – he had cared for her for three years – and she had turned into a beautiful woman. Why should she not be his? She would make an ideal wife. The fact that she might see it as a betrayal of trust was utterly beyond his comprehension. Had he not educated her so well he might even have been right: the survival instinct of the village girl would have brought her round to his way of thinking, the echoes of voices of generations of village mammas would have whispered to her from across time, telling her that he was a good catch, would feed her, clothe her, take care of her children, she would be protected, safe – what more could a woman want? So what ingratitude to God's bounty was eating at her soul?

Precisely, like thousands of teenage girls throughout the English-speaking world down the generations, the Brontë sisters were eating at her soul. The same teacher who had been involved in the scandal with the headmistress had tried to open the girls' minds with her favourite childhood novel from the English convent where she herself had been educated. Her own life of emotional frustration and disappointment invested her teaching with a power that took with her even the most sluggish of the girls in her class. Twice a week in the heat of Africa, thirty emotionally charged adolescent breasts sighed and heaved beneath moistened eyes as Miss Ndum transported them to the windswept moors, the rugged masculinity of Heathcliff and Rochester, the towering female passions, the great sacrifices, the poor girl rescued from poverty by pure love. Other teachers longed for the classes after Miss Ndum's: the girls were always starry-eyed and docile. However, the more perceptive amongst them sometimes wondered if she was not cruel in her brilliance, opening the girls' hearts and minds to that which was out of their sphere, filling their young hearts with hopes and aspirations that could never be fulfilled. Miss Ndum, however, maintained that the right to dream was essential. It was true, most of the girls would be disappointed in life, but if they had no dreams then there was truly no hope, and if only one girl made it, then it would all have been worthwhile.

It was the day of her thirty-ninth birthday when she herself finally accepted that she was one of those girls who would never find her great passion outside of the pages of the Brontës. After school, she retired to her little room with a bottle of gin and the school's only copy of *Great English Poetry*. She was curled up on her bed with her toothbrush glass nicely filled with gin, torturing herself with John Donne and wondering whether he had looked anything like Heathcliff, when the headmistress, a fellow spinster, knocked on the door and walked in. "Judith, what are you doing?"

"Crying!" she replied, and suddenly she was, uncontrollably.

The headmistress, her old friend, sat down beside her and hugged her.

It was twenty years to the day since her Heathcliff had been bringing her nineteenth birthday present. She had been all dressed up in her best church frock, her mamma had plaited her hair and they were waiting for him together on the front porch. As he climbed off the back of the motorcycle taxi, smiling and waving, he was hacked down with a machete.

It was a case of mistaken identity.

He died in her arms. The heart that had beaten so strongly against her chest when he held her close and made sweet promises in her ear pumped the last of his dark red blood in weakening spurts over her well-starched white church frock.

Judith clung to her friend and sobbed. Twenty years of frustration bubbling over, twenty years of living life unloved, feeding her need for passion through the pages of nineteenth-century novels. She looked up at her friend and kissed her.

There are no secrets amongst women, and African women are no exception. The affair was only a few weeks old when it was discovered. Miss Ndum should have been ruined; in fact it was the best thing that ever happened to her: she had finally left the emotional cocoon of education and rediscovered her life. After six months of outrageous promiscuity of which she would never have felt herself capable, she spent her last savings on a plane ticket to Libreville in Gabon. She quickly found a teaching post and, not much later, happiness, with a widowed lecturer in French Literature. She never again read the Brontë sisters.

Had it not been for the passions and dreams of Miss Ndum, Chioma might well have accepted the role cast for her and for a while it was true, she did. *Survival.* Deep down inside her, though, she knew that it would not last. She knew that there was something more.

Ike announced to his parents that he intended to marry her, and that was when the trouble started. Ike's mother descended like the wrath of God. There was no way her son was going to marry this homeless housekeeper, he should marry a woman who would bring value in keeping with his hard-won status. Chioma spent another two months under Ike's roof. Then one day, after a particularly unpleasant tirade from Ike's mother, her own reservations took control. She packed a small bag and walked out the front door. She left Ike a short note in her elegant round handwriting – the money spent on her education had not been wasted after all.

She never saw him again. Years later, though, she was to hear that he had indeed married the woman of his mother's choice who had proved lazy and unfaithful, and he was now selling vegetables at a roadside market whilst his gigantic ex-wife lived in fat luxury with a Chadian businessman in Abuja.

In walking out of the door she was terrified, but liberated. She was taking control of her life. And she did what teenage runaways do the world over. She took the first bus for the big city, which in this case happened to be Lagos.

Chioma's first view of Lagos had been the bus terminal: people bustling, running, shouting – all the typical noise of an African city. She made her way to a newsagent and bought a local property magazine. Ike once told her, "Find the rich and you will find work," so she looked up the most expensive rented accommodation she could find listed and took an *okaada* (motorcycle taxi) to the address. She went to the estate management office and within four hours – after all she was polite, pretty and literate – she had found work as a maid.

The compound was full of oil company workers who were mostly, but not exclusively, expatriate. Chioma was working in the house of a Nigerian oil company executive, his wife and children. The man of the house, a Urroba, was rarely present. Chioma found that she and his Hausa wife got on well together, and the children were well behaved. Her duties were not onerous: ironing, cleaning and sometimes riding in the taxi with the children to take them to school. Jamila, the lady of the house, would often come and sit with her while she worked, glad of an intelligent female to talk to and a break from the company of five and seven-year-olds. She did not share Chioma's passion for books, but was more than happy to provide them occasionally, hoping that the influence would rub off on her children and counteract the never-ending stream of TV and video games. Chioma felt that her luck was changing.

She found the work easy and the company pleasant. Somewhere, though, it lurked in her mind that there was something else, something more. This was not her future. It was almost as if there was a snatch of a half-remembered song that eluded her memory, haunting the recesses of her soul just enough to annoy, but never clear enough to be identified.

One day Jamila came home early. She worked part-time and had been given a bonus and some time off; on her way back to the estate she had stopped in at a bookshop and brought Chioma a present. It was one of the classic novels of Nigerian literature; she herself had read it at school and had been surprised to discover that the well-read Chioma had not. She saw it in the window and on impulse bought it for her new friend. Chinua Achebe was himself an Igbo and had single-handedly revolutionised Nigerian literature. Whilst never as prolific or as politically controversial as the executed Ken Saro-Wira, it was Achebe who had opened the doors of African writing in English.

Jamila was pleased with her purchase. She liked Chioma and, whilst she was not particularly bookish herself, she had enjoyed Achebe at school and was happy at the thought that she could introduce something new to her friend. But she could never imagine the effect it was going to have on Chioma. The novel was entitled *Things Fall Apart*. And that was exactly what happened to Chioma.

Chinua's characters are Igbos clinging to a disappearing culture under threat from the incoming white man, with his religion plucked from the harsh deserts of Arabia and then modified over centuries to justify his own supremacy. If God created man in his own image, the religion that the English brought to Africa was created in the image of man. Forged at first in the repressive homoerotic confines of the Pauline traditions of the Vatican state, in more recent years it had been honed with scalpel-like sharpness on the equally homoerotic playing fields of Eton. The Igbo villages of Chinua's world are relentlessly crushed beneath the wheels of history. Like an African Thomas Hardy or a malevolent deity, he creates his rural characters, breathes life into them and then allows fate to slowly and inevitably drive them into oblivion.

Chinua's prose immediately captivated Chioma: he was speaking to her of her own peoples, her own traditions, using words that only their people new. He was removing the sense of inferiority: the lush green jungles of Africa could produce literature as legitimately as the windswept Yorkshire Moors. She read eagerly, but the author did not ever mention the truth. The heritage that she had been brought up to treasure, that she had learnt at her mother's knee. Never once did he mention Israel. His Igbos were simple Africans, believing in false gods, living in an age of ignorance, no better than the Hausas, those descendants of the Arabs, with their tendency to violence and superstition. The Biafran War had been a recent memory, an open wound to Chioma's parents; they had never allowed a spirit of reconciliation to interfere with their children's education.

It was whilst she was suffering this unexpected assault on everything upon which her identity had been founded that she suffered the fate that afflicts attractive female domestics the world over. Jamila's husband made a pass at her. Her encounter with the works of Chinua Achebe had already left Chioma feeling uncomfortable; it had also revived in her a need to know, that dangerous itch that Miss Ndum had awakened in her, before Ike dashed the chalice from her lips. Now, the unwelcome – though not entirely unexpected – advances of Jamila's husband were all the push she needed. Jamila was, and had been, a good friend to her as well as a considerate employer, and Chioma wished no ill to her friend. So she said nothing, hoping against hope that Jamila's husband's actions were an aberration, a moment's insanity, the behaviour of a man under stress, and that her removal from the foyer would heal any underlying rifts in their marriage. Jamila, she knew, would not survive separation: the shame of divorce would be more than she could bear and Chioma suspected that Jamila was already over-dependent on the whisky and sodas that she sipped so elegantly every evening and sometimes in the afternoon.

So once again the nomad in her soul triumphed. Without a word to her friend, she packed her small bag and left.

Bereft of home, company and even identity, she was now no longer even able to blame her blood. Achebe had stripped her of that solace.

And this was when Azzi came into her life. A gaunt, gentle, intense young man, he was full of ideas and ambitions – that he would one day own his own car and a house. Chioma had already seen such things, but Azzi's naive enthusiasm was inspiring and touching, and he was not Igbo. At that moment it was important. Being Igbo had brought her nothing but shame and disappointment, and an Igbo writer had destroyed the very beliefs on which her identity had been founded.

Their meeting was unspectacular. After leaving Jamila's, Chioma did not want to return to domestic work, for in a family there were too many emotional pitfalls. She had some money saved up, and after some wandering she found a room not far from the Adamac Yard in Port Harcourt. She then managed to find employment, washing overalls and work clothes outside one of the shipyards. Every evening she would wait outside the rusting plate-steel gates and the single workmen would hand her their overalls as they walked out. She would stay up all night washing their clothes and return them damp but clean in the morning. She would then go to work in the houses of one or two women, again washing clothes, until she finally hit her bed at midday.

Azzi had been one of her first customers as she stood touting for business outside the gates. She was pretty and had an engaging smile, so he told his friends about her, and then regretted it. He would collect the overalls from his friends and bring her more and more work.

Their courtship was uneventful and marriage ensued several months later. They had both been young and lonely, and were happier for it.

They moved into a room slightly bigger than the room in which Azzi had originally lodged, in a slightly nicer compound. Azzi worked hard and after a while, they purchased some land not far from the yard. Then, slowly, brick by brick, they started to build on it, using anything they could find, from bricks to milk crates. The birth of Chidi brought happiness and respectability: they looked like a family. Then the price of oil went up and George Bush invaded Iraq. Oil prices soared and the fires of capitalism needed to be fed. The war machine needed fuel, and so everything they owned was crushed beneath the blades of a bulldozer sent by the federal government.

Chapter Seven

Harrison, with time, learnt to live in his unresponsive body, not that he had a lot of choice. It was a learning process, a readjustment of the senses, a review of perspective and a new type of comprehension. He learnt, as a result, to find pleasure in unexpected details. Small things that previously would have passed by unnoticed now fascinated him, and he took whatever comfort and stimulation became available and was grateful for it. He found a measure of peace within himself; the gradual improvements in his mobility held less importance to him as his mind rediscovered deeper satisfactions, long forgotten. The sonorous sound of Chioma's voice as she read to him from the Old Testament every day had begun to convey far more to him than the mere words that she read so beautifully. He lived alongside her and experienced the highs and lows, the pleasure she took in her son, her anguish over his future; he felt the passion of her tortured soul through her cadence and intonation for five years. Sometimes, when Sarah was out, Chioma would cross herself and confess to him; she would tell strange tales of Chukwu, the Igbo name for the one true God that she had learnt as a child. She would tell him of how she had had Chidi circumcised, in the Igbo manner, without telling her husband. She told him of the exodus of her people, as she had been taught it by her mamma, and of the destruction of her faith by Chinua Achebe and his clever little book. She told him how she had hated Chukwu (God) for lying to her all these years – and how she was asking for forgiveness, wanted God to take her back.

As the years passed, Harrison's slow progress allowed him to respond in small ways that seemed to comfort her. As his responses developed so did her openness; she talked more and more about her fears for her son and her doubts about her faith. Despite his confinement and the singularity of his congregation, there were times when Harrison felt himself responding to the intimacy of that sonorous voice with an empathy he had never previously known. He came to believe that being struck down had rendered him a far more sensitive and intuitive pastor than he had ever been as an active, able-bodied man. His own faith had suffered trials and tribulations, but it had only been in the searing heat of the vision granted him that he had felt with absolute certainty the hand of the deity whom he had served for most of his adult life. Now that his world was defined by the walls of his home and the pictures painted of the outside world by Sarah and Chioma, he realised the paucity of his own knowledge of even his immediate surroundings. His ignorance of his country pained him as much as the frustration of his immobility, compounding the sense of missed opportunities. He wished with a desperate futility that he had been less blinded by the prejudice of his own traditions, and had, whilst he still had the power of mobility, learnt more about the rich culture of his neighbours. He was now brought to confront through his own ignorance the fact that the legacy of Biafra remained hanging heavily over the region and indeed had formed many of his own perspectives. Even though he would never have supported any kind of prejudice himself, the Igbo were still a separate entity, almost a nation within a nation, occupying the same time and space but somehow existing almost entirely separately. Whilst it was true that they seemed to own most of the shops and businesses, he now saw that commercial transactions had been about the only contact he had ever had with them.

As the years slid almost unnoticed from one to the next, Harrison found himself no longer confined to the sofa and would spend most of his days in the shade of the porch, back in his favourite chair outside the house. He could even walk short distances aided by Sarah and Chioma. He had regained mobility in his right arm but not his left. The right side of his face too was mobile and, though he could not speak coherently without great effort, he could at least indicate pleasure and discomfort.

Not far from the compound that had so unexpectedly become her home, Chioma had discovered an elderly Igbo man from Anambra state. He ran a small trading post, supplying the port community with items purchased by his sons in Onitcha market and delivered on a monthly basis. Uchendu looked forward to Chioma's visits; he was an elderly man, apart from the monthly visits by one or other of his sons, he rarely had the opportunity to speak Igbo. That Chioma was pretty made the visits that much more pleasant, but it was only when one day she mentioned Chinua Achebe that the relationship progressed beyond mere formalities and the simple pleasure that an old man might derive from the presence of a pretty young girl.

It was a great pleasure to him that she knew something of the 'old ways', as he liked to call them. She seemed to have a deep affection for traditions that seemed to have offered so little to his own children, who were, as far as he could see, more interested in the glitz, violence and fantasy of American television than anything Nigeria had to offer. It was many years since he had been taught by his father of the eternal struggle between Chukwu and Agbara, the spirit struggling to wrest control of the Uwa, the visible universe.

It was a grey and humid Friday, like so many days in Port Harcourt, when the greyness of the sky melted into the grim buildings and the grime smeared itself across the garden of Africa, as if Lowry had taken the colours of his palette and attempted to imitate the violence of Van Gough's brushwork, and then in frustration had thrown a bucket of water over the easel and let the greys merge in defeat. Port Harcourt, though, had become almost invisible to Uchendu, who, over the years, had found less and less cause to leave the comfort of his shop. This particular Friday he had been expecting a visit from his young friend, who would appear like a slash of light, a vibrant colour daubed beneath the darkling skies. It had become a ritual: she would always buy palm oil and *garri* from him. They both knew that she could buy it closer to home, but they shared the pleasure of speaking in their own language. At the back of what he laughingly called his 'emporium', Uchendu had his special room, where he would sit quietly when there were no customers. A mirror, mounted by the door, allowed him to see if business (or, as he put it, 'hot bread') was approaching. Today he had placed a large pot of heated water on the low table and a couple of little sachets of Lipton's on a plate beside them. Two tall glasses and a box of sugar awaited the arrival of his young friend.

In Chioma he had found an intelligent and thoughtful student. Gradually, they had explored each other's knowledge of their culture and history, each sizing up the other before laying bare their soul. It had been a long, slow, but deeply enjoyable process, and now it had arrived at a crucial moment, one that Uchendu had decided he could not forego. He was not a young man, and this might be his last chance to do good, to earn real credit with his God and his ancestors before he died. He did not, nor ever had believed in chance. Chioma had come into his life for a reason: he had a message, or a duty, brought about by the burden of knowledge, that he must discharge.

He had been thinking about this meeting for some time. He enjoyed discussing Igbo history, the old systems of jurisprudence, the legends of intervention by affronted ancestors. These things were after all public knowledge: *Nollywood* was full of tales of vengeful ancestors and village feuds amongst the Igbo. Chioma, however, had kept returning to a theme that was clearly bothering her. That she knew anything of the subject at all told him a lot about her family background; he had gained the impression that it was largely her mother who had taught her these things. That

75

was enough, it was a theme dear to his heart, and it tortured him that his sons had shown no interest in the subject.

The old man raised himself from his seat. There was still time, she would be another few minutes. He left his special room and went back into the small, neat house behind the shop. A few moments later he returned bearing a seven-pronged candelabra, which he placed carefully on the small table that formed the centrepiece of the room. He smoothed out the chequered plastic tablecloth that had been slightly disturbed by the heavy foot of the candelabra and brushed an imagery speck of dust off the seventh arm of the immaculately clean icon. He sat back and surveyed it, and felt strange: his mouth was desperately dry, yet his eyes were becoming moist. How was that possible, he wondered? He sat still, waiting, the faint sounds of the city barely audible except for the occasional car horn. He wondered if she would think it rude of him if he started the tea before she arrived.

As if released by the grey humidity of the outside world, the colour that was Chioma glided into the room, then collapsed into the old armchair that had recently become so familiar and comforting, which they both now thought of as her seat. The total contrast in the two actions struck Uchendu immediately: the smooth control of her graceful entrance and then, like a marionette whose puppeteer had suddenly lost interest, her flopping on to his chair, just a simple Igbo woman fresh from the village. Seated, her almost intimidating beauty, though still evident, was somehow less oppressive: the edges were softened and the gleaming smile that so often had made the hair on the old man's neck stand on end was the sloppy, almost embarrassed smile of a tired daughter before a much-loved father. She intrigued him. If only he had been forty years younger, he thought – what a woman to have had by his side. With such a woman he could have done anything, he would not have finished his days in a dusty old store selling cassava. It was true that he was in fact a wealthy man, but had been a widower for as long as he cared to remember, and the mother of his sons was now just a warm glow in a distant past. His children had their own lives, so he did the only thing he knew: he ran his business. It filled his days, kept him in contact with people, and now it had brought this dazzling light to his fading eyes.

Chioma took a deep breath and looked around, as if assuring herself that nothing in her secret sanctuary had changed. Her eyes alighted briefly on the candelabra on the table; there was a slight movement of her eyebrows as she acknowledged it.

"How far oh Ogaaa di? *Olee ka i mere?*"

"*Dő mma nn.* I am fine. You are welcome."

She reached over the low table and started to prepare the tea, selecting a bag and lowering it into the glass, then carefully pouring the hot water. She liked doing little things for the old man. It was strange, she thought. Her whole life was spent taking care of Harrison, a man of similar age, and she had become fond of her charge, but here she found doing even simple things for Uchendu was almost therapeutic.

They sat for a moment in silence, allowing the hot liquid to do its job. Chioma noticed that Uchendu was sitting with what appeared to be a ram's horn across his lap. On the table, near the candles, was a short, delicately engraved rod that looked to her as if it were made of bronze, almost like a small ceremonial baton.

"So you goin' to tell me what is dis t'ing? I t'ink I do savy oh. Dis ting is from Israel and Father Jacob, no?"

Uchendu switched into Igbo; broken English was not, he felt, a suitable language for such noble matters.

"Yes, my daughter, you are right. I know you have been wanting to ask me about our history and now I will tell you what little I know." He paused and looked at her thoughtfully, then, taking a deep breath, he continued. "Listen, my child, we bear a great heritage and a great burden. You are right, it is a tree of the seven fathers of Israel. Jacob, may he feel the mercy of Chukwu, was one of them, and was, as you know, the father of the twelve tribes. Of the sons of Father Jacob the fifth was Zebulun and he begat all our ancestors, may they watch over us with pleasure, because it is said that his son, named Zevulunu, on the advice of a certain Levite or priest, married a woman from Oji who was herself from the Tribe of Judah, and from this union was born Ozubulu Ben-Zebulunu, the father of all the modern Igbos. It has been passed down by our ancestors from generation to generation that this ancestor, Ozubulu, did beget four male children who became the fathers of the true Igbo regions."

The old man paused and rearranged himself on his chair. He fingered the ram's horn in his lap. Then, still looking at the horn, almost as if it was dictating to him, his brow furrowed with concentration and he continued.

"Now, this is the part that concerns us directly, so please be patient with me that I tell it right. One of these four sons was named Amakwa, from whom your mother's and my blood runs, and they settled in Neni in what is now Anambra. It is from them that we inherited our trading traditions, and it was they that first built the great markets of Onitsha. Of the others I am ashamed to say I know little; one of the sons was I think called Egbema, and it is he who fathered the Egbema Ugwuta clan in Imo State and the Ohaji Egbema clan in Israel, but more than that of the sons of Ozubulu ben-Zebulunu I cannot tell."

Chioma regarded the old man in silence. His eyes were rimmed with tears; pride in his heritage and shame at his ignorance mingled in damp trails on his cheeks. She reached into the sleeve of her lace and drew out a small embroidered handkerchief, with which she gently wiped the tears from his face.

"Thank you, Papa," she said quietly.

"There is more my child, much, much more, but I am an old man, my memory is not all that it should be, and our people have forgotten much that was important and replaced it with pagan nonsense. The woman from Oji who was descended from the

Tribe of Judah, I recall being taught that she was Ndiigbo of the line of Afra, the descendants of Abraham by Ketrah, his wife after Hagar and Sarah. So the blood in us is strong. It comes twice from Abraham; it is our blessing and our curse."

Chioma sat in silence. Slowly absorbing what she had heard, unbending the heresies of Chinua Achebe from her consciousness, and praying that the spirit of her mother might forgive her for having doubted her teaching.

She stood up – it would be kind to leave the old man for a moment. She picked up the painted steel jug that he used for hot water and carried it through to his little kitchen. She lit the stove and waited for the water to boil. She did not hurry with the water; she needed to think and wanted to give Uchendu time to compose himself.

When she did return to the room, the old man was looking much more relaxed and there was little trace of the moisture in his eyes. She prepared him another glass of sweet tea. He smiled at her, an ageless smile.

"Sit, my young friend, and have patience with a foolish old man, it is many years since I have spoken of such things. But it gives me pleasure and it is good for my soul, may our ancestors be pleased with me!"

He took a long swig of his tea. Chioma worried that he would scald himself, but he wiped his mouth on the back of his hand.

"Ah, that's better, now where was I?" He paused.

"Amakwa?" Chioma suggested.

"You know the Old Testament well I think?"

He did not wait long enough for her to reply, though her mind leapt back to the crippled Harrison.

"Has it never struck you the number of Igbo words we find in the Old Book? The whole thing begins with an Igbo word, 'Genesis' – remember, child, our ancient ancestors did not write, so these stories were passed down orally – and what do we say to someone in Igbo when they are going to tell us a long story? 'Jee *n'isi isi*: start from the beginning' and when we have heard that story and do not wish to forget it we say, '*Detuoro nu mu ya:* write it down for me.' Which over the years has become 'Deuteronomy'."

He paused for her to absorb his words. "And even our name, 'Igbo', is it not strikingly close to 'Hebrew'?"

This she had heard before.

"Who else but us and the other acknowledged children of Abraham circumcised in the first eight days?"

Chioma sat back in her chair. The old man was clearly excited now, it was many years since he had had a chance to discuss such things.

"You see, my dear, it is us alone who carry the true bloodlines of the patriarchs, and this is where it all began, here in Africa. It was here that Eve betrayed the trust of God, and yet the stories have been hijacked by our Oiybo descendents, who now inhabit the Holy Land. Really, though, the Arabs built no pyramids, it was the Nubians, our black brothers. Abraham himself was Eboan, a black man, the father of the Igbo!"

Uchendu was animated by his excitement; he could barely sit in his chair. Chioma was enthralled, it was true, by the old man's speech and enthusiasm, but she was worried that he might make himself ill and despite his obvious passion and conviction, she was not absolutely convinced.

"Please, Papa, calm yourself. I need to think."

Uchendu stopped. "I understand it's a lot to take in. And please forgive an old man for getting so excited, it is many years since one of our kind has taken an interest in our history, and if they only understood it, our future."

"But Papa, if all this is true, why?" She was struggling for words. "Just look around us, Papa, is this the Promised Land? Are we the chosen people? Is this filth in which we live our reward?"

"Alas, yes, my daughter, it is! For our ancestors committed a

80

great sin. 'Let the sins of the fathers be visited upon the sons' – and so it has been. It was us that broke the covenant, not God."

He paused for breath.

"I know what you are thinking, my child; you look around, you see the corruption, the poverty, the evil. It was our people who made the golden calf at the foot of Mount Sinai, the sin has been bred out of our cousins the white Jews, they are so far from the blood line of Abraham that they are without sin, and our grandchildren the white men, they know little of all this; they are but infants on the face of the earth, newcomers. What do they know of all this but fragments of legends we have handed down to them?"

Uchendu paused again, and wiped his brow with a neatly folded handkerchief.

"My daughter, when the temple was destroyed, our people were scattered. They lost their faith in the one true God and they ran from their lands. Only the Igbo returned to where it all began, it was only our ancestors who in atonement for their sins redeemed themselves by coming back to Africa."

Chioma felt doubtful.

"Child, think of the Igbo tradition. You will remember I am sure – your mamma will have taught you – that it is against our ancient tribal law to speak badly of a spirit. We have always been taught that those of our ancestors who lived well, died in honourable ways, were buried correctly according to the traditions that we have followed since Adam our father left the Garden of Eden. Those ancestors, and only those ancestors, live in one of the worlds of the dead, those worlds that are mirrors of the world of the living. But there is between us and God an unsettled skull. The debts of our ancestors must be paid. In every generation we are given the means to rectify our situation, to pay the debt, and still we squander them. Nigeria should be one of the richest countries in the world, our people are amongst the most ancient, yet our brothers and sisters are starving. Chukwu has given us all we need, but we have not the eyes or the faith to see it."

"It is so true Papa, we have everything and nothing. So where are our ancestors in our time of need?"

"They are here, my child, they are here! Are you not familiar with the term *'ndichie'* – 'those who return'?"

Chapter Eight

Sally had been forced to revisit her understanding of capitalism. When they first arrived in Lagos, she saw poverty which, even to a Palestinian, was shocking: the gross differences in income and quality of life, the expressions on the faces of the street children that reminded her painfully of Gaza. Then she saw Mo's company flat. Hot and cold running water, a real, deep bath, the huge hardwood table – her soul was torn in two between the conscience of the activist and the desires of the woman. It was true that this was all paid for by an exploitative, capitalist neo-imperialist American oil company that was quite clearly racist, almost certainly misogynist, and undoubtedly funded by fortunes made on the back of the slave trade. Then she looked at little Houda sitting on the huge white leather sofa, smiling quietly as Mickey and Minnie flicked across the TV's plasma screen. She thought of the same little girl standing on a pile of rubble as a heavy machine gun cut her mother in two. For Houda's sake, then, she told herself without much conviction, she would learn to live with it. She poured Houda an orange juice (product of Israel, she noticed), then retired to the bathroom.

The flat was situated in a large well-guarded compound; Mo had dropped them off and then left for the market – there was little in the way of provisions in the apartment. He had been in Gaza for three weeks and when he was in Lagos he had a bachelor's approach to housekeeping; urgent supplies were required. Sally had decided that the bathroom would be the place to reflect: hot baths were a guilty pleasure. But when she saw the number of bottles lined up on the side of the bath she was stung with sudden jealousy – was there another woman here?

She immediately embarked on a search of the wardrobes. There was no sign of any female influence except a photograph of Mo's mother; after all, he was still a Palestinian. She returned to the bathroom and started to run the bath. There she began a more thorough examination of the plethora of bottles and potions. They all bore the same legend, which she was enough of a linguist to read: 'pour homme'. She laughed quietly at herself, then decided to teach him a lesson and emptied most of them into the bath. *What a pampered bourgeois little tart he is!* she thought to herself as she lowered herself into the steaming water. She lay still, the excessive bubbles almost over her head and spilling down on the floor, and felt her principles being slowly washed away. *It is nice being rich,* she thought. *I'll do it for the little girl's sake.* But she knew that wasn't strictly true either.

Hanging on the back of the bathroom door was a thick white towel. She wrapped herself in it and padded through to the salon where Houda was still transfixed by the way Mickey's voice seemed to come from all over the place through the surround-sound system. She went back to the fridge: chocolate. She took the chocolate and went and sat down with Houda.

By the time Mo got back two hours later, the bourgeoisification of Sally was complete. The two girls were sitting next to each other on the floor, engrossed in the adventures of Pluto, with chocolate smeared about their mouths, oblivious to the world. Mo smiled to himself; he still wasn't quite sure what he had got himself into, but he thought he was going to like it anyway. His mother had always been nagging him to get married and, while he didn't think Sally was quite the sort of girl his mother would had in mind, Mo, as many sons did, frequently underestimated his mother's intuition.

Chapter Nine

"You know ah still young for take in anodder bikin, look at my girl my Terry. Because my daughter is big don't go stop me for born anodder one. It don't mean ah'm all dried up."

Azzi looked over the table at Amanda, who was busying herself with the stove. It is unusually circumspect for Amanda, he had thought. She was, in his experience, generally more direct than that. For a moment his mind leapt back across the years: Chioma's slender form and quiet beauty were so different from Amanda's larger-than-life personality and battleship proportions. *Chioma,* he thought, *had been almost reed-like.* She would bend and sway in the breeze, offering little resistance to passing tempests, but would always uncoil having weathered the storm. Amanda was an altogether different story; if the door wouldn't open she would walk straight through the wall.

He remembered how much his own mamma had treasured him – he had learnt as he grew up that he had had many brothers and sisters, all of them stillborn. He had passed the term of Chioma's pregnancy in abject terror lest the curse be revisited upon him; bad blood flowed in his mamma's veins, he had been told by many – including his own grandmother.

There was warm bread on the table and a bowl of olive oil. He tore a lump out of the bread and dipped it in the liquid. It was thick and golden extra virgin oil, a little treat that his exalted salary allowed him. He had learnt the habit from an Egyptian chief engineer aboard one of the barges they had been supporting, and watched the oil drip slowly off the bread, causing heavy ripples in the bowl. He remembered the engineer teaching him about olive oil, spending hours talking about the consistency. It was possible, he had assured Azzi, to ascertain the quality of the oil by the speed with which it dripped from the bread and the size of the droplets. The engineer had dreamt of one day retiring to his father's olive groves, giving up the sea and leaving the heaving streets of Alexandria for a quieter life. It was, Azzi suspected, a dream, and would always remain as such. He watched as a golden droplet formed beneath his morsel of bread. He squeezed the bread slightly and watched the drop swell till its weight was too much and it fell back to the bowl. *Deep down,* he thought, *maybe that's what we all want, to go home to our own kind?* He thought about the engineer and his unrealisable dream. *We need our dreams,* he thought, but did he, Azzi, *have* a dream? What did he really want?

Another drop of oil was beginning to form beneath the morsel of bread. He looked up. Amanda was watching him. Her posture was stern, her hands rested upon her wide hips and there was a detectable arch to her eyebrows, but when she spoke there was a softness to her voice that took Azzi by surprise, and turned the words that could so well have been a reprimand into an expression of concern.

"You didn't hear a word ah said, did you?"

"Yes, I did. I was listening, honestly. I just…" His voice tailed away, the sentence and the sentiment remaining unfinished. There was a lump in his throat.

Amanda walked over to the table and sat down. She brushed her hands on her apron.

"Now, stop playing with your food, get it down you and tell me what's vexin' you."

The words were strong, as was the tone, but the work-hardened hand with which she reached out and held the empty hand that had been resting idly on the table seemed to be full of warmth and gentleness.

Azzi swallowed his bread. The action was a bit too strong and his eyes a bit too moist.

"You still missin' your bikin boy oh?"

"It's been a long time I did miss my bikin."

"Ah knows, say it no' easy for you, but me an' you if we stay togedder can make one family. It's never too late, we're no so young again now it's true oh, but we can make up for lost time no? We can pick up where we left off all those years ago, if you had only been a more grown up ah wouldn'y have had to shoot all those stones at you and we be havin' a nice big family all ready oh!"

Azzi turned his hand over slowly so that it fitted into hers, and squeezed it gently. He looked at her; there was a certain beauty about her face – perhaps handsome more than beautiful – and she loved him, had always loved him, since he was a child. The stones thrown from the roadside were still bouncing off him, but at least he now knew what they meant.

"Shine your eyes Mr Azzi, you has a woman dat loves you like no odda woman can, you 'as a good job like you never did dream o' havin', oh an you has money in yo' pocket an ah never took a single naira from you 'cause ah has my bar an ah don't be needin' yo' money Azzi. Ah just needs you, and ah needs yo' bikin, ah need to feel somt'in' livin' inside me, make me a proper woman. Terry she be a good girl but she ain't never had no proper papa. An ah want you Azzi to gi'me the baby you should ha' gi'n me years ago. Let me tell you Azzi, ah was nine years old when ah knew ah wanted yo' baby."

Her hand gripped Azzi's tightly; the strength in her fingers was phenomenal. He looked across the table at her, and as he did so he felt the intensity of the emotion that was gripping Amanda's features. The pain and loneliness of the stone-throwing little girl, the sadness and compassion of the grown woman, seemed to reach out to him from some forgotten back road of childhood and he suddenly realised how absorbed in himself he had been, and felt guilty. He knew that despite her totally uninhibited and indeed often shocking forthrightness, this sort of emotional nudity was rare for Amanda and it did not come easily to her.

Her display of emotion was infectious. Azzi stood up and walked round the table. He put his arms about her and she squeezed him like a bear.

"Ah love you Azzi, ah really love you. You savy dat ah ain't never said dat an' meant it to no odda man Azzi."

He held her tightly to his breast. He could feel this strong woman collapsing in his arms. She looked up at him. Her face was streaked with tears.

"I know," he said softly, stroking her hair. "I know." And he realised that he too was crying.

They sat clasped together for some time, feeling the warmth from each other's bodies and taking comfort in their shared tears.

That was how they were when Teresa walked into the room. She smiled to herself and then backed quietly out.

Chapter Ten

Despite the flawless blackness of her skin, Chioma seemed to Uchendu to fill the room with light. When she left it was as if a shadow fell across his soul.

And out of the darkness came light, he mused to himself.

He could hear her in his little kitchen, washing up the tea service and singing quietly to herself. He enjoyed her company; the house and shop seemed full of life when she was present. Even though she said so little, her gentle personality seemed to seep into even the darkest corners of the building. He wondered whether or not he was doing the right thing in telling her these things; after all, the world was now a changed place, she had her own battles to face, the daily chores of putting food on the table, of educating her young son to survive in a hostile world. Should he really be burdening her with these stories and the implied responsibilities they carried with them? Maybe, in the final analysis, they were no more than that. Perhaps his sons were right. "Would it be better if these things were left to die with the older generation?"

Uchendu was thus musing, staring vaguely at the candelabra on the table, when he sensed Chioma returning to the room.

She sat down opposite him again. The lace she was wearing was a rich green and dark blue; it was tightly wrapped about her, and in the shadows of the room it seemed to blend into her. Uchendu looked at her closely. *There is,* he always thought, *something unearthly about her.* He had of course heard stories of great Igbo queens of the past – they must have looked something like Chioma. She smiled at him as she rearranged the fabric of her lace more comfortably. A slight rustling sound. When she smiled he felt something in himself being drawn towards her, and could not help but smile back.

"I think I should go home," she said.

Uchendu felt the light fade. "But you have only just arrived! Please humour a lonely old man and stay for another cup of this Lipton's, and I will tell your more of the old ways." His voice, he knew, was almost pleading.

She laughed. "No, I meant I think I must go back to Igbo land. Back to Onitsha. It is not right that my son is educated without his history, without his heritage. You know, Papa, my mamma used to say, 'If you neglect the pot, it boils over and extinguishes the fire'. My son has rights that I grew up without fully knowing. I want Chidi to know about all this. Would you mind if I bring him to see you sometime? Perhaps you could help teach him Igbo and something of our people's history."

Amanda's pregnancy was a major catalyst in Azzi's life. Suddenly, the feelings of transience left him, and his relationship with Amanda was at last truly consummated. He now had every thing he could want, the job, the home, the family; he knew Amanda loved him in a way that Chioma never had. Chioma he had given Chidi, and Chidi's birth had prevented her from loving any other: every ounce of her being was devoted to her son, and any sentiment she had for her husband was founded in her gratitude for having provided enough semen to bring Chidi into her world. Amanda loved him absolutely and had done so for years in his absence, but much as he loved her, he knew that deep down in the hidden recesses of his soul he would never be able to love her as he had loved Chioma.

Throughout the pregnancy, though, Azzi lived in fear. He carried bad blood. His own dear mamma, who had cared for him and raised him, had lost so many children. He himself had lost his own son through his own inability to provide for them.

Even though Azzi tried hard to conceal his discomfort, Amanda knew he was scared. And yet, in general, the household was a happy one. Her pregnancy also brought Azzi and Teresa closer together, and for the first time in her life Amanda felt like the real family mamma she had always wanted be. It hurt her deeply to see Azzi's fears; she knew they were unfounded. The bar would provide a good enough income for both of them if it should happen that Azzi lost his job, not that that seemed likely. More importantly, she had worked for Azzi's mother for most of her childhood and knew the truth about his blood and from whence it came. She had known of the adoption since not long after she had arrived, through an overheard conversation between Sarah's mother and her employer. After all, she had been his mamma's maid for years.

She had gone to the household when she was seven, the youngest child of a large family that was struggling financially. Her parents had put her into service in the hope that she would get a better education than they would have been able to provide themselves. They had, all things considered, done the right thing. She had a stubborn, frequently obtuse personality and, hidden in the chaos of a large, undisciplined household, she would almost certainly have run amok. The more focused existence with Azzi's mamma had instilled in her the discipline that had enabled her to make a success of her bar, and brought the even more notable success of her own daughter's education.

Chapter Eleven

Blinding flashes of lightning mean an impending storm
Nigerian proverb

Aunty Julie is perhaps the most attacked structure in the global petroleum industry outside of Iraq. That is not its only unique feature. Aunty Julie is what is known in the oil industry as a jack-up barge. Basically, it's a floating platform with three legs that can be pushed down on to the seabed to jack the barge up out of the water and create a temporary platform. A few years earlier, in what passes in the oil industry as ancient history, Aunty Julie was jacked up. Then, as a matter of convenience and cost saving, its owners decided that, rather than foot the bill for a new permanent platform, Aunty Julie would fulfil the function, and so, with the signing of a few pieces of paper and some borderline ethical behaviour by the classification societies, she said farewell forever to her sea-going life: the necessary risers and conductors were installed and Aunty Julie was elegantly transformed into a permanent production platform.

The oil company and the engineers congratulated themselves on the money they had saved. Promotions and brown envelopes were handed out, and all seemed well, until the permanent staff aboard Aunty Julie began to notice that drinks poured into glasses did not lie as level as drinks poured elsewhere, and that the glasses started to slide off tables.

The surveyors had neglected to look into the seabed formation where they had pinned down Aunty Julie and she was slowly sinking on one side. It was not long before the incline was noticeable from shore. Many remedial solutions were proposed, but all of them would have entailed the shutdown of production for several weeks at least and, for an installation that was pumping over ten million dollars a day in crude, that was not an option. So there she stayed, sitting like a wedge of blue cheese some 200 metres off a stretch of Nigeria's most beautiful coastline. More significantly, however, Aunty Julie sat at the mouth of a river that serviced one of the poorest and most neglected communities in the country.

It was during the Biafran War that the community belonging to the Ijaw tribal group under the leadership of General Isaac Adaka Boro had, along with many other Niger Deltans, fought alongside the federal government. The war had been fought against the largely Igbo secessionist Biafrans. The Yoruba-dominated federal government had gushed forth promises of a better future, but as soon as the collapse of the Biafrans had been assured Adaka Boro was assassinated by Nigerian federal troops just outside Okrika. With the iconic leader out of the way, the federal government proceeded to systematically crush the region, both economically and militarily. The last thing the federal government wanted was a well-armed, well-disciplined force to turn upon them. The promises were soon forgotten and the oil flowed into bank accounts in Lagos and Abuja.

Captain Lee R. W. James Jr was from Louisiana and his ravined and nicotine-stained face looked like a relief map of the state. He was laying pipe from Aunty Julie to a satellite well with a barge that, anywhere other than Nigeria, would have been condemned as un-seaworthy. Captain Lee had long given up trying to understand. He had spent time in Angola, a country that had been shredded by civil war with a fraction of the oil reserves of Nigeria, and there he had had facilities and safety standards to rival those back home, yet here in the Niger Delta he was laying millions of dollars of pipe with a barge that would have raised eyebrows in a Mississippi swamp.

Captain Lee was a chain smoker. Wherever he went he was shrouded by a pall of exhaled smoke to the extent that non-smoking employees used to fight amongst themselves to avoid going into his office, so bad was the smell. Captain Lee was smoking a lot, even by his standards. He was facing a dilemma: his employers had paid their dues to the community and the community was still affording protection, so he was, in theory, safe. And yet things in Nigeria were never quite that straightforward. Aunty Julie had been attacked three times in the last week and a British surveyor and an American 'tool pusher' had been kidnapped. The week before, the security boat had mysteriously suffered a generator failure and blacked out. During the blackout, militants had attacked the vessel and the Nigerian Navy personnel on board had apparently been over powered. The Philippino master had foolishly resisted and been shot; he survived, but would probably never walk again. Two of his crew had met their ends on the edge of that traditional African equaliser, the machete. A large quantity of weapons had been taken from the vessel. The following morning there had been an armed bank robbery in Port Harcourt. The official line was that the same weapons had been used. The federal government always preferred to write off attacks as piracy rather than political militancy, but they weren't fooling anybody.

Captain Lee lit another Marlboro and inhaled as deeply as his tar-caked lungs would allow. From his office window he could see Aunty Julie, her tilted decks deserted. The platform had been blacked out all night; no flare-stacks burnt. All around the field there was silence. Officially the personnel had been evacuated for safety reasons: 'Other pirate attacks might be imminent.' This was not true, as Lee well knew: the local 'community' had withdrawn its 'protection'. Basically, that meant that all workers from that community (which was most of them) had withdrawn their labour and anyone who was not from the community, if they had a healthy fear of machetes, would withdraw their labour too. It was, to all intents and purposes, a strike, although that was not a word that would be used officially, as Nigeria does not enforce protective labour rights, as do more unionised Western countries. The effect, however, was the same: a total stoppage of production. The Obra field had been choked. The Delta community was flexing its muscles. It was a dangerous game they were playing; if they did nothing, their region would continue to be exploited; too much, and their wives and children would find out exactly how much human rights were worth compared to the price of oil. The army did not waste time with machetes, and the Western democracies that so loudly trumpeted civil rights were known to grow strangely silent on the subject when the precious supply of oil was threatened.

Captain Lee felt the weight of his responsibility; it was not clear what was expected of him. Should he stop work voluntarily? In sympathy? That was certainly not the way his employers and shareholders would see it, but they were thousands of miles away on the golf courses of Miami, not bobbing up and down on a rusty old lay barge a short canoe ride from an enraged and heavily-armed militant community. The majority of his riggers were local hire; he had had no choice, the community dictated whom he could and could not employ. They were largely inexperienced, and that deficiency had already led to one fatality and a mutilated arm in otherwise avoidable accidents. This, however, did not seem to faze the community leaders: as long as his employees came from the right villages there was no problem. Unionism in the Delta state had not evolved beyond the right to be employed; safety and conditions were not seen as an issue. The reality of the situation, as Lee well knew, was a scam, or a '419' as the locals would call it. The Council of Chiefs collected a subscription from every man who worked on the field, and lived well on those subscriptions; they sold the labour of their villagers with no regard whatsoever to their welfare. The parallels with slavery were not lost on Captain Lee, who had grown up in a town where the Ku Klux Klan was as respected as the Rotary Club (in fact the two organisations were virtually indistinguishable). It was true that, sometimes, after an accident, the community would try and extort compensation from the company, allegedly for the victim's family; in reality, though, the money found its way into the coffers of the Council of Chiefs as compensation for loss of earnings. All this played on the captain's mind as the smoke settled onto his nicotine-stained face and bloodshot eyes, adding another stratum to the tar-caked ravines that characterised his jaundiced complexion.

The barge would soon be running low on potable water and food and, as all the local ports were locked down by the industrial action, supplies would be hard to come by. One supply boat had left Port Harcourt with food, fuel and water on board for the barge, but not long after it had sailed it emerged that the captain and crew of the supply boat had not been paid for six months, so they had simply commandeered their cargo and had sold it.

As Captain Lee ruminated, the new supply-boat-cum-anchor-handler, the MV *Aberystwyth*, lay at anchor some 200 metres away. She, too, was running low on fuel and potable water, and was riding high, bobbing like a cork in the long swell. Azzi had the bridge; his mentor and friend Capt. Evans was down below trying to sleep.

The small boats came out of the river mouth at an incredible speed. It was true: they were not much different from the boats that were regularly seen fishing in the oil fields, but the fibreglass hulls and the addition of 115 horsepower engines hurled them over the rolling swell. They swarmed over the sparkling surface of the ocean like a cloud of long black insects. Azzi had no doubt about what was coming; even without the aid of his binoculars, he could see the AK47s (Communism's only lasting gift to Africa) and the sun glinting gently on the machetes as the bows of the canoes lifted smoothly over the swell. After seeing the weaponry, the black, white and red flags that adorned the boats seemed an unnecessary statement of the occupants' intent.

The Nimbe community in Bayalsa State is one of the most militant of all the Ijaw Niger Deltan communities. They live along the rivers, their infrastructure is minimal (which makes them a difficult foe to attack), and they have an armoury that makes the national army think twice.

Labo was a thickset young man. He had been involved in violence before, but mostly nothing more than inter-village squabbles. Because of his size (and perceived lack of intelligence) the community leaders had frequently used him to enforce local debts. Although this rarely amounted to more than the giving of a beating, he had been shot once, and this shooting began the chain of events that led to his being in the boat that sunny morning.

It all started when the elders sent the strong arm of local law to retrieve a sum of money owed by a young man for whom they had found work. The youth had decided that, as he had only had one month's work out of the arrangement instead of the anticipated two, he would thus only pay half the agreed 100 000 naira. This did not sit well with the Council of Chiefs, and a polite request for payment was sent to the village. When this did not meet with the desired response, Labo and his colleagues were dispatched to retrieve the money and make an example. The young man was not to be found, so they burnt down the family home. As they returned to the speedboat in which they had come, someone, probably the missing young man, opened fire on them with an automatic weapon. Labo was hit in the leg and the bullet passed right through his calf.

In the hours that followed, every man, woman and child was killed, the village burnt to the ground and effectively wiped off the map. The Council of Chiefs expressed concern that the boys might have 'slightly over-reacted', but no direct action was taken.

Labo was, however, quietly pinpointed as one of the instigators of the excess and he gradually found himself being marginalised. He was perceptive enough to realise that things could eventually turn against him and so, when the opportunity arose, he retreated into the bush and joined the militants.

Now he was sitting in the front of the canoe as the boat skittered over the long swell, his own AK47 clasped in his hands. His blood was full of the homemade *Kai Kai*, which was strong enough to run an outboard, and his nervous system pulsed with his first ever taste of crack cocaine. Like everyone else in the boat, he was dressed in an assortment of rags, red, white and black, and his face was smeared with white powdered clay and earth from the sacred land of the Delta. He was protected by the gods of the land and, more importantly, the Owuamapu or *Mammi Water* (mermaids) of the creek.

The barge filled his vision, its eight anchor wires stretched out like a spider's legs slicing in and out of the water as the swell passed beneath the boat. Hanging off one of the anchors was a supply boat. No one appeared to be on deck. She just pitched gently in the swell.

Mo was in the engineer's office of the barge, staring blankly at an *auto-cad* presentation that had frankly lost his interest. He wondered whether anyone ever read his carefully prepared reports. He suspected that if, at the end of the job, the valves were opened and the oil flowed, nobody really cared how the pipes had been laid, or even where they were. It was fast money for a few and hard, dangerous and underpaid graft for many; graft that frequently resulted in a proliferation of widows and cripples.

A Palestinian childhood teaches many things. One talent essential for survival is the ability to recognise the sounds of incoming munitions. As the first rounds of the heavy, general-purpose machine gun hammered into the sides of the barge, Mo was probably the first to recognise them for what they were, and one of the fastest to react. It proved, however, to be one of the rare occasions in his life when he made absolutely the wrong decision, as he ran straight into captivity.

Azzi had no doubt what was coming. He knew that the militants would take any white man that they could find. He released the automatic brake on the winch that was holding the vessel on to the anchor buoy of the barge, fired up the engines hard astern and watched with relief as the mooring line disappeared through the fairlead into the water.

He swung the boat around and headed for open water. As the vessel started to pick up speed, the first bullets hit the wheelhouse, sending glass flying across the gleaming new instrument panel. Azzi hit the floor as fast as he could. With his right hand he reached up, grabbed the VHF radio set and started to transmit the first Mayday message of his career. The lack of water, which just a few hours ago had been a major worry, was now a blessing: the M.V. *Aberystwyth* surged ahead unencumbered by weight. It also occurred to Azzi that the heightened freeboard might make the vessel harder to board from a canoe.

At that moment, Captain Evans' head appeared through the wheelhouse hatch that led up from the galley. A round ricocheted off the roof supports and caught the old man in the shoulder. Azzi watched his friend and mentor crash to the floor, blood pumping from his shoulder. Azzi ripped off his own shirt and stuffed it over the open wound, with his other hand he felt the back of the captain's shoulder for an exit wound.

There was none. The bullet was lodged inside. Azzi dragged the captain's body towards the wheel so that he could hold the compress in place with his knee, operate the wheel with one hand and the radio with the other. The Mayday message was now also for an urgent helicopter evacuation.

Mo pushed his way through the fire doors towards the stern of the barge, planning to run up the outside stairs to the helideck.

He had previously noticed that there was a space between the roof of the accommodation block and the helicopter landing pad that would make a good hiding space. The reinforcement of the helideck also meant that it was probably the most bulletproof area on the barge. *He had not,* he thought, *survived a Gaza childhood to die from a ricochet in Nigeria.* God's humour was cruel, but not that cruel.

As the thick fire door swung open he realised that God's humour was in fact far more sophisticated than he had previously credited. The man standing in front of him was attired in a parody of Middle Eastern or biblical dress: on his head was a cloth draped like a traditional Arab *kyfaya*; the rest of his body was covered in torn rags of red, white and black cloth. His skin was smeared with white and grey powder, and a huge eye had been drawn about his own left eye. There was nothing in the least biblical, however, about the assault rifle that he rammed into Mo's stomach. That was definitely twentieth-century Eastern European.

Bullets were hammering into the side of the barge, people were shouting, and then, ominously, single shots began to ring out from the deck area. Transfixed as he was by the barrel pointing at his navel, the single shots coming up from the deck drew Mo's blood away from the parts of his body that needed it most. His body felt heavy and cold as he pictured the militants walking the deck, executing the cowering riggers with whom he had spent the last two months on board.

A heavy machine gun opened up on the back deck. There was, as Mo well knew, a dive-spread situated on the stern. Large quads of pure oxygen were stored there to service the decompression chamber. *All it would take* he thought, *is one bullet into the O^2 quad and the entire vessel would be history"* This was definitely not a good place to be.

By now the rag-clad apparition was pushing Mo towards the side of the barge, shouting as they went. Mo looked over the side; a small boat was below him, sporting a ridiculously oversized outboard motor. Three men were already aboard, all similarly dressed – like mud-stained shepherds from a school nativity play – and brandishing automatic weapons. Mo's captor gestured to him to climb down into the boat. Its occupants were also shouting and gesturing. One of them seemed to be telling him to stay put whilst the other was telling him to go down. Mo froze: whatever he did next, he would be disobeying a man with a gun, something that his experience in the West Bank had told him was not a healthy proposition. The boat was about two metres from the barge. The man in the bows was strafing the side of the vessel, trying to manage a heavy machine gun the way Rambo did in the movies, ignoring the bipod on the barrel and holding the gun at hip level while the belt feed dangled into the canoe. The recoil was too much for him and it flung him backwards into the boat. As he fell, bullets sprayed out of control, slamming into the rusty steel superstructure. Mo flung himself to the deck just in time, as the high-calibre rounds smashed into the accommodation block behind him on a trajectory that a few seconds earlier would have taken his head off.

He realised, in panic, that the biggest danger here was being killed by accident; these people did not know what they were doing. Mo had grown up in a culture of guns; he had been around armed and angry men all his life. It was true that the Palestinian militias also had a penchant for public displays of firepower and would discharge rounds liberally into the air. The difference was that they trained endlessly and when they fought (other than amongst themselves) they fought against one of the best-trained, most battle-hardened militaries in the world. The men before him in their rags, being thrown about by their own weapons, would have been ridiculous in his eyes had their incompetence not made them so dangerous. The safest place would be in the boat, and they clearly wanted him down there but were scared of the gap and probably couldn't swim. They were afraid he would disappear under the waves. He vaguely remembered hearing something of this kind from the local riggers – the idea that white men could disappear under the waves.

In the end the decision was made for him. The boat came close alongside and he was pushed from behind. He slid down the side of the barge onto the large Yokohama buoys chained to the side of the hull and into the boat. He was shortly joined by two other white men, one of whom had obviously been off shift been awakened from his sleep by the shooting. This man was in shorts and T-shirt, and the other in overalls and rigger boots. Mo's captor then joined them and the boat backed off, the occupants still pouring rounds indiscriminately into the accommodation block. Mo felt sure there must be casualties.

The boat turned in a surprisingly impressive arc and lifted out of the water as 115 horsepower of Yamaha outboard flung it across the waves. One of the men – Mo thought it was the man who had first captured him but he was not sure in the confusion – leered at Mo and dragged his finger in an unmistakable gesture across his throat before throwing a clear liquid in Mo's face. The liquid seared his eyes. Mo stuffed his hands into his eye sockets in a vain effort to ease the pain. He was pushed down into the wet bottom of the boat, the guns opened up again, hot spent cartridges rained down on him, the smell of cordite was pervasive and he was bounced unmercifully by the movement of the boat as its over-powered engine hurled it over the crests of the long swell. As an engineer, Mo's brain was telling him that these boats were not built to withstand this sort of treatment or handle this much power. He wasn't sure whether capsizing was something he should be wishing for or not. He was now sure these people could not swim.

As the boat containing Mo and his fellow captives pulled away from the barge, Azzi's pursuers gave up the chase. The militants saw their colleagues swerve away, three terrified white faces in the boat; had they continued to follow the supply boat, they would have been embarking on a pursuit alone into deep water. Azzi saw the canoe power away; it seemed unstable as it hit the wake of the straining supply boat. The helmsman throttled through the turbulence, stabilised the craft and then flew back towards the tree-lined coast and the deep mangrove swamps.

Azzi's radio crackled into life: a *medi vac* was on its way. There was suddenly a lot of radio traffic, the airwaves were alive with sit reps, requests for assistance, updates and simple exclamations of relief. Slowly, someone started to take charge: it was the radio room at Aunty Julie. Radio discipline was gradually re-established and people started to switch to other channels, freeing up Channel 16, the international hailing channel. The radio room called Azzi and directed him to bring his casualty to Aunty Julie: the heli-deck was operational – was his casualty fit for a basket transfer to the platform? Azzi replied that it would be best avoided. A few minutes later he was redirected. He was to take his casualty to the recently attacked barge where they too had casualties and the transfer would be easier.

Aboard the barge, Captain Lee was gasping for breath like a fish floundering in the sun. For once his lungs were starved of air, not smoke. His normally yellow face was grey and the ravines were filled with sweat as his body twitched and convulsed, the muscles spasming with the unfamiliar exercise. It was not a bullet that had laid Captain Lee on his back; the stress had been just too much for his nicotine-overloaded coronary system, and after years of abuse it had finally given up.

When the bows of the boat had first hit the side of the barge, Labo had been one of the first up on board, climbing like a demented monkey. He knew he had to make a good impression: this was his first raid, and he hoped that the commander who had been in the canoe with him would be impressed. It was a privilege to go out on the raids. There were men who had been in the camp much longer than him who had never been chosen to go.

Labo had never before set foot on a barge. In fact, he had not been on a vessel much larger than a canoe. There were machines, winches and compressors everywhere. The deck was dominated by two cranes: a fixed crane that was the largest man-made structure he had ever seen and a crawler crane that was not much smaller. There were people running everywhere, mostly Africans, and some yellow people whom he assumed must be Philippino. He had never seen people who looked like this before, but he had been told to leave them, their governments would not pay, they were worth little. There was so much going on that for a moment he was lost; then he heard a weapon open up behind him and there were things to shoot everywhere.

He turned his Kalashnikov on the accommodation block that towered over one end of the barge. Windows exploded as he strafed the peeling white walls. The crawler crane had a huge control cabin, with massive panes of glass that erupted satisfyingly as he turned his weapon towards it. The sun had been shining on the glass and he had not been able to see inside – indeed, he had given it little thought – and he was shocked when an African body flew through the side door and fell twenty feet on to the steel deck below. He felt empowered, he was a god on this steel island of running men; the crack and *Kai Kai* boosted by adrenalin forced his heart to drive the blood even harder though his pulsating arteries. He screamed at the top of his voice, and his lungs seemed to find unlimited air. He had never felt so alive. He looked at the arms that held his gun: bulging muscle-bound with the strips of red cloth that would protect him from bullets and machetes. The commander-in-chief himself had tied them to his arms, giving Labo his own personal blessing.

He ran towards the accommodation block; guns were firing all around him, but none in his direction. It was just like the movies: people were hiding, cowering, running before him. He opened the first door he came to in the side of the large accommodation block. The corridor was dim and it took a few seconds for his eyes to adjust. He had been told about these places: this was where the '*ben aye u*', the white people, lived. He tried the first door he came to. It was locked, and he ran down the corridor banging on all the doors in frustration. All locked. He howled in anger: this was not the way it was supposed to be, he wanted a white, a prisoner of his own so that he too could be a hero.

He knew what to do, he had seen it done in the movies: shoot the lock off. He raised his gun and pointed it at the last door and fired. The thin plywood splintered as the American-made armour-piercing rounds tore their way through. It took longer than he had expected, but eventually the door swung open. He charged through in excitement. He had found one, a white man. Even Labo did not need to look very hard to know that neither the white man nor the African who had shared his cabin would be coming with him. The bullets he had used to open the door had pulverised both of them, and they were now nothing more than a bloody mess the floor. Had he been of a more perceptive or philosophical nature, he might have noticed that their deeply oxygenated blood was mingling, and it was of the same colour. Thinking, though, had never been Labo's forté. The only thing that passed through his brain at this moment was that he had messed up. Adaka Boro himself had said that expatriate workers were not to be harmed. His mission had been to catch them and take them hostage. Make the oil companies pay money for them, make the world's media (not a concept he really understood) listen to the plight of the Niger Deltans. Suddenly he did not feel so god-like anymore. It was not the killing that bothered him, but the disgrace.

He rushed out of the corridor straight into Mo. His luck was changing. He shoved Mo hard with the barrel of his gun, with the level of adrenalin flowing through his veins he would have been incapable of any less brutal manoeuvre. He herded Mo back to the canoe. Had the *ben aye u* seen what had happened? Had this strange-looking white man seen which cabin he had come from? This white might save him from disgrace, but he might also pinpoint him as the killer of white men.

He arrived on deck. He thought about shooting the white man there and then just in case: dead men don't point fingers. Other militants were coming towards him, driving cowering whites before them. It was too late. The whites were loaded into the boat. Labo felt the familiar surge as the canoe rose up on to the plane, the huge Yamaha lifting it clear of the water. Usually it gave him a rush, the same high he had had when they had raped the girls in the village before burning it to the ground. Now, however, Labo felt no exaltation; he was terrified. If the general were to find out, he could only begin to imagine the consequences. He looked back at his prisoner. He tried to look into his eyes: there was nothing there to say that he had seen, no smug sign of knowledge. Labo drew his finger slowly across his throat: a warning. Damn those eyes that were looking back at him! He grabbed a bottle of *kai kai* and threw it in the man's eyes. At the entrance to the villages newcomers were anointed with *kai kai* to prevent them from bringing in evil spirits; perhaps the *kai kai* would remove the sight of evil from his eyes. Labo had never been so scared in his life.

The 'big picture' was anathema to Labo; his vision rarely extended beyond his own immediate physical needs and their immediate gratification. Maslow's pyramid of needs had been based on a being far higher up the emotional evolutionary scale than Labo, with Labo the ghost was not a fluid abstract entity haunting the machine, the ghost had been firmly in the driving seat since Labo's first breath. Now it was in distress, screaming and stamping its feet inside Labo's over-calcified cranium, like a petulant child facing punishment that deep down he knew he deserved. Labo knew that his life had been good. Now he had killed a white man, and if he were found out it might not be good anymore. Distant, abstract notions like morality or the 'cause' were beyond both his intellectual and emotional development. To Labo, 'federal government' was something that you said a lot before words like 'motherfucking' and 'bastards', and it sounded good and made the bosses happy enough to pat you on the back. He had no understanding of what went on in Lagos or Abuja. That since the kidnappings had started, the leadership of MEND had come to an unspoken agreement with 'the bastards from the motherfucking federal government'; that these displays of wrath would invariably end on a peaceful note, with MEND setting the oil workers free unharmed. Niger Deltans would be permitted to air their grievances on the world stage, as long as the oil workers periodically taken hostage were not harmed. A status quo had been established. The leadership of MEND were well aware that if foreign oil workers (especially British or American) started dying in numbers that could not be explained away as accidents, things would change. And MEND could not win an all-out war. They could inflict significant damage on federal troops who tried to come into the creeks, it was true, but no one at MEND headquarters thought seriously that, if it came to war, the federal government would worry about issues such as human rights or collateral damage; the Geneva Convention does not apply to civil war, and is rarely applied to African wars of any kind. The creeks would be carpet-bombed and the militants would be burnt out of their hideouts. There was no census of the creek people, so no one would ever know how many people had died. It would be a hidden genocide and the Ijaw people would, quite simply, cease to exist. Oil money was involved and that brought a lot of international silence, even in a relatively developed country like Iraq. Many of the oil companies operating in the Delta region were American, and the MEND leadership were well aware of the myopic vision of the Statue of Liberty. When it came to it they were African, and there were good reasons why the Statue of Liberty had not been placed in Texas. The presidential failure to sign the Kyoto agreement had so successfully shrouded her in smog that she had trouble seeing beyond her own state, and certainly the only light her torch cast in Africa was the yellow glow of the illegal flare stakes that acidified the once life-giving rain and had introduced asthma to the children of the Delta, as if they didn't already have enough to worry about with malaria, typhoid and malnutrition.

None of this would have been comprehensible to Labo even if anyone had tried to explain it to him. He just knew that whatever was in the mind of that strange white man with African-looking hair might spell glory for him, or disaster. It was in the hands of the gods, and for the first time in his life Labo was not quite sure how much he actually trusted them. He took another swig of *kai kai* and fired his gun into the air. It made him feel better. "Asawanaa?" he shouted.

"Wanaa!" the other militants chorused. "Asiminia?" "Ascee iy aay!"

It was a chant that over the next few weeks was to haunt both the dreams and the waking moments of Mo and his fellow captives.

The boat continued to scream down the coast, hissing as the bows cut through the glassy surface, almost becoming airborne as it crested the ever-present lazy swell that typifies the region. Mo lay huddled on the wet boards, bouncing painfully every time the vessel hit a wave. The muzzle of a gun was pressed into his side, and the man holding it had his finger on the trigger. Mo was terrified that, with the next bounce of the boat, the weapon might accidentally be discharged into his side.

The pain in his eyes was receding and his mind was becoming clearer, more aware of the discomfort of his cramped position. There was sudden activity in the boat. He felt the speed reducing. The gun was removed from his ribs and the man who had been holding it leant forwards and told him to sit up. With some difficulty, Mo straightened up and manoeuvred himself on to one of the bench seats.

It was his first chance to look around. They were still at sea but a long way from the barge. They had travelled along the coastline, and were now bobbing up and down with the motor idling just outside the surf zone. The helmsman was clearly waiting for a lull in the swell to negotiate the potentially traitorous braking waves, many of which had faces of over two metres. He was rearranging the weight distribution in the canoe before running the waves. Mo guessed they were going to try and surf the canoe and ride the wave over the sand bars that were causing the waves to peel elegantly from left to right. In front of them, about twenty metres beyond the breaking waves, there was calm, clear water where the wave energy was dissipated by the tumbling foam. Calm, clear water, and a river mouth: Mo knew well what that meant, he had flown over this region hundreds of times in helicopters, being ferried out to barges and platforms. It meant they were going into the creeks, the endless, unfathomable maze of mangroves.

The helmsman picked his moment and gunned the engine. He perfectly matched the speed of the following wave, then eased off just a fraction. Mo felt the stern of the canoe start to lift, then gravity took over: the engine idled and the canoe rode the wave perfectly over the sand bar. Even under the circumstances Mo was impressed: it was the first sign of competence from these people that he had seen.

Chapter Twelve

Under other circumstances, Mo would have enjoyed the trip through the Delta. The scenery was breathtaking and, having grown up in the urban devastation of Gaza City and the camps, he had a pronounced, almost mystical sensitivity to natural surroundings as being something sacred. Had his intellectual commitment to engineering not barred the way, his heart would easily have drawn him down the path of Sufism.

The oil industry has caused ecological damage in the Niger Delta region; that is indisputable. But as the little boat twisted and turned through the swamps, the only visible sign of the modern world was the outboard motors and machine guns. The ride was fast and fluid, and lasted about forty-five minutes. They passed through several villages, and whenever they did so shots were fired and villagers came out to cheer. The inevitable cries of "Swanaa? Wanaa!" would go up.

Mo found himself concentrating on details, though part of his mind was telling him that even this was a form of denial to prolong the journey, since he feared that the journey's end might be just that. He knew that, theoretically, MEND did not execute its hostages, but he had grown up in the culture of Fattah, Hezbollah and Hamas. The Palestinian movements had never been squeamish about the loss of a few hostages. It was not so long ago that the Iraqis had blasted the decapitation of the American hostage Nick Berg across the internet. He hoped that MEND had not been taking lessons. Despite American protestations to the contrary, the great days of international terrorism were long gone. Al Qaeda had spelt an end to all that.

There had been a time when different groups from all over the world with totally different causes would learn from each other, aid each other. Baader Meinhof, ETA, the IRA and the PLO – they would often meet up, like multilingual alumni returning to the alma mater of Gaddafi's desert training camps. Those days were all gone, the angry middle class intellectuals such as Carlos the Jackal and the Minute Men were dead, imprisoned or rehabilitated, and now even Ghadafi himself had been reconstructed as a model African leader.

But MEND had their own agenda. Their links were more to crime organisations than political extremists. And Mo was on much less familiar territory than he suspected. In most parts of the world, being a Palestinian was a bad thing. Except when it came to radical groups – nobody kidnapped Palestinians; the mere idea was ridiculous. Mo doubted that there was a radical group anywhere in the world (outside the Likud) that was not in some way sympathetic to the cause; besides which, hadn't they, the Palestinians, been the pioneers? Who had hijacked more planes than Leila Khalid and the early Palestinian Marxist liberationists?

As the small boat swung around along a bend in the river, the helmsman eased back on the throttle. A white banner was stretched across the water between two tall trees. Before him, Mo saw a rough wooden jetty; men waved guns from it and from the land alongside; improvised red and white flags flew from huts. They wore conspicuous red and white ties knotted around their arms.

Labo had learnt when he first arrived that the ties and flags were symbols of Egbesu, the Ijaw God of War. Warriors, he knew, wore the knots as protection against death, believing that, having taken an oath of submission to Egbesu, no metal weapon could harm them. Bullets and machetes would bounce harmlessly off them. 'Odeshi', it was called; a complex interplay of spiritualism and herbalism.

He looked around the boat. He felt part of something, but also alienated by what he had done; the dead bodies in the cabin haunted him, their spirits would already have returned to the sea, may even be swimming after the boat. The *Mammi Water* that inhabited the rivers that swirled around the camp should protect him – he hoped. He had, however, a nagging doubt: if she had heard the supplications from the spirit of a seafarer unjustly slain, that protection might no longer be afforded.

He preferred not to think about it. He looked towards his comrades-in-arms, proud young men, many of them much better educated than him, some of whom had even been to university. As the boat approached their camp, their demeanour had begun to change. They were returning heroes. The shouting subsided and they sat upright in the boats, like kings returning home from war, their weapons propped upright on their hips and their expressionless faces painted with white chalk to signify purity. Leaves were tucked into bands and folds in their clothing so the enemy would see trees rather than men approaching, and each man wore a tiny white seashell about his neck to show his allegiance to the *Mammi Water*. Labo looked across at Commander Jackson, a slight figure sitting in the bows of the boat with the heavy machine gun. The ammunition belts were draped across his bare chest like some strange mechanical snake coiling down to the plaid skirt called a 'George', which covered his skinny legs.

Mo had noticed with a shiver that Jackson had painted the Star of David on his stomach to signify the lost tribe of Israel. Mo knew intellectually that, for these people, the Palestinian conflict was a far away war in a far away place, and that for them, the Star of David was more likely an adopted symbol of some convoluted and misunderstood Christianity than a passion for Israel. Though the subliminal imagery stored up from a Palestinian childhood was hard to suppress, the images were a collection of living nightmares; it was as if some sick, twisted, malevolent mind had trawled the darkest recesses of mankind's ancestral memory and assembled everything that is terrifying to the human psyche, then handed it out to these young men in bucketfuls. *So different,* Mo thought, *from the intense young fanatics of Hamas and Islamic Jihad with their pristine white robes, cultivated beards, philosophies and sophistic arguments and mobile phones.* These men had stepped straight out of the soul of the continent. Creations of the id of modern humanity, un-tempered by change and the grinding progress of history.

As Mo looked at them sitting in their modern speedboat, with their Russian-made machine guns, he felt the tendrils of history reaching out from a time when there was only Africa. For a fleeting moment, he had the briefest of glimpses past the sophistries of cultural evolution into the darkness of his own soul. The raw and brutal nature of human existence, unfettered by the comforts of revealed or imagined faith, reared up in front of him. It was as if the whole of time and creation was slipping away into the swirling vortex of a history based on man's persistent denial of his own mortality, and in the mouth of the vortex sat the silhouettes of these armed men, much as their ancestors had done before recorded history began. The spears had been replaced with guns, the jungle had been poisoned, acid rain had corroded the life from the trees, but now the jungle was fighting back; these wiry black messengers from the dark heart of Africa, the Eden of humanity, were exacting Abel's revenge. Cain had gone forth into the barren wilderness and to keep himself warm he had raped the land, plundered the seas, sucked the black blood from the arteries of the planet, and now Eden had had enough and she was sending forth her children, because something must be done. *Hezbollah,* he mused, *had much to learn.*

Mo looked at them again, black figures against the sunlit green of the jungle. *No wonder,* he thought, *Nigerian soldiers have been known to just drop their weapons and run when confronted with these jungle wraiths, these ghouls from the swamps.* It was not the guns or bullets that made these men strong, nor was it the charms and amulets; it was the combination, the ramshackle collection of confused imagery that sent frightening echoes cascading round long-forgotten recesses of the human psyche.

As the boat pulled into view of the jetty, the men started to shout and cheer. Guns were fired into the air and the shouting and cheering intensified. Mo had a momentary vision of cannibalism. The helmsman gunned his engine, a victorious surge of power and a sign of authority to the dancing men on the shore, causing the boat to surge forward and almost unsettle Mo from his seat. As the boat hit ground alongside the jetty, the returning warriors climbed out of the boat with their weapons again propped upright on their hips and their white-painted faces immobile and expressionless as cast masks. They didn't look at Mo or his fellow captives, but stepped proudly from the boat whilst eager and less restrained hands helped Mo and the others scrabble across the unstable and unfamiliar vessel.

Mo could feel the adrenalin playing havoc with his nervous system; the back of his right leg was vibrating uncontrollably. The shouting and shooting seemed to be in a separate reality, glimpsed through a sepia veil that moved with him, protecting him from the truth of the situation. The skin on his face seemed to have rubberised and his mouth was a desert: his tongue seemed to be swelling, engulfing his mouth, preparing to cut off the precious supply of air that kept him living through this nightmare.

The path he was herded up was short and muddy. A Nigerian, shorter than him, with slanted, almost Asiatic eyes and horrific scars on his face, took hold of his arm and manoeuvred him gently to one side. Just to the right of the path was a particularly gnarled and ugly-looking tree. The tree was adorned with strips of cloth, red, white or black. Just in front of the tree was a roughly constructed wooden tripod, about waist high to Mo, and on the top of the three short protruding spikes sat half a coconut shell.

The scarred man gently manoeuvred Mo till he stood directly in front of the coconut grail. The man lifted two palm fronds and dipped them in the half shell, then used them to sprinkle Mo with a liquid that he immediately recognised as having the same smell as that which had been thrown in his eyes during the boat ride. The scarred man muttered something in a language that could have been anything; it was so slurred that Mo doubted that even a native speaker of whatever tongue it was would have understood. The man looked him straight in the eye. There was no expression on his damaged features, but there was a look of deep intelligence that shook Mo for a moment.

"You can go now, you have been blessed."

There was just a hint, Mo thought, *of sarcasm in is voice.*

Labo looked around. Everyone appeared happy, except the *ben aye u* – but that was to be expected. He made sure he was dancing and cheering as loudly as everyone else, *but not too loudly,* he thought to himself; *after all, better not attract attention.* Jackson was clearly drunk and out of control; the heady mix of adrenalin, crack and alcohol too much for him. He had a reputation for being weak where alcohol was concerned and it was rumoured that it was that which had stopped him from progressing within the movement. Otherwise, when he was sober, he was a clever and considerate commander. He had been at university in River State studying English Literature when, at the end of his second year, he had run out of money and dropped out into the waiting arms of MEND. The revolutionary movement had provided a voice and a purpose for the angry, disillusioned young man. Now, though, Labo noticed, the regular Jackson who greeted him every morning and led the early-morning prayers and dancing was nowhere to be seen. His face was drawn and there was foam about his mouth as he danced and cavorted, hurling himself into his soldiers and occasionally discharging his pistol into the air. He was naked except for a life jacket.

Labo watched as Jackson grabbed the hostage that he, Labo, had found, caught him by his short, almost African hair and threw him to the ground. The clearing was hushed; everyone except Jackson himself had stopped singing; it was as if the entire camp had collectively breathed in and held it, as Jackson and Mo acted out a macabre piece of drama. Two performers so deeply enwrapped in their scene that they had become utterly oblivious to their audience. Jackson capered about, his whole body twisted, almost embroidered into the performance, his spittle-laced mouth ranting lines written by some embittered playwright far above and beyond his comprehension. He knelt down on all fours like a dog and pushed his face up close to the hostage and spat in the man's face.

"I can kill you if I want," he shrieked.

Labo noticed The Secretary, as the camp residents called him, walk quietly up behind Jackson. The Secretary ran the camp. He never went on raids and rarely carried a gun. He was responsible for the management of the camp, the provisions and the payment of salaries. He was a direct appointment from MEND central. Jackson was snarling and hissing in the captive's face. The Secretary quietly bent down and picked up the pistol that was beside Jackson's left hand, quietly removed the magazine, checked the chamber and replaced it in Jackson's hand. Labo had heard of Jackson's excesses, stories told in hushed voices by other newcomers to the camp who themselves had probably never witnessed Jackson at his worst. Jackson placed the gun alongside Mo's head.

"I could kill you!" he screamed, and pulled the trigger.

The gun clicked, the firing pin shot into an empty chamber. Jackson rolled over on to his back, his feet and legs waving in the air, hooting and screaming with laughter. Mo, still on all fours, had not moved, but was visibly shaking. Labo got a better look at him; he wondered whether Mo was a half-caste. Labo had never seen a real half-caste before; he had met loads of albinos of course, the Delta was full of them. Many people blamed the chemicals being pumped out of the oil refineries for the increased number of albino births; other deformities were also on the rise, though many of them did not live long enough, for one reason or another, to make an impression on the statistics.

Mo looked up slowly. Jackson was lying on the floor in front of him, arms and legs waving frantically in the air like some helpless upturned insect, the useless pistol still clutched in his hand. Mo wanted to urinate. He could feel his body shaking, losing control; he almost wished that they would just shoot him and get it over with, put an end to this terrifying charade. Jackson leapt to his feet and started screaming and shouting in his own tongue, still naked but now streaked with mud and saliva. He called out again, clearly much angrier now, his temper inflamed by the impotence of his weapon. Someone brought him an AK47. He cocked the weapon and pointed it at Mo. He pulled the trigger, and again nothing happened. Mo looked up behind Jackson. The Secretary was standing there looking Mo in the eye; he raised one hand out of sight of Jackson and shook a finger discreetly from side to side. Mo understood that the gun was empty; this was all show, the quiet man was reassuring him. Mo was only partially comforted.

Labo watched intently. He was enjoying the show and was hoping against hope that Jackson would kill this man, the only man who might be able to finger him as having killed the two whites in the cabin. It would solve all his problems. He would be a hero for having captured a hostage, there would be no witnesses to his transgression and, if Jackson himself killed someone, there were less likely to be repercussions against him for an accidental killing during a raid. If there were no witnesses, he could even say that they had been armed.

The man they called The Secretary looked on. These displays

caused him unnecessary stress. He knew from experience that, once the crack and *kai kai* were out of his system, Jackson would return to his normal quiet, efficient self. He also knew how to deal with Jackson as he went through this chemical comedown. The problem was the men; most of them he considered to be unutterably stupid. They would look on and enjoy and admire; they would regard this as entertainment, and even as something to be emulated. But Jackson was constitutionally unsuited to drug abuse: the combination of mild epilepsy and, The Secretary suspected, some deeper form of personality disorder, induced a frightening schizophrenia. At times The Secretary considered Jackson as a friend, someone he should support; indeed, when Jackson was in a chemically 'normal' state he was one of the few people in this godforsaken place worth talking to.

He caught himself – 'godforsaken'? Whilst it was true that he needed to speak in such terms in front of these superstitious savages that made him ashamed to be Nigerian, it irked him to find himself still using such ignorant vocabulary. God was, in his opinion, something the English had found useful in suppressing dissent. Religion encouraged ignorance and as soon as the black man could shake off the yoke of faith, he would be able to compete on an even footing with the Europeans. The Secretary had convinced himself that there were no longer any white people who actually believed this rubbish. It was true that there were many who professed faith, but that was just part of the bourgeois colonial conspiracy to oppress the black and brown. The whole papist charade was a form of oppression, designed by the ruling classes to oppress the poor. It was a subject that he and Jackson frequently discussed, the cultural oppression of black Africa by white Christianity. That their brothers and sisters still clung so fervently to such delusions was an eternal frustration to the two young idealists. They had started off as angry young men, fugitives from the white-dominated (as they saw it) higher education system looking for a native truth in the heartland of oppressed black Africa, believing that they would find some higher path through their struggle against injustice. And, like the thousands of white middle-class hippies who had taken the road to Marrakech, or the existentialist Marxists who had mobbed the streets of Paris in '68, they had found little but poverty, ignorance, corruption and prejudice. There was only a simple struggle for subsistence, the daily pain anaesthetised by faith and alcohol. They also found that, whenever they wished to discuss such matters, their native tongue was deficient in the ideologically loaded expressions they need to clear their consciences. Ijaw lacked the post-structuralist vocabulary on which they had come to rely. Fishermen have little need for words such as 'dialectal', 'existentialist' or 'deconstructionalist', and even the basic structures of the language limited revolutionary thought. More and more, they relied on the Greco-Roman heritage of the postcolonial capitalist education system that had built the universities that had given them the language and philosophy with which to reject them.

It is ironic that the path to disillusionment is so frequently trodden by those blinded by the search for truth. Thus the two comrades had arrived as avenging anti-missionaries: preaching against what they had come to see as the oppressive ignorance through faith that surrounded them. With the passing of time, however, they had come to realise that they were swimming against the tide and that, in fact their soldiers' simple faith had made them much easier to control, and consequently the lives of Jackson and The Secretary, as their leaders, much easier. At first they had had heated discussions about the subject, attempting to justify their ideas of a form of necessary evil, something that could be morally acceptable if done for the greater good – or were they simply embracing the shackles of slavery? Eventually the practical reality of attempting to run a guerrilla movement manned by illiterates had triumphed over ivory-tower idealism, and inevitably they had colluded, and Jackson had declared himself a prophet in direct communication with the gods of the earth and the *Mammi Water*. The Secretary could see the bitter irony of what they had become, but sometimes he wondered whether Jackson could. These were the moments when he lost sympathy with his friend – maybe Jackson was starting to believe this mumbo jumbo? Maybe he should give up the whole thing, make peace with his family and go to America, join the capitalist rat race. Unlike many of the soldiers, he was not from the fishing villages. Yes, he was a Niger Deltan, but he had grown up in a large compound in River State. His father, a successful businessman, had a collection of Mercedes and little time for his children.

Mo felt hands beneath his armpits. He was being lifted up and guided to the nearest hut. Here, he was pushed on to a bench in what passed for a room, in that it had a corrugated iron roof and four walls partially made of planks. If it had not been so integral to the whole structure, it would perhaps have been a veranda. The wall to Mo's left was the only one that was solid and went all the way to the roof. Behind him was a waist-high wall fashioned out of the same crude planking as the rest and ahead stood a wall with an opening that led into some sort of narrow corridor with rooms off either side. To his right was an open space with a single wooden stake acting as a roof support. In one corner of the space was a new Sony TV and DVD system, alongside a tattered cardboard box, into which had been flung a large quantity of CDs and DVDs, none of which looked in a fit condition to be used.

Mo was pushed back against the wall. Men in various states of dress and undress started to crowd into the space, most carrying weapons. There was a lot of shouting and jostling. The quiet man with the Lenin-style beard, who had signalled to Mo earlier, pushed his way to the front. He was wearing camouflage fatigues and looked more as Mo would have expected a jungle guerrilla leader to look. Mo noticed that in his presence the men became quieter and more subdued. He carried what appeared to be a child's exercise book. He handed it to Mo.

"Write your name, your nationality, your date of birth, your position on the vessel and your company's phone number."

He gave Mo a pencil, short and chewed, with which to write.

For the first time Mo noticed the steady chug of a diesel generator. That explained the TV. He looked down at the book. It was indeed a child's exercise book, and the required details had been laid out for him in a strong script, creating a crude form to be filled in.

He hesitated for a moment over 'Nationality'. His Lebanese passport was not strictly legal, but he figured that, what with the ongoing war, birth certificates were unlikely to be unearthed at short notice. He wrote 'Lebanese', and hoped that the government that had unknowingly adopted him would not disown him now.

When he had finished, he handed the book back to the quiet man, who asked him if he had been injured and if he needed any special medication. The crowd was beginning to lose interest.

Jackson reappeared in the opening that looked out on to the river. He was still naked and his body was smeared in mud and white chalk. He was carrying the heavy machine gun that had thrown him off balance in the boat. Now there was no ammunition belt thread to the gun, but one was draped around Jackson's shoulders. He was clearly still extremely drunk and out of control, and was struggling beneath the weight of the gun.

He pushed his way though the men, some of whom were looking alarmed, while others seemed to find this a turn for the better. While Jackson ranted in his own tongue, Mo noticed the quiet man in fatigues deftly catch the weapon from Jackson's hands and check that that the chamber was empty before an enraged Jackson snatched it back.

Jackson shouted at The Secretary, then turned back towards Mo. He stopped shouting and stared hard at Mo. Even without understanding a word of what was being said, Mo knew what had happened: Jackson had forgotten what he was talking about. He stood still for a moment, threw the weapon angrily on the floor and walked out.

The scarred man who had 'blessed' Mo on his arrival came in, carrying a glass bottle of something that looked suspiciously like diesel and a paper cup. He poured some of the substance into the cup and handed it to Mo. Mo's hesitation must have been obvious. Scarface hesitated, smiled, demonstrating that the damage to his face extended to his dentistry, took the cup back, swallowed it himself, poured another shot, and handed it to Mo.

Scarface smiled again. "It's good, make you feel better, feel free!"

Mo drank the liquid in one draught. He expected it to be strong, and did not want to splutter on it; nevertheless, he had been totally unprepared for the searing reality. It was, he guessed, a similar sensation to drinking lighted napalm.

Scarface smiled and slapped him hard about the shoulders, in what Mo assumed was meant to be a friendly gesture.

"Feel free," he said and wandered off.

The burning sensation slowly ebbed from Mo's throat and whilst he felt anything but free, it was true that he had started to feel detached from the goings-on. He had no idea what he had just drunk, but the effects were definitely numbing. This, he realised, was probably a good thing.

Now Jackson re-materialised. He was wearing an inflatable life jacket again, and had found an AK47. A small group of men stood behind him, wearing white war paint on their faces.

"Stand up, white man!" he shouted, leaning forward, so close that Mo could feel Jackson's spittle on his face. "Stand up you fucking white man."

A hand appeared from nowhere, grabbed the fabric of Mo's coverall and dragged him to his feet.

"Outside, white man!"

Mo was thrust back outside. His bare feet slipped in the mud, he stumbled and caught his toe on a root; the pain cut through the anaesthetic effect of whatever it was that Scarface had poured down his throat. The muzzle of a rifle was thrust in his back and there was excited shouting and screaming behind him. Hands, feet and rifle butts pushed him forwards, the mud kept trying to rear up and smack him in the face, but somehow his body would not let him fall, however much he wished it. Maybe if he fell they would put a bullet in the back of his head and it would all be over. He saw that he was being herded towards the jungle. Brutal, unfamiliar territory. No place for an educated boy from Gaza.

The trees seemed to rush towards him but never came closer. His feet slipped in the mud. Small twigs, roots and God knows what else tore at the flesh of the soles of his feet. Then, finally, it happened: he slipped, the oblivion of the greyish mud beckoned, the very substance of Adam's creation, the essence of the flesh of mankind calling him home. Here in the heart of Africa where it had all begun, where a lonely God had breathed the essence of life into a heap of mud and unleashed hell on earth; here in the oil-infested, acid-scorched, dying forests of Eden, Mohamed, the child of Abraham, was going home. He could hurl himself deep into the welcoming mud from which he had been formed; he could find the consummation of nothingness in the womb of the world. His hands reached forwards, breaking his fall or reaching out to embrace oblivion, he could not tell.

As the wet and slimy earth reached out to return his kiss, her soft flesh ready to mould itself about his body, strong hands reached down and caught him. Harsh fingers dug into his body as they hauled him back up on to his bleeding feet.

"Take 'em over dat place," a voice called from somewhere in a different world. "Against de trees."

The air seemed to have taken on the density of mud, in sympathy for his loss. Mo moved slowly forwards. The trees were harsh and twisted; they offered no solace, they knew he was an alien. Mo knew that this was the end, that he was going to die here.

He tried to pray. There was nothing.

He tried to think of Sally and Houda.

Again there was nothing, and he knew that he was totally and absolutely alone.

Chapter Thirteen

The bullets tore into the bark of the trees above Mo's head. He flinched, hunched his shoulders, as if that would have any effect on the thousands of bullets that all his senses told him would soon be tearing through his flesh. His only hope was that it would be quick and that he would not scream.

Laughter broke out behind him.

"Move, white man, you're too expensive to kill now!"

More laughter.

"Move! Your government will not pay for a dead body. Feel free!"

Scarface came up to him. Mo could feel his body shaking furiously; his whole being wanted to break down and cry. His pride alone was keeping him on his feet. Scarface took him by the elbow, paused, and looked at him quizzically. There was gentleness in the grip that surprised Mo.

"Come on, *ben aye u*, we move now, dey nomake dis ting again. Have deir fun. Is over now."

Scarface took Mo forwards, deeper into the jungle. The path was uneven and rough, and bits of rubbish were scattered about, little coloured specks of plastic, like the shed skin of some synthetic snake. The jungle opened up suddenly into a clearing. There were two rough-hewn benches around the edge; in the centre were the remains of a tree.

The tree was clearly dead: it had been cut off at just above head height, and what was left of the trunk showed the marks of many machete cuts and not a few bullet holes. Mo dreaded to think what it was used for.

Seated on the benches were more militants and, to Mo's surprise, three white men from the barge. His mind was still struggling to deal with the events of the last half hour, and the attack on the barge seemed a lifetime ago. He vaguely recalled being loaded into the speedboat and watching other crewmembers being herded over the side. They had been in the boat next to him. Only one did he know well, a deck leader-man by the name of Tommy; the other two he knew were divers, but he had had little to do with them. The two divers were sitting next to a tall, thin militant wearing the most inappropriate blue blazer imaginable. The stress showed in their faces; it was as if their skin had been stretched across their skulls. They were both well tanned from spending too much time on the helideck, though the colour they both had now Mo had rarely seen outside a morgue. Even so, the way Mo felt, he was sure they looked better than he did. Tommy the deck leader-man was in his sixties and had that physique frequently associated with Americans of his age: not with the best will in the world would his skin ever be drawn tightly across anything, at least not whilst he was still living inside it. Blood ran down his face from a gash across his nose, and one of his eyes was beginning to swell. His complexion had taken on the grey, waxy look that morticians work so hard to disguise.

Opposite Tommy and the divers sat the man in the blazer. To Mo, the inappropriateness of his attire was almost frightening in itself. He was wearing pointed white snakeskin ankle boots and very baggy calf-length black trousers with the Prada logo displayed near the hem. The trousers, Mo was sure, had been designed for women. Beneath the immaculately pressed, gold-buttoned blazer, he wore a white roll-neck Lycra vest similar to the type that surfers and cyclists wear. He was almost painfully thin, and as he spoke he constantly stroked the side of his shaved head with a small black pistol. Another five militants stood around the clearing; all were carrying machine guns. There was a strong smell of ganja. The thin man seemed to be giggling a lot. Mo was pushed into the clearing.

"You are welcome," giggled the thin man. "Feel free."

His voice was high and there was a faint trace of a lisp. One of the other militants leant forwards from behind him and handed him a large joint. The thin man placed the pistol between his thighs, removed a Zippo lighter from his blazer pocket, lit the joint and inhaled deeply.

"You smoke?" He offered it to Mo.

Mo didn't know what to do. To refuse may cause offence; to accept may be a trap that would result in a beating. He hadn't touched marijuana since his university days, and was quite sure that one or two puffs on whatever it was they were smoking would leave him rolling on the floor vomiting.

"Its good, make strong," said the thin man, making a theatrical gesture of flexing his biceps.

Mo looked around his fellow captives. No eye contact, no clue what to do, no recognition at all. Their body language sung out to any one who cared to look: *defeat*.

One of the other militants took the joint, inhaled deeply, and breathed the smoke in to Mo's face.

"Too strong for the white man!" he laughed.

"Sit, what's your name?" said the thin man.

"Mo."

"Ah, Mo feel free, Mo I am 'Youth Shall Prosper'. I am the chosen leader. These are my men. You are here because the federal government are killing us. They are robbing our land, look around."

He made an expansive gesture with the hand holding the pistol. The joint was in his mouth, and he took what appeared to be a bottomless lungful. As he continued to speak, the smoke gushed out through both his nose and mouth.

"Can't you see we are suffering? We have nothing, and in Lagos and Abuja they drive around on good roads in Mercedes."

As a resident of Lagos Mo knew better, but he decided that this was not necessarily the moment to redress the misconceptions of a man with a gun and a lot of drugs flowing round his bloodstream. He stood – there was no obvious place for him to sit – with his head down, trying to look attentive and submissive at the same time and desperately trying to avoid any eye contact that may be taken as confrontational.

"You can see we are suffering? You think this is normal we live like animals?"

There was an edge to the voice now. This was exactly what Mo had feared. He decided some response was needed. He looked up, made brief eye contact, then looked quickly away again. "What they are doing is wrong," he said quietly. "We all know that."

There was a general murmur of agreement. The militants were passing among themselves plastic bottles of the green liquid that Mo had tasted earlier. He had always been of the opinion that guns, drugs and alcohol did not mix. He didn't think things could get much worse.

A militant with an immaculately coiffed goatee beard, carefully pressed clothes and similar snakeskin shoes to the thin man, made a gesture to a scruffily attired militant to move from his seat and make way for Mo.

"Please, sit down, do no be afraid. Feel free," said the smart looking man.

Mo found himself between one of the divers and the fat American. The American's breath was permanently audible: a harsh, rasping sound, as if the air was having to force its way past an ever-constricting windpipe. Every time he made the slightest movement, a small gust of air would be forced from his mouth, breaking up the otherwise rhythmic sequence of rasping exhalations. It was like sitting next to a mildly malfunctioning industrial pneumatic device. Mo could see that the blood on his face was drying. The actual wound appeared to be a gash across the bridge of his nose, though due to the generally bulbous morphology of his features, a broken nose would have been hard to recognise. Mo vaguely recognised the diver to his right as being the South African diving supervisor from the barge. Under normal circumstances people had a tendency to point out that he looked remarkably like Tom Cruise. Mo looked across at him and caught his eye, and received a slightly raised eyebrow in acknowledgement. They both went back to looking at the ground.

"Mo, what's your job on the boat?"

It was the thin man, 'Youth Shall Prosper', who was speaking.

Mo was not sure what to say. Did being an engineer make him sound too important? Would that make his ransom more expensive? If he were to give himself a too menial position they might consider him not worth keeping alive and shoot him out of hand. He could feel all eyes on him; the silence seemed to stretch out like a long strong hand, feeling for his throat.

He decided to play safe, to answer truthfully but in a manner that would mean little to them. This would give him a chance to see which way the wind was blowing.

"I am a technician," he replied. There was some muttering in Ijaw from the group.

The South African had obviously picked up on Mo's dilemma. "He repairs our diving equipment for us," he volunteered.

Mo felt an immediate sense of relief. He wasn't alone. The South African continued: "He has to fix anything our supervisor wants."

Mo understood straightaway: he was being filled in on the story that they had already told. The South African was letting him know that as far as these people were concerned, he was a diver and not a supervisor. So his fellow captives had been thinking along the same lines as he had.

There was some more conversation in Ijaw. Mo began to try and take in his surroundings a little better. It was becoming clear to him that there were two groups here. Youth Shall Prosper, was obviously the most important person present and, Mo guessed, the fashion-conscious militants were his bodyguards, or at least constituted some sort of elite, judging by the way the other men reacted to them. Not only were their clothes in noticeably better condition, the weapons they carried were cleaner, newer, too, and to Mo's eyes more sophisticated. He guessed that they did not live in the camp like the others, based on the cleanliness and general inappropriateness of their clothes for the jungle conditions.

The smartly dressed man jabbered something in rapid Ijaw and pointed to the South African. Two words were recognisable: Tom Cruise. Mo felt the South African stiffen beside him. There was general laughter amongst the well-dressed militants. The others appeared bewildered.

Chapter Fourteen

Labo had been left in the main compound. When the senior men had led the hostage away, the hope he had experienced during Jackson's exhibition and the mock-firing squad had slipped away, and now they were distant memories leaving barely a ripple on the dark surface of his consciousness. Now that both the entertainment and the chance to impress the top men with shows of enthusiasm were over, the soldiers were breaking up into little groups that were defined as much by education and age as anything else. The more experienced and long-term camp residents retired to sit and smoke in the eves of the compound's rough buildings. Another group half-heartedly kicked a partially inflated football around the cleared area that served as a parade ground. The younger and newer members of the camp gravitated to the little jetty where not long ago Mo had been unloaded. Back behind the main hut, the generator was running; rap videos were playing on the TV screen and the rhythmic sounds of black America's urban discontent were pumped incongruously into the African bush. Down by the still waters of the jetty, bottles of *kai kai* were being passed about, joints were being rolled and smoked at a fantastic rate, and the atmosphere was one of joyous celebration. There were *ben aye u* in captivity: good times were on the way.

Labo found himself the focus of attention of a group of newer recruits, who themselves had never been on a raid. He was plied eagerly for war stories, of what the barge had looked like and whether or not he had actually killed any federal government troops. Normally he would have revelled in the attention, demonstrating how he had fired, hidden behind obstacles and generally given dramatic (if not strictly accurate) accounts of his own daring exploits. Now he was not at ease; his eyes were forever drawn to the line of trees behind which he knew his destiny was being decided.

Why had Jackson not killed the white man? It was clear that Egbesu, the Ijaw God of War, was playing games with him. Labo knew that the gods could be capricious, but what had he done to deserve this, a warrior of a true Ijaw bloodline? There were times when sacrifices were demanded, but they were being oppressed. The gods should be helping him.

In a rare moment of introspection Labo thought back to the events that had brought him to this pass: the raid on the village that had got out of hand, the screams of the girls he had raped, the smell of the burning homes and the sickly stench with which they had mingled with as the bodies had started to burn. The concept that what he had done might be morally offensive to the gods was beyond his comprehension, but what if one of those women had been destined to give birth to a great Ijaw warrior, even the reincarnation of Adaka Boro himself? This train of thought was terrifying, and it was a train that was careering out of control. The babies and children that had died that day and they were, it was true, Ijaw – any one of those male children could have been the bloodline of Adaka Boro himself.

The gods, it was clear, were angry with him. The funny-looking white man was his nemesis incarnate – the gods, Labo knew, could be cruel in exacting their vengeance. They would play with him, torment him, prior to his destruction. There was only one way that an angry god could be appeased and that was through the shedding of blood. It might be his own that was required, but he reasoned that if he could offer up enough blood of quality, the gods may be appeased. After all, Egbesu was not like the white man's Christ, some weakling in long white robes – he must be vigilant. This was his quest, he had heard of warriors in the great days being sent into the jungle to bring back valuable trophies, an enemy's head for example; if they failed they would be put to death if they succeeded they would become great warriors, heroes to the tribe, even kings. This, he began to convince himself, was what was being done to him. He was a warrior, he told himself; Egbesu was a hard master and would test him to the limits, but, if he proved himself, even the likes of Jackson and that condescending bastard The Secretary would one day bow down before him.

The thought stirred his loins. He must be careful, though: if these traitors to the gods, these false prophets, were to find him out he would have failed, and Egbesu the true God of War did not protect failures.

The crowd of young soldiers, waiting on Labo's recollections, were surprised at his reticence; but no one dared speak, they knew he had killed before and his muscular physique was intimidating. His eyes seemed far away; he must be in touch with the gods, they said amongst themselves. He was a great warrior, they knew as he had told them himself – perhaps Egbesu was appearing to him directly at this moment.

They waited by his side as his stunted mind wrestled with itself. Still waters do not always run deep; they are sometimes deceptively shallow and frequently stagnant. But Labo's silence made more of an impression on his circle of young admirers than any graphic account, however gruesomely exaggerated, would have done.

Had The Secretary been aware of what was passing through the minds of his young subordinates, he would probably have given up the struggle once and for all and applied for a job with Exxon Mobile.

133

Chapter Fifteen

Dricus Van Neuveldt looked at the Arab engineer sitting next to him. He tried to do it without raising his head too much; he did not want to loose the submissive posture that he was attempting to maintain. He was very conscious of the fact that the slightest change in body language could radically alter the outcome of the situation. So he battled to control his deep-rooted instincts, to prevent them from surfacing and influencing his posture.

Dricus was old enough to remember apartheid. Though the greater part of his life had been lived post-Mandela, his soul still carried deep roots in the Transvaal and his five years' military service, much of which had been spent fighting in Angola, had formed most of the emotions that were coursing through his body. He could not evade the fact he was being held by black men with guns. And worse than that, they were untrained, uneducated, ill disciplined, intoxicated black men with guns.

He regarded the engineer carefully. Like most offshore divers, he regarded field engineers with a mixture of contempt and suspicion. Field engineers were people who had never done a real day's work, had no idea how things worked in the real world and came up with stupid ideas, pointless procedures and generally made the job more difficult than it was, by getting in the way.

And this one wasn't even white.

Dricus checked himself. He knew that it was the stress that was making him think like this. He was not his father, he belonged to the new generation, was part of the rainbow nation and was proud of it. *Adapt and survive.* He had looked around as the old regime crumbled and seen the future; he had watched his army colleagues sitting about in Boer bars lamenting the passing of the old days and he had seen dinosaurs complaining about the changing climate. He wasn't going to finish like that, South Africa was his home, he was African and he was planning to stay. He would adapt to the new realities and bring his children up to survive in the new order.

It was helpful that he belonged to a liberal church. In fact it was there that he had met his schoolteacher wife, who taught in an almost mixed school. He was proud to think of himself as progressive, the new model white South African. He was also astute enough to know that even thinking like the old guard could get you killed. They weren't stable, some of these *kaffirs*. One wrong gesture and they would waste you as soon as look at you.

As far as the Nigerians were concerned, the engineer was white, Dricus reminded himself. The man looked terrified, which was not surprising under the circumstances. He probably didn't look much better himself. Anyway, the man appeared to have taken the hint he dropped, so he was probably reasonably bright, for an engineer.

Dricus looked back at his feet and concentrated on appearing submissive. He vaguely remembered being taught about situations like this when he was at the military academy. The instructor had told them that, if they could think themselves into the mindset their captors wanted to instil in them, they could control their own body language. It was a sort of method acting for soldiers. At the time, neither he nor his classmates had taken the instructor seriously: it was an easy class that was held after drill, a chance to relax before the afternoon run. Now he tried desperately to remember what that man had told them. There was a lot about controlling the situation through submission, which in those days had seemed ridiculous (there were much easier ways of controlling blacks: shouting, for example, had usually worked). But the memory that came most readily to mind was of being back in the academy classroom, his freshly showered body, aching from the drill session, rubbing against the starched uniform shirt and the ever present smell of polish.

"Hey, Tom Cruise, you have to make phone call to your company. Tell them if they don't pay money we will shoot you."

It was the thin man speaking. Dricus did not trust him. He did not trust any of them, of course, but there was something about the way this man lisped slightly. He had always associated lisping with weakness, and weak men in power were dangerous: they reacted like women, irrational and emotional. And this one had a gun.

"What you want me to tell them?"

"First you tell them that you are alive. Then you tell them who is here. Then you tell them you are prisoners of MEND." The thin man paused and looked at him quizzically. "You understand who are MEND?"

Dricus had a moment's panic. Of course he knew who they were, they were a bunch of black militants. He could not, however, remember for what the initials stood. That admission could easily be taken as a sign of disrespect and this effeminate *kaffir* might take offence.

Fortunately for him, the thin man was far too stoned to notice his hesitation and carried on, obviously enamoured by the sound of his own voice.

"We are the Movement for the Emancipation of the Niger Delta," he explained.

Dricus silently thanked God for the ego of the black man. It never crossed his mind that the thin man might actually be considerably more perceptive that he had credited.

"Do you know the phone number of your company?"

Dricus watched whilst the thin man composed the number, following his dictation, feeling the eyes of the other captives upon him. He knew at that moment that he was their only lifeline.

The thin man handed him the phone. It was already ringing. Dricus held it to his ear – no phone had ever seemed to ring so slowly. Was there no one in the office? At long last some one picked up the phone, and immediately the signal failed.

A flash of anger crossed the face of Youth Shall Prosper, as if he thought Dricus had sabotaged the signal. The thin man re-dialled. This time the connection was good.

Dricus did not know what to expect when he finally got through – some sort of exclamation perhaps, and expletive expressions of concern? The phone continued to ring; it annoyed him slightly that under the circumstances the office weren't hanging on the phone waiting for his first contact. He could hear just from the ringing that the line would not be good, that there would be an echo. Eventually the phone was answered.

"Hello, Darren? It's Dricus. We've been captured."

There was silence on the other end. Dricus could hear his own words echoing back to him. The silence continued, too long for the delay in transmission. Darren must just be sitting there.

"Darren! It's Dricus! Can you hear me? We are hostages! Are you listening?"

Again he heard his own voice echoing back to him across the open line. Then eventually: "Dricus, is that you?"

The voice was flat and lifeless.

Dricus could feel the stress rising in him. "For fuck's sake, Darren. Are you drunk?"

No reply.

Dricus shook with rage and frustration. "Listen, if you can't cope with this, pass me to someone who can."

There was again silence on the line.

"There's no one else here. I am all alone in the office."

At last there was some emotion coming into the voice, but it was not the emotion that Dricus wanted to hear.

"I'm here alone."

There was a pause. Dricus could hear the voice shaking clearly. "I'm scared, Dricus."

Dricus could imagine Darren's fat little body quivering with

137

fear in his air-conditioned office. If he was that frightened he had probably been drinking. It was all too much for Dricus and his normal imperturbability began to give way.

"You're scared! You're not the one with a fucking gun at your head! For fuck's sake pull yourself together and get me someone who is at least half competent and sober."

Youth Shall Prosper had been listening with bemused interest. Now he grabbed a Kalashnikov from one of the nearby soldiers, cocked it, and loosed a burst into the air.

Darren clearly heard it. Dricus could hear him sobbing on the other end of the line.

"Will that help focus him a little, do you think?" Youth Shall Prosper enquired politely.

Dricus knew he had to control the situation. The state Darren was in, he was quite capable of going into complete denial: putting the phone down on the desk and walking away from it.

"Darren, listen to me carefully. Now take the phone and go upstairs and find someone in the directors' offices, do you understand me, Darren? Say 'yes' if you do."

Another delay.

"I can't, Dricus. I will have to walk past the windows, they might shoot me."

Despite the stress, or perhaps because of it, Dricus almost laughed. He suddenly had a clear vision of the tubby little Englishman hiding under his desk, shaking with fear in the middle of a busy city.

Dricus controlled his voice. He knew what to do. Darren was clearly drunk. He was going to have to control him like a child.

"No, Darren, they won't shoot you, they are all here with us. Anyway, why would they shoot you? They want you to take the phone upstairs. So listen, we'll do this together. Now are you with me?"

"Yes."

"OK. We'll crawl across the floor, keeping away from the

windows, make our way to the door." Dricus could hear the scraping of furniture and Darren's laboured breathing. It was just like being at work, directing a diver in black water over the comms system.

Youth Shall Prosper was watching in amazement. Dricus could imagine he must be wondering how the white man had ever managed to colonise Africa. He felt he should say something now, establish a rapport with the thin man. He put his hand over the phone so that Darren would not hear what was said.

"I am sorry, but he's a fucking idiot," he said.

Youth Shall Prosper smiled. It unnerved Dricus: he was not sure whether or not the thin man had understood, was humouring him, or was simply condescending; it was a smile that implied everything and conveyed absolutely nothing.

For the first time Dricus wondered whether he might have grossly underestimated the thin black man standing in front of him, Kalashnikov hanging loosely in his right hand, his head tilted back slightly so that the smoke from the joint hanging from his bottom lip would not blow into his eyes. But he returned his attention to the phone: he could still hear Darren's laboured breathing, which he thought might be interspersed with sobs.

Chapter Sixteen

Sally sat on the edge of the sofa, an uncharacteristic glass of whisky gripped in her hand. The cell phone, horribly silent, lay lifeless beside her like the corpse of a recently deceased but much loved pet. She kept glancing at it, willing it to light up, ring, indicate some sign of life, but it lay there, silent and inanimate.

She heard a key in the lock; a few moments later a young woman walked in. She was tall, elegant and her long, dark brown hair hung free about her shoulders. It was not often that Sally thought about the past these days – she had decided that was best left where it belonged – but as the young woman stood before her, happily chattering away about some amusing triviality that had occurred at university, Sally's mind fell back across time and space to a pile of rubble and a little girl and a headless teddy bear. They still had that bear, she and Mo had found a tailor and had a new head made, and then had slowly weaned the traumatised child off it. It now lay carefully wrapped in tissue paper, in a box hidden at the foot of a wardrobe in their bedroom. For years they had protected the child that had brought them together through pain; they had tended to her every need, sat through her nightmares and slowly watched as she had emerged from darkness and flowered into an exceptional young woman. Now, Sally thought, she was going to have to put it all in jeopardy.

She took a deep breath. "Darling, come and sit, down. I have something to tell you. Daddy's," she paused almost scared to speak the words, "been kidnapped."

Saying it out loud, articulating the awful reality, was too much, and Sally at last burst into tears.

Houda put her arms around the woman she had called 'Mother' for fifteen years. Mo and Sally had not only saved her life and given her opportunities that would never have been available to her in Gaza, but they had also been good parents to her. Theirs was a strange family, forged in the dust and fumes of a warzone. There had been no other children; not for want of trying, but when it had been discovered that the problem lay with Mo, both had, in a way, been relieved: the intensity of the bond that held the little family together was so strong it would have allowed little space for a newcomer, however much he or she might have been wanted. The consequences of violence echo across the decades and the ripples are felt in many places. Said's bullet had ripped apart a community, decimated several families and now, in a flat in Lagos, its echoes were still cascading as the two women he had joined together held each other and wept for a man whose life it had changed forever. Said, too, had been a victim; he had not chosen to be born in an occupied land, with an elder brother whose already unstable personality had been simultaneously poisoned and nurtured by the violence that surrounded them. The roots lay deep in the forgotten and spiralling sands of time when a young slave girl had taken up her young boy child and walked into the unknown. Surrounded by the blasted stony desert of Arabia, the two forlorn figures had almost succumbed, as the harsh desert sky had seemed to press down upon the dead earth as if to squeeze the last drop of life-giving water from the rock-strewn dust. Mother and child had stumbled helplessly from one burning yellow rock to another. The light and heat that leapt from the stones had dried and burnt their bodies, until finally it was clear that both woman and child were close to an agonising and lonely death.

And yet, in what might perhaps have been the most barren place on earth, ringed by the most brutal-looking mountains imaginable, the god of wrath and anger had taken pity on them. The young child had struck the ground in infantile desperation –

or under the guidance of the archangel Gabriel, depending on one's perspective – and water had gushed forth. Mother and child had been spared and the future of the Arab race had been decided. The exodus of Haga the slave girl and the infant Ishmael, driven from their home into the wilderness by Sarah, the mother of the Israelites, had created one of the most bitter family feuds to which the human race had ever been exposed. Then, centuries later, Sarah's jealousy had helped apply the gentle pressure to the trigger of little Said's American-made rifle and sent the bullet spiralling through the brain of his gentle cousin, Lieutenant Samuel Ashraf of the IDF. A man whose last conscious thought had been for the safety of the young woman who sat now on a sofa in Lagos, holding her adopted mother as she cried for a man who bore the name of the last prophet to emerge from the sands of Arabia.

A few hours away, across the oil-sodden swamps of a lost Eden, Chioma sat looking at her only son, the child for whom she had placed all her worldly possessions on her head and walked into the unknown. Chidi was now a young man and her life, she could sense, was about to move on. It was true that Joseph had said nothing of true significance to her, but she had somehow sensed that even her receptiveness to him was indicative of a change in her life. Joseph might not be the man who would change her life, but he had reawakened in her the desire to be a woman, to live beyond the scope of her child. It was time to change; the chapters of motherhood were drawing to a close; new responsibilities awaited her.

She knew that, in some ways, what she had done to Azzi was wrong, but her child had come first. She had served her penance, those years of tending to an elderly and infirm man. She had raised her child and the debt had been paid.

Ron Forrester was not liked by many people. He was short, curt and officious. He had a bullish air about him that beguiled many people into thinking that his tendency towards corpulence was in fact musculature. He had achieved his position in life through a combination of cunning, aggressive bullying and general intimidation and, when necessary, toadying. To him life was a competition in which anyone taller, better looking or more educated than him was out to get him. He had always worked on the principal that offence was the best form of defence, and he was a master at being offensive. He was a very successful manager. And right now he was annoyed.

Forrester hated divers, and now two of them had gone and got themselves kidnapped. It was going to cost money and time, which in turn was more money. In his view, divers were all a slightly elevated form of pond life, and if he had his way he'd let the militants shoot them and that would be two less over-inflated salaries to pay. The fact that that was not good business sense annoyed him even more. The divers would get sympathy for this, they might even get pay rises. What was really galling was that the company needed them and in a small industry, he well knew that if the company was not seen to behave correctly towards the divers it would become harder to get more. And much as he hated to admit it, they needed divers to keep him in the lifestyle he had come to enjoy. God he hated them. The very fact of having to go downstairs to the diving department sickened him; but he was getting no answer on the internal phone and he needed the personnel files for the respective embassies.

Unfortunately for Darren, the office door opened inwards. Ron Forrester on the other hand was not in the habit of opening or closing doors gently – unless of course he was snooping. The door caught Darren in the side of the head, and sent the mobile phone flying across the floor.

Darren Seaton was always terrified of Ron and in his current state Ron's aggressive presence was just too much for him. He rolled over on to his side, curled up into the foetal position and started to sob. Ron could see that the screen on the phone was lit, and sparing little thought for the blubbering wreck in front of him, he bent down and picked up the phone.

"Ron Forrester, Niger Marine. How can I help you?"

"Thank fuck for that!"

Ron did not need to ask for the caller's identity: from the strong Afrikaans accent and the stress in the voice he knew immediately who he was talking to.

"Dricus. Are you OK? Who is with you? Is anyone hurt?"

"It's just me and Mark from Niger Marine. There is a foreman from the barge, and a field engineer, but they have been told to speak directly to their own employers. The bargeman is slightly hurt but it's nothing serious. Ron, you've got to get us out of here."

"Of course we are going to do everything we can. Now let me talk to the man in charge."

Ron was in efficiency mode: he knew that the company's and his own personal reputation would rest on a rapid and successful outcome to negotiations.

"This is our boss, he's called Ron, he wants to talk to you."

Dricus handed the phone to Youth Shall Prosper. Youth Shall Prosper removed the joint from his mouth and handed it to one of his well-dressed henchmen.

"Hello, Mr Ron, I have your people here. I am from the Movement for the Emancipation of the Niger Delta, I speak for the Niger Deltans, we are very annoyed."

There was something bizarrely understated, Mo felt, in the thin man's choice of words. 'Annoyed' seemed a totally inappropriate word to cover the maelstrom of munitions that had so recently engulfed the barge. It occurred to Mo that Youth Shall Prosper's tone was almost deferential, almost apologetic, even though he was making demands and threatening murder.

"You can call me 'The General', it is easier to say, I think, than 'Youth Shall Prosper'."

The captives sat in transfixed silence, trying to fill in the blanks, to guess the other side of the conversation that was determining their fate. Youth Shall Prosper did not help things by strolling around as he spoke, phone to his ear and head tilted back. His stance was so casual he might have been chatting to his girlfriend on a quiet summer stroll.

"Mr Ron, You must pay five hundred million naira or we will, I am afraid, not be able to release these men. We will have to shoot them."

Mo watched as Youth Shall Prosper handed back the phone to Dricus.

"Speak to your boss man. Tell him we are serious people. Tell him he must pay and that our people are suffering." He held out the phone. "Take it! Tell him!"

Dricus took the phone. As he did so, Youth Shall Prosper took back the joint from the well-dressed militant and took a long inhalation. Then he cocked the machine-gun that still hung in his right hand. There was something entirely languorous about the whole action. And he was still smiling at Dricus.

Mo was convinced he was about to witness an execution. And the change in Dricus's posture seemed to imply that he was thinking the same thing. When he spoke there was a tightness in his voice.

"Hello, Ron, It's Dricus again. Yes, I am here with Mark, for the moment we are both O.K. but it's not going to stay like that for long if you don't do what they want. Listen, they have real guns with real bullets. Ron, these people are not playing games. We are somewhere in the swamp, there are mosquitoes like helicopters and there is no malaria medication. These people are living in terrible conditions, and I don't want to die in another man's freedom fight."

Youth Shall Prosper swung his machine gun in the air and fired a burst one-handed into the trees. Leaves, twigs and dew fell from the shattered branches like confetti amongst the hostages. He reached over, grabbed the phone from Dricus, and broke the connection.

"That was very good. Now we will wait."

Ron Forrester heard the shots and then the line went dead. He knew that this was a show of strength, a bit of psychological theatre learnt from Hollywood and designed to upset him, to frighten him into thinking that someone had just been shot. Deep down, he rather relished the idea of a bunch of divers being slaughtered; but it would be disastrous for business and not, therefore, in his fiscal interest, however much short-term gratification it might give him.

He looked down at the quivering Darren Seaton on the floor. The shots had been loud enough for him to hear. He was still in the foetal position with his hands clasped about his head, sobbing gently. Forrester looked again and toyed with the thought of kicking him, driving the heel of his shoe into those white flabby features. The thought stirred him between his legs. He could feel his jaw setting involuntarily as he imagined the nose erupting in blood as he pounded that useless head into the mud-and-beer-stained floor.

"Get up, you useless piece of shit!"

But he needed Darren. Darren was his mole, his gopher; he needed the relief that bullying Darren gave him.

Had Ron Forrester been of a slightly less Machiavellian disposition, his approach to the situation would have been the stuff of self-help books and motivational speakers the world over. 'There are no problems, just opportunities,' he was wont to remark when there was enough alcohol in his system to loosen his tongue. Unfortunately, what was apparently an admirably positive approach to life actually interpreted itself as 'a problem for *someone else* means an opportunity for Ron to make *more* problems for *someone else*.' He liked power, it excited him, as the bruised faces of many of the local bar girls would testify. *The situation he now faced must,* he thought, *be turned to his own advantage.* The diving department was under stress; he could use the opportunity to gain a foothold, bring them under his sway.

Darren was slowly picking himself up off the floor, still snivelling, and avoiding looking at Ron. Ron watched with ill-concealed disgust as Darren wiped his nose on the end of his T-shirt. Soon he would be rid of people like him, but for now they served their purpose.

Chapter Seventeen

Mo was taken with his fellow captives back to the shack where he had first been interrogated. This time, they were taken to a room at the opposite end of the building. There were two mattresses on the floor, both rancid. The floor itself was rough-hewn timber, as were the walls. There was a window over which a corrugated iron shutter had been tied.

"This is where you will sleep," the Secretary informed them. Then he left them to their own devices.

Mo found himself sharing a mattress with the American. *Although, given the size of the American, 'sharing' might not be the most appropriate term*, Mo reflected as he perched precariously on the edge. He had not been prepared for the mosquitoes. Many times in his life Mo had been bitten by mosquitoes, midges and various other insects, but they were as nothing compared to the persistence and sheer pain of the mosquitoes that feasted on him now. He thought back to Dricus's comment on the phone comparing them to helicopters. As a child in Gaza, Mo had learnt to fear helicopters; then, in the oil industry, he had come to see them as a convenient taxi service. Though even after years of walking across helidecks to be strapped into Sikorskys, the thwacking of the rotors as they carved through the air would occasionally send his mind reeling back to childhood days, when he had hidden in the cellars with his mother as the Israeli helicopters slammed missiles into the neighbourhood.

Occasionally he would feel a stab as his skin was penetrated; but worst was the irresistible itch that would start up, especially in the soles of his feet. The temptation just to touch it with his other foot was almost overwhelming. It did not take long to learn, however, that this was a very bad move. The pain that shot through his legs would last all night. "They are brutal," The Secretary later remarked to him, "Everything in the Niger Delta," he went on with the slightest hint of a smile, "is brutal. The mosquitoes, the land, the people, the animals, they are all brutal. We are a brutal people, in a brutal land." Then he stopped for a moment and looked at Mo, and smiled. "But yes, you are right: the mosquitoes are the most brutal!"

The American was already asleep. His breathing was even more audible in sleep than in waking, though his activity levels were about the same. Mo lay on the edge of the mattress; he had only been wearing overalls when he had been captured and he had no shoes. He looked around the little room; if only there was some cloth he could tie about his feet that might protect them a little from the incessant assault. The American was sleeping in his work boots, as was Mike the English diver. Both appeared to be asleep. Across from him on the other mattress, Dricus seemed to be suffering similar problems with his feet by the way he was constantly rubbing one against the other. Even over Tommy's snores, Mo could hear the sounds of the jungle, the cicadas chirping in the night, the murmur of voices from other rooms, the occasional muffled laugh.

He tried to curl himself up in to a foetal position to limit the amount of flesh that was exposed to the marauding mosquitoes. But the position was not comfortable and he found most of his body resting on the floor. The American continued to snore besides him, apparently oblivious to the incessant high-pitched whine of the mosquitoes and the sharp assaults they launched against his body.

There was a pattering sound on the wooden floor not far from Mo's head. He looked up. Less than a metre from his head was the clear outline of the largest, hairiest spider he had ever seen. His tired and bitten body tried to jump to its feet, but another instinct told him not to move lest he attract the creature's attention. Mo was no lover of spiders of any size, and certainly not of spiders that appeared to be at least the size of his hand. He watched in horror, transfixed, as the thing continued its journey across the floor and then squeezed its enormous body through a crack in the lower plank of the wall by the head of his mattress and the floor. *That was it,* Mo thought, *things could not possibly get any worse.* Another part of his brain intervened, he knew that that was nonsense; he was a hostage surrounded by armed men and he was worrying about arachnids to which he held no interest whatsoever. Then, against all his instincts, he lay down again on the mattress and fell into a deep but troubled sleep.

The first thing he noticed when he awoke the following morning was the pain in his head, and he wondered whether it had not been the pain that had awakened him. It seemed to start at the base of his neck and to be pulsing pain through his cranium. His entire body ached; he felt gritty and dirty, and the mosquito bites were itching unbearably. His face was pressed against the oily mattress. He was sure that as soon as he moved it would feel worse. Tommy was still snoring beside him. A metre away from him, he could sense, as much as see, Dricus beginning to stir.

"Jesus, bru, my fucking head." The South African was clasping his head and groaning. His stirring had awakened Mark. "How you feeling bru?"

"Like a crock of shit, fuck off and leave me alone." The Englishman's voice was groggy with sleep.

"What do you think happens now?" Mo ventured.

"I guess we just wait, bru. They feed us an' take care of us to a point, I should think, we're worthless as damaged goods!" Dricus almost laughed, but stopped short. "Jesus, bru, my fucking head, what the fuck is wrong with me?"

A drum started to beat not far from the front of the hut.

"Jesus, that's the last fucking thing I need."

Mo lifted himself up, but as soon as his legs took his weight he wished he hadn't. The mosquitoes had decimated his feet. He eased himself over to the window and pushed back the side of the corrugated iron shutter.

About ten metres away, at the edge of the clearing, a plank had been lain across two smaller logs to form a sort of small table about three inches off the ground. An emaciated man wearing no clothes at all was sitting on the plank, holding a large wooden drum with an animal skin drawn across it. He was beating out a simple rhythm with a piece of wood. Other men were slowly approaching the drummer. By their movements, it was clear that most of them were still waking up. The drummer was joined by another man, he wore a Liverpool football shirt and started to play a counter-rhythm on a Coke bottle with a nail. A third man joined in with a smaller animal skin drum.

Mo had grown up with the rhythms of Arabic music and he quickly recognised that there was some very complex syncopation going on. For a moment he forgot the pounding in his head. The music held him enthralled, much the way the spider had the night before. He barely noticed as he was joined by a bleary-eyed Dricus at the window.

From where they stood, they looked straight on to what served the camp as a parade ground. They were not to know, but all MEND camps were built on similar principals laid down by Adaka Borro, the spiritual godfather of the movement. What Dricus and Mo saw was almost textbook. There was a clear space surrounded by tall trees. The camp had been built in the crook of a bend in the river; at the apex of the bend was the rickety little jetty where Mo had landed the previous afternoon. There was a gentle slope down towards the jetty. Just beyond the ridge sat the little coconut shrine where the hostages had been anointed on arrival. All around the perimeter of the clearing, the trees were adorned with strips of cloth in red, black and white, the same adornments as the kidnappers had worn during the raid, though now saturated with dew they hung limp and heavy against the bark.

As the two men watched, unsure of whether or not they were wise to do so, another drummer joined the group. Men were still shambling on to the parade ground from the huts on the perimeter and, it appeared, beyond. Some were dressed in shorts, others were wearing paramilitary apparel and others were naked. Mo noticed that they were forming a group focused around the man who had been his chief tormentor the day before. Jackson was wearing a pair of Union Jack boxer shorts and had a strip of white cloth tied about his head. There was a leaf tucked into the front of his bandana. The group seemed to be starting gradually to move in time with the constant beating of the drums. No order was given, it was almost a metamorphosis or awakening: as the rhythms were absorbed into the group and took hold, they gradually animated them into one pulsating, organic mass. Each man's shoulders slouched forwards, moving to the rhythm, while their hands hung loosely at their sides. Some were so stooped that their hands dangled below their knees. They stomped their feet to the beat, slowly forming into two lines, which began to trudge rhythmically up and down the parade ground.

Jackson danced between the two lines. He would cry out in his high, clear voice, "Swanaa?" to which the group would chorus, "Wanaa!" Another voice would then cry out, "Asiminia?" eliciting a great guttural heave of, "A ssee aye ay!" Occasionally, one of the men would break off and dance alone before Jackson, a violent gyrating maelstrom of arms and legs; this would carry on, till the next time Jackson cried out, when the dancer would return to his place in the trudging line, his chest heaving and his skin glistening with sweat. Even during the fits of activity, Mo noticed that all the dancers had the same bland, almost blank, expressions: it was hypnotic.

The only person who seemed unmoved and detached from the spectacle was The Secretary. Still dressed like an African Che

152

Guevara, he leant against one of the trees watching and quietly smoking a hand-rolled cigarette. A flicker of emotion passed across his face – almost, it appeared to Mo, a look of contempt. The Secretary drew again on his cigarette. He looked across the compound and caught Mo's eye. He held the gaze slightly too long for Mo's comfort. Breathing out a huge swathe of smoke, he flicked away the stub of his cigarette, pushed himself up off the tree against which he had been leaning, and shambled off into the bush.

The exchange of glances had pulled Mo's attention away from the dancers, but still they danced. Still the drums played. Clouds rolled overhead, thunder rumbled across the sky, stirring the heavy damp atmosphere, and then the heavens opened up. Rain fell as only African rain can: pounding into the trees, churning up the earth like bullets, raising a noise like an angry crowd as it battered down on the corrugated iron roofs of the huts. African rain is different from rain everywhere else in the world. African rain doesn't fall; it hurls itself at the ground like the spite of a vengeful deity.

The rain fell so hard it cut the skin, like thousands of warm razor blades. It fell on the sills of the window as Mo looked out and ricocheted up off the coarse wood, stinging Mo's face as he watched the militants. And still they danced.

The rain and the dancing stopped almost simultaneously; the parade ground had been churned to a mud bath. Tommy was awake; the swelling across his nose and around his eyes was becoming a deep, imperial purple. He sat in the corner of the hostage room, legs straight out in front of him, his stomach resting on his thighs.

Dricus took Mo by the elbow and guided him out of the room. They stood on the muddy ground, the air still moist from the heavy rain.

"Listen, bru, I don't know how well you know Tommy, but he's a liability. We needed to keep an eye on him if we mean to get out of this alive."

Mo looked uncomprehending.

"Look, he's not too bright. He's not fit, and he's got a big mouth." Dricus paused, and held Mo's eye. "Look, bru, I don't know much about you, but you look quite fit and you must have passed some exams to get your job, so despite being an engineer you must be quite bright. With Tommy what you see is what you get. He's just a big, fat, thick yank. Have you been in the military?"

"I grew up in the Gaza strip. It's hardly necessary."

"Right. So I guess that wasn't the first time you heard gunfire, then?"

"Hardly."

"Listen, I was in the Recce's in South Africa, in the old days, when we still had a country. You should understand what that means, if you're Palestinian. They take our land and say it's their divine fucking right!"

Mo looked sharply at Dricus; there was a sudden change in his voice as he uttered, or rather spat, the last few words: the accent became harsher and his face was almost unrecognisable as the soft-spoken man Mo had so often greeted on the barge but to whom he had never really spoken.

Dricus took a breath. He seemed to change before Mo's eyes back into the man he had been a few minutes before. Even so, Mo was left with an uncomfortable feeling: Dricus had stirred up long-forgotten memories of angry, bitter men with beards, some with scarves and others with skull caps, demanding each other's blood over a barren land. That such disputes could still arouse such emotion, even here, where different men with the same guns were fighting over a very different land, was a tragedy in itself.

"Listen," Dricus continued. "Mike and I have been talking. I don't know how much you know about these kidnapping situations here in Nigeria, but usually they hold the guys for a couple for weeks, then the money is paid, and that's it. But it can go wrong, and we have to be ready. That's why we need to agree about Tommy. Look," he stared Mo hard in the eyes, "if we have to run we're not taking him with us. That leaves us no choice. When we've gone they will torture and kill him; he will tell them anything he knows about our plans, and he will die horribly. So if we have to go we will have to kill him first."

It seemed to Mo that Dricus rushed out the last sentence, uncomfortable with what he was saying. "Also, bru, he's got a lekker pair of boots and you ain't gonna get far in the bush with bare feet!"

Dricus winked and squeezed his arm turned, and walked back into the hut.

Mo stood quietly watching the slow movement of the river.

Dricus was about to enter the hut when he thought better of it. Tommy would be sitting there, and Dricus found him revolting, his fat spilling out all creased with stretch marks like an old woman. Dricus, though, was not quite as brutal as he had been trying to convince himself he was: he did not want to look Tommy in the eye, even if they were weak and watery eyes. Instead he carried on walking along the front of the hut.

As he approached the open section he heard raised voices and slowed his approach. He walked slowly, staying close to the wall so the protagonists might not notice him, trying to look casual enough that, should someone come upon him from another direction, it would not look like he was eavesdropping but simply walking carefully, that his bare feet might not slip on the muddy surface.

What he saw, to his surprise, was Mark sitting on the bench where he had been seated the day before when he was asked to write his name and details. He was smoking, the cigarette held between thumb and forefinger and cupped inside his right hand. The generator behind the hut was running noisily, and the TV was on. 50 Cent was playing, welcoming to the 'Candy Shop' anyone who cared to listen. In front of Mark a young militant stood, gun in one hand, joint in the other. He was wearing nothing but a pair of denim shorts that were pulled down below his buttocks, as if he had been surprised whilst in the act of going to the toilet and then forgotten about them.

Dricus wondered how he managed to walk.

Mark looked comfortable and was nodding occasionally as if in agreement. It occurred to Dricus, though, that Mark looked as if he was far more interested in his cigarette than in what was being said to him. As Dricus's ears adjusted so that he could identify speech from television, he began to hear what the half-clad militant was saying, and the sentiment sounded strangely familiar.

"Dem Biaffran dey id de one what cause all de problem in diis country, dey steal from de real Nigerian, 'tis dem wid dey 419 what do cheat everybody. Dey is everywhere, every city you do go you do find dem dere. Dem Muslim in de north have de right idea and did kill dem like cockroaches. An you know what white man, it is dem what bring you here, not us 'tis den dat love de money so much, they has de oil companies in America wid dere Jewish broddas from America! They fuck us and bring you here so we has to kidnap you people, to make dem listen. Now dey is clever people dem Igbo cockroaches dey is not de government cause dey do not like people to see dem have de power in de land, but dey have de money and de business and dey demselves tell de government what to do so it be good for dem an' deir Igbo children."

Mark nodded and asked for another cigarette. It occurred to Dricus that the only thing that had changed was the accent; he had heard the same rant from impoverished and embittered Afrikaans farmers about the rich Jews of Johannesburg – for fuck's sake they even called it 'Jewburg' – and he had watched it on grainy black and white footage on the history channel, the German vitriol translated into pristine white letters at the foot of the screen.

He guessed there must be a table just out of his sight, because the militant who still had his back to him ducked right and then leant forwards towards Mark, lighting the cigarette with a green plastic lighter.

"An' you know what dey is doing now?" The speaker continued, sure in the knowledge that the cigarette would have sedated his audience into attention. "You know what they do now?" The voice developed an edge that was clearly not lost on Mark: he looked up from his cigarette, the uncertainty on his face evident to Dricus. He could imagine what was going through Mark's mind: *was that a rhetorical question? Was he expected to know? Was he about to be beaten about the head with a rifle for not paying attention?*

The young militant took a long draw on his joint, then threw his head back and exhaled forcibly, sending a plume of smoke above his head. He looked back down at Mark. "Of course you don't know!" He laughed and took another long drag off the joint. "You see," he continued, passing the gun from one hand to the other like a ball, the joint hanging from his bottom lip, "dat is 'cause dey is so clever! Dey fool de people it is only us, the fighters of MEND. You know MEND? Yes? We are MEND! The Movement for the Emancipation of Niger Delta! It is only MEND dat sees de truth! You know what is Nollywood? It is de films made in Nigeria, Nigerian people make many films, sell everywhere in Africa, number one films, make big big money! Any way you look at dem Nollywood films now dey is all made by Igbo people. Igbo people actors, Igbo people write dem, Igbo people produce dem, Igbo people tell stories to whole world 'bout how good Igbo people are! I tell you white man when my fadda fight again' dem Biafran Igbo scum kill millions of dem. Even de white people cut off de food for de cockroaches for dat dey die! But not kill enough, Nigeria still infested wid dem bastards."

"Yeah right! It's pretty bad huh?"

Dricus recognised a platitude when he heard one, even if the young militant did not.

The militant seemed pleased with himself; he leaned forword again and slapped Mark on the shoulder. "Hey, Mark, you good white man we not shoot you! You go home you family when company pay money, tell them, pay quick so you go home. Here," he gestured wildly with his arm at the surrounding bush, "here no good for you people! Too much mosquito, too much malaria no good for you! Your blood not same black man blood, good you go home my friend; feel free! You sure you no want smoke ganja?"

Mark smiled and shook his head. The militant swaggered off chanting to himself: "Swanaa? Wanaa!"

Mark waited till the young man was out of sight, shook his head, then proceeded to carefully pinch off the end of his cigarette and tuck it behind his ear. Dricus noticed that he had hardly smoked it. *Cunning bugger*, he thought. Mark stood up, looked around again, put both hands in his pockets and stepped outside. He laughed.

"Jesus! What was that all about? I just sat there and nodded, didn't have a friggin' clue what he was on about. Seemed to make him happy though!"

The pair of them started to walk a circuit of the parade ground. They had done two laps, neither of them speaking, when Mark said, "Dricus, I don't get this: he kept going on about '*eeboos*', and killing them. I thought that was what they called us."

"No, bru, I keep forgetting you're new to Africa. It's an easy mistake to make. '*Oyibo*' is what most Nigerians call white people. '*Igbo*' is a tribe, I think the second biggest in Nigeria, and one of the biggest in West Africa. '*Oyibo*' is I think an Igbo word. Down here they don't use that because they hate the Igbos because of the Biafran war and a load of other shit. Here they call us *ben eye ewe* or something similar – not quite sure how they pronounce it."

"Yeah I gathered he wasn't too keen on the Igbos! Funny, innit, back in the UK you get all the black lobbyists going on about how racist the whites are and how black people can never be racist, then you come out here and they're at each other's throats. I tell you, listening to that little fucker, I might as well have been listening to some right-wing thug in the UK going on about the Jews! And he was talking about his so-called black brothers! Does my friggin' head in!"

Dricus snorted. "You say that to a white South African! Let me tell ya, bru, when the Zulus and Xhosa start going at one another, man, you wouldn't believe it! I was no fan of apartheid but it kept them apart from each other as well. Now it's a never-ending fucking body count!"

They walked on for a bit, then Dricus interrupted the silence. "You know, it's funny you should mention the Jews, 'cause that was exactly what I was thinking when I was listening to him, and I was remembering something, you know? A few years ago, we had an Igbo chief on board, looked after the Nigerian galley, you know, made the *garri* and all that gooey stuff they eat, and he was all right. Well, he was telling me one day about how the Igbos are in fact the real black Jews, the famous 'lost tribe of Israel'." He walked on. "Well, at the time that got me thinking: you knew I've been working here for years, and I know them quite well, and you know what? All the business people I know here are Igbo, and during the Biafran war it was quite well known in S.A. that Israel was supplying weapons they had seized off the Arabs in the Yom Kippur war to the Igbos for free! South African government at the time even recognised them as a state! Makes you wonder? About the same time there was a terrible famine here amongst the Biafrans, and it was the South African Jews who were behind some of the fundraising."

"Well, they should friggin' love old Mo, then: he's a bloody Arab, in 'e! Probably hates the Jews more than this lot do!"

"Got reason, though: he's Palestinian! You know they have a saying in Nigeria: 'A place is not fit for human habitation if no Igbo man can be found there.' And I remember once a rigger telling me a joke about them. He said: 'The Americans weren't the first people on the moon, it was the Nigerians.' Obviously every body looks at him like he's a fucking idiot, then he carries on: "When Neil Armstrong walked around the big rock he found an Igbo man with a souvenir stall selling cheap sunglasses and imitation watches."

As the two men approached the river end of their circuit, they noticed that Mo was now sitting on the little bench where the drummer had sat, and was watching them thoughtfully. The walkers joined him, and Mo caught Dricus's eye.

"Yeah, Mark and I have already talked. What about you? You cool with it, bru?"

"Well, I don't like it and I hope it doesn't come to that, but you're right, I suppose. But we wait? I understand that most of the time these things are sorted quite quickly for cash, isn't that right? We don't want to go creating a worse situation than we're in already."

"No, we have to agree," Mark replied, "that's all. None of us want it to come to that."

"Good. But yes, I agree with you. Anyway, how are you guys feeling? I've got the worst headache I've ever had in my life!"

"Me too, I feel like shit, like someone stuck my head in a vice and kept cranking it up," said Mark. He pulled the partially smoked cigarette from behind his ear and stuck it between his lips. One of the militants was standing not far off, keeping a casual eye upon them. Mark held out his arm and made a gesture imitating the use of a lighter. Seconds later, his cigarette was lit.

"Thanks, dude!"

"No wahalla, feel free!"

The militant ambled away.

"If one of them fuckers tells me to *feel free* again I am gonna fucking scream. They come on to our barge, shoot the fuck out of the place, drag us into the swamp, stick us in front of a firing squad, hold guns to our heads, and then they tell us 'feel free' and want to be friends – who the fuck do these people think they are?" Mark kicked angrily at a tree stump, spat, stood up and started to walk off, his whole body taut with suppressed rage.

Dricus made to follow him.

Mo reached out and placed a hand on his arm. "No, leave him!"

There was almost a command in his voice, which took Dricus aback. He was not used to assertive engineers and, he acknowledged guiltily to himself, he wasn't used to taking orders from a coloured – not unless they were holding a gun.

Mo squeezed his arm; it was uncomfortably intimate, but Dricus was well enough travelled to recognise it for what it was.

Mo looked at him for a moment as if thinking what to say, as if weighing up whether he was doing the right thing, whether or not this sub-sea manual labourer from the home of racial segregation, from the other side of the barbed wire fence, was ready for what he was going to say. Dricus found the pause excruciating; he hoped his ethnocentrism had not been too obvious.

Mo appeared to come to some sort of decision. "You must leave him, my friend. If you follow him, he will fight you. He is in shock and needs to lash out at someone. Just watch him and keep him away from them, we don't want him snapping at them. And we must not fight amongst ourselves if we are going to live." Mo shrugged and gave a wry smile. "Remember I grew up in Gaza! I have seen people in this state so often it is almost routine; at least here he cannot go out and blow himself up! But then I suppose that he has something to live for. We didn't."

The end of his sentence trailed away, almost as if from a man falling slowly over a cliff. Dricus noticed that Mo was no longer looking at him but staring deep into the earth, to some distant hell that Dricus could not begin to imagine. Suddenly he felt a great respect for Mo. Generally he regarded engineers with little more than contempt, at best they were an inconvenience, people who had never done the job, full of theory and no practical common sense. But he had begun to see Mo in a new light.

"You know," Mo continued, "I used to work with a Rhodesian barge foreman."

The choice of the word 'Rhodesia' was not lost on Dricus.

"It's funny, we had such similar backgrounds."

Dricus's face must have expressed more shock than he intended. Mo almost laughed.

"Really, bru," he mimicked the South African's accent perfectly. "No, you must understand, this Rhodesian, he grew up on a farm his parents and grandparents had built from nothing, into which they had poured their lives, their sweat and their blood. Then one day people came and took it away from them, murdered them in their beds, because they believed that God, through the prophecy of Mugabe, had told them the land was theirs! I used to look through the wire fence with my grandmother when I was a child and watch the Israeli machines on the farm that *her* family had farmed for over 800 years, and now it was taken from them by force 'because God said so!'"

Dricus had never heard the word 'God' uttered with such venom before.

"I guess I had never thought of it like that, I mean."

"You mean you never had a kaffir make you feel uncomfortable like that before."

Mo's smile took the sting out of the truth. "No, wahalla, my friend. I have worked with many South Africans before. There is no problem, but it just shows how crazy the whole thing is. You know, we gave you the word 'kaffir', it is the Arabic word for 'non-believer', and now here we are together being held at gunpoint by some more people you would probably call kaffir, to whom God has promised land. You know what I think?"

"No?" Dricus was flabbergasted, he had no idea where this was leading and found Mo's equanimity unnerving. "No. Go on. What do you think?"

"God should learn to keep his mouth shut!"

Despite having spent years off shore and having heard about every conceivable form of blasphemy and obscenity imaginable, Dricus was still at heart a well-brought-up, God-fearing Afrikaner and, however much he tried to rationalise it, blasphemy still shocked him, especially coming from an Arab who, he had assumed, was a Muslim. Dricus did not know where to turn.

"Ah! Now I have shocked you! No, I am not a good little Muslim, I am an engineer, a scientist, an empiricist. I believe in what I can see and measure, not old stories written down thousands of years ago, full of hate and murder. And yes, I do know what divers think of engineers; but some of us can think for ourselves you know."

A shadow fell between them and they both looked up from the low benches. Mark was standing in front of them, a fresh cigarette unlit between his lips.

"Feeling better?" Mo enquired.

"Yeah, I guess so... it's just so goddamned frustrating, and I've got such a fucking headache, and these little fuckers keep being *nice*... makes me wanna scream. And you know they can't see what's wrong! Gave me some more fags though!"

Chapter Eighteen

Chidi stepped forwards. His opponent was taller than him and a few years older. They both bowed to the umpire, then turned and bowed to the three judges, and finally they faced each other. With their hands held together as if in prayer, impeded only by the laced-up gloves, bowed again. The gum-shield filled his mouth and the protective helmet smelt of years of stale sweat and blood, hope and despair, the history of fights long forgotten.

The gloves had been a present from Aunty Sarah for his fifteenth birthday. He had always thought it strange that the two such different women in whose company he had grown up had been so supportive of his passion for kickboxing. His mamma, who had always been so protective when he was smaller, was sitting just a few metres away from the edge of the mat, where a much bigger boy was about to do his best to hurt her little one. Yet there she sat. As always, she wore traditional lace. He could not remember seeing his mother in modern clothes; all his friend's mothers wore modern clothes, except the ones who were clearly villagers. Mamma, though, was not a villager; she was better read than many of his teachers and she had helped him all the way through school. There had been times when he had almost felt ashamed of her: all she seemed to do was clean up after Uncle Harrison and wear old-fashioned clothes. But she had always been there for him and as he grew older he had come again to rely on her companionship. She didn't look like the mothers of his friends, nor did she sit and gossip with them. She knew them all, it was true, and she would smile and pass the time of day with them, but she always seemed different. Taking care of

Uncle Harrison took up much of her time, and she did have other friends, but Chidi always felt that his mamma was somehow special, somehow more in focus than the rest of the world.

One day his maths teacher had been teaching the class about eccentric and concentric circles. He had thought of his mamma, and the word had taken on a new meaning for him; that was his mother: eccentric. He wasn't sure if she would have appreciated the idea, so he never said anything, but that was how he had come to think of her, and he was very proud of her now, with her long lace and straight back and silent way of smiling. He desperately wanted to win this fight; he wanted her to be as proud of him as he was of her.

Chioma sat watching. A man opposite her, the father of the boy her son was about to fight, leant towards the woman seated at his side. This woman, who was the older boy's mother, was also wearing lace; but on her it didn't look comfortable, Chioma felt, more of a statement than a natural way to dress.

"Have you seen the way she watches him? It's like watching a cat waiting to pounce," the man said to his wife.

"What is you doing lookin' at dat woman?" She jabbed her husband hard in the side with a comb that might have been in her hand for just that purpose. "Der some tin' not natural 'bout dat woman, she be doing da voodoo or somet'ing. You keep your eyes to yourself before she go doin' some o' dat magic on you an' ah be doin' something far worse to you!"

The lady crossed herself and tried hard to look righteous. She jabbed her husband again, though not quite so hard this time, just to make sure he had got the message.

Chioma caught the movement out of the corner of her eye and looked over at the woman. Their eyes met. Chioma smiled, the woman crossed herself again and looked straight ahead, concentrating on her righteousness. She shivered; she found she desperately wanted to urinate.

Chioma continued to look. *People were strange,* she thought to herself, then went back to watching her son and immediately forgot about the tubby woman who looked like she needed the toilet.

Chidi eyed his opponent. The boy was older than him and now, up close, Chidi could see that he was strong and looked confident. The muscles in his arms were prominent. Suddenly Chidi was scared. He didn't want to be there in the ring facing this man. He could throw off his gloves and cry, run to mamma, bury his head in her skirts and cover his shame. She would stroke his head and tell him that it was O.K.

The fear tugged at him; his throat was dry, his eyes felt moist. He was going to get hurt.

The two young men faced each other, appraising each other, trying to dominate, adolescent hormones releasing confusing pheromones, their bodies controlled by instincts so deeply buried in their essence that they were hardly aware of them in themselves but deeply aware of them in the other. Their conscious minds told them to adopt the stances their trainers had taught them; evolution drew the blood away from their faces, constricted their pupils and lowered their heads so that their eyes were protected. Domination was everything. Slowly, they began to circle each other, in the manner prescribed by the sport. And beneath the surface, something far deeper was happening, something that stretched back across time, that touched the very core of all those males present in this converted church hall, not far from the polluted seas that thrashed the litter-strewn coastline of Port Harcourt. Their very chromosomes were sparring, testing each other out, judging who, when it came to the ultimate test, would survive, whose DNA would be passed to the females and whose would slowly decompose and be forgotten. The eternal quest for the alpha male.

Chioma watched intently as the beloved fruit of her womb measured himself against his rival. She could see rivulets of sweat forming on the skin she had created and she was proud of her child; she knew he was becoming a man. *There was*, she reflected, *little of his father in him; Azzi had been a gentle man who had struggled through life without flare or inspiration*. Though now, as she watched their Chidi, she suddenly and for the first time in years found herself standing by a dusty roadside again. For a moment her mind left the ring, and she was watching not Chidi but Azzi as he placed himself in front of the fat man from the federal government. She could feel little Chidi bury his head against her breast as the huge, rusting yellow bulldozers smashed into the side of their home.

Chidi's right foot left the floor and slammed in to the side of the older boy's head. The older boy's parents flinched as their son's head twitched sideways; the mother with fear for her child, the father with the unconscious shame that this fatherless pup was violating the hierarchy of male dominance, as if he himself had taken the blow. He did not rationalise it as such, but an attentive observer would have noticed the slight shift in his body language as he leant forwards, his body partially shielding his woman from the hostility, the shame, the threat to his manhood, his head lowered ever so slightly and his jaw set.

Chioma, on the other hand, watched with pride.

To her right sat an elderly man whose grandson had been fighting in the younger age groups and was now, with a thick lip for a trophy, out playing football behind the hall with his recent opponent, all thoughts of the competition forgotten. For them, the violence was over, and the most important thing in their universe was to kick a partially inflated football between two milk crates. The old man, sitting there in his best Sunday suit, was tired, but the hall was cool and he enjoyed the competition – there had been nothing of the sort in his youth. The British had established boxing clubs, but they had been few and far between and somewhat elitist; here, he could pass a pleasant afternoon. He watched as Chidi, emboldened, planted the heel of his left foot hard in his opponent's chest. His foot returned to the mat to provide a pivot for his body and his right heel impacted hard on the other boy's cheekbone. Blood sprayed from his nose in a crimson shower, little droplets of scarlet rain irrigating the arid mats. The referee stepped in and separated the pair. They stood, staring at each other, the body language now quite different: the older boy's shoulders were sagging while Chidi seemed to grow in stature, a David metamorphosing into a Goliath.

For some reason he could not adequately explain, the old man suddenly wondered if Cain and Abel had looked like this as they faced each other on some desolate plain at the birth of time.

Chioma felt herself swelling with pride.

Chidi's fight did not last long. His opponent's eyes were starting to swell and his nose was bleeding badly.

The referee put a stop to it – after all, they were children, and this was supposed to be a sport. He had been a coach for many years. He had worked for much of his life in Paris, doing various jobs – hospital porter, chef – and eventually he had had his own window-cleaning business which, after twenty years away, he had finally sold and come back to Nigeria. During his exodus he had learnt much, and one thing that had particularly impressed him was the success of the martial arts clubs in the Arab quarters of Paris. These small clubs seemed to give meaning and discipline to young boys and girls who would otherwise have roamed the wreckage and needle-strewn waste grounds between the HLMs where they were invariably housed. He himself had been introduced to the martial arts by a young, intense Algerian, whom he had met working in a hospital laundry. He never looked back: through all his years in Paris he had trained, and it had provided him with friends and a sense of identity. When his window-cleaning business started to grow, it was from his martial arts club that he recruited his employees. They were fit, hard working and, he figured, highly unlikely to get mugged.

He had returned to Nigeria with his Vietnamese wife. Their teenage and extremely beautiful daughter stayed behind in Paris, to study and hopefully find work. There was no future for her in Nigeria, she said: she was a half-caste and knew little of the culture or any of the language. She thought in French and could communicate well enough in Vietnamese, but her English was appalling.

On his return, he and his wife found themselves well off. They lived in a nice house and his wife opened a restaurant. He wanted to give something back to the community that had nurtured him as a child, recreate the success he had seen in Paris. So he opened a dojo.

There was some success, and he enjoyed it. It gave his life in retirement some meaning. He had forgotten, however, that he was now dealing with his own people in their own country. In Paris he had been dealing with immigrants who clung together for support in a hostile cultural environment. Here, there was a level of fierce competition amongst the parents that far outstripped anything that took place on the mats.

As he watched Chidi and his vanquished opponent bow to each other, he felt a sense of pride. This, to him, was one of the most important aspects of what he taught: respect. What happened on the mat stayed on the mat. Both boys bowed to him and then to the judges. He was proud of them. It did not escape his attention that the father of the defeated boy was scowling and staring hard at Chidi, while avoiding the glances of his own son. If the boys were to grow into viable members of society, they needed their parents' support, and that did not involve punishing noble failure. He had seen boys come to training after losing a fight, with bruises that he was sure they had not sustained on the mat. He thought he might try and speak to the father. Or maybe not. There was only so much he could do.

Chidi stepped off the mat and walked up to his mother. Considering the violence in which he had so recently been involved, he now seemed somewhat shy and awkward. He was immensely proud – even more so, given that his mother had seen him win – and he was proud, too, of the way she looked. He knew he had the most beautiful mother in the room. When fighting, he had been totally and utterly focused, his body and being had been one, and it was that which had assured him his victory. As soon as it was all over, though, he was again Chidi. It was as if his mother had seen him naked, seen his raw adolescent soul exposed. Part of his mind leapt on the thought and told him how ridiculous it was – of course she had seen him naked, she was his mother! There was, however, something else: she had glimpsed a side of him that he did not want her to see, the emerging man. He struggled to explain it to himself – a feeling, something so deep and primordial that he could not put it into words; it was almost as if she had seen him having sex. And in a way he was right, she had, she had witnessed the metamorphosis of an alpha male.

The next round in the league would be a week later. Chidi left the hall and made his way to the crude changing room. Chioma sat through the next fight, not really concentrating, waiting for Chidi to re-emerge; she knew it was a long process. He had started to worry about his skin and general appearance, and she had teased him that he used more cream on his body than she did. He had reacted badly and she had dropped the topic, just hoping he would get through this particularly hormonal stage of growing up quickly.

The fight ended and Chioma used the opportunity to slip out of the hall. She would wait for Chidi outside: *what with the vanity and gossiping, teenage boys were worse than women*, she thought to herself.

She waited in the rough waste land that served as a car and motorbike park and general dump. She had been there long enough to start to daydream when the parents of the boy Chidi had beaten came out, closely followed by their son.

The two boys had retired to the changing room, all animosity forgotten. They had shared a can of coke and their shampoo, and then had fallen into a discussion on the merits and otherwise of the girls in the latest Two Face video. The coach would have been proud of them.

The father of other boy, Chris, had strutted fitfully up and down outside the changing room, unable to stay in his seat at the ringside, the scene of his public humiliation at the hands and feet of a fatherless Igbo. His wife stayed seated, fanning herself with her head held high, doing her best to appear as regal as she could. They were above this barbarism; her son was made for better things. This was simply too uncultured for him, her body language seemed to say.

The referee had watched them with a mixture of pity and disgust. This new emerging Nigerian middle-class epitomised to him, in a way, everything that was wrong with his country. He loved Nigeria with a passion, but there were times when he despaired. Chris was a good kid and he was fond of him; he hoped devoutly that the child would not pay too heavy a price for the father's shame.

Eventually it was all too much for Chris' father and he burst into the changing room. When he saw his bruised offspring chatting happily with that filthy little Igbo, that pretty boy who was so unmanly that he looked just like his mother, it was more than his injured pride could bear. The scene he created further humiliated Chris in front of Chidi, who, in the final analysis, was his friend. Tears began to roll down the boy's face and Chidi turned away out of respect for his feelings. But the rampaging father had seen it as a sign of contempt and it only served to aggravate him further. The blood pumped into his flabby cheeks and they shook over the collar of his expensive, over tight shirt.

Chris could feel his own humiliation rising inside. The fight had not upset him; everyone in the club knew Chidi was good – he was a natural and he was also popular and Chris was proud to be known as Chidi's friend. He knew deep down that kickboxing was not for him; he enjoyed the training and he had good friends at the club, but the club to him was far more important than the competitions. Chidi was different: he moved like a cat, and the skills seemed to come effortlessly. Above all, he was not big headed about his talent; he almost wore it with indifference.

Chris stood against the chipped and flaking yellow changing-room wall, his long body submissive before the strutting elder male. He felt his world collapse; pain burned behind his eyes and crushed his chest. Finishing his abusive tirade, his father turned towards Chidi and, with a contemptuous gesture, snarled, "An' I don't know what you think you are looking at! You people don't belong here!"

He started to turn away and reached for the door. Chris could feel something rising inside himself, it was a feeling he half recognised. It started as shame and humiliation, but it was behaving strangely, twisting and turning inside him, pumping adrenalin to unfamiliar parts of his body, shaking his legs, his jaw, his whole frame. It formed words in his throat that he did not want to release, but they too were taking on a life and a will of their own. Slowly and quietly, as if unsure of themselves, like a new hatchling facing for the first time the heat of the sun, they struggled out: "Don't speak to Chidi like that, *he's my friend*."

Chris could not believe what he had done. His father spun on his heel, his hand raised to shoulder height, preparing to deliver a vicious backhand across his son's face and crush both this dissent and his own shame once and for all. But his hand stopped. Something was happening. He watched in disbelief as his son's shoulders rose up and backwards, and his tear-stained face looked up. Not only had he been answered back, but he had been defied. He could not believe it was happening.

A voice in Chris' head was telling him to stop, to cower – how dare he do this thing? But something far stronger was gripping his soul, moving deep beyond his control, something that told him he felt good, that now this thing had started he could not step away.

Words are like bullets: once you have fired them you can never call them back. He loaded the second chamber, and this time the words came with more force. They had grown inside him and they came out fighting. "I said, *don't speak to Chidi like that, he's my friend.*"

He felt strong, he felt free. His father stood still, a stupefied expression fixed on his features, his hand suspended uselessly in mid-air, and suddenly Chris understood that if the blow came, his training would give him the ability to stop it. Yes, the knowledge and the training were there, but even more importantly so was the belief. His whole body was pumping now. "Don't ever humiliate me in front of my friend again, and if you think you could have done better, you get out here and you fight him, he is one of the best and he beat me, but at least I had the balls to get out there and face him, knowing that he *could* beat me. All you can do is bully your wife and children – get *out*!"

The father looked into his son's face. There was something in Chris' expression he had never seen before. He knew that something had changed between them absolutely, and that, in some way he could not explain, he had been beaten, deposed.

He lowered his hand, turned and left.

The old lion was toothless and usurped. His roar no longer trumpeted fear and respect. He was beaten and he left, his tail between his legs, his head slumped between his shoulders.

Chidi breathed out. He felt as if he had been holding his breath throughout the entire confrontation. The atmosphere lifted and suddenly they were just two teenage friends again.

"Sorry about that, dude!"

"Hey, wow! I mean… Jesus, do you realise what you just did?"

"No, but it sure felt good! Bet I catch big wahalla when I get home."

"No, you won't," replied Chidi, with a sudden flash of insight that he could not begin to understand. "I'm sure glad you didn't look at me like that out there, though. I would not have stayed on the mat long enough to beat you, I'd have been halfway to Lagos by now!"

It was enough to release the last of the tension, and they both collapsed in uncontrollable laughter.

It was some time latter that the family came out of the door and walked past Chioma. She saw them coming, and straightened herself up.

"Good evening," she said politely.

Chris's father twitched and forced himself to grunt something that might just pass as a greeting, then lurched towards his Mercedes. His wife looked at Chioma and the sides of her mouth twitched too, as anger surged across her face. Chioma smiled and Chris' mother huffed away, hitching her lace skirts up out of the mud and stumbling inelegantly after her usurped husband.

Chris followed languorously, his face swelling. Chioma knew him well; as one of Chidi's friends she had often spoken to him, and he was always polite and respectful. It was a friendship she encouraged.

"Good evening, Ma Chioma, Chidi is just coming."

"How far, Chris? Are you OK? I don't know what to do with you boys. Is everything all right?"

"Yes, thank you, Ma Chioma. Everything is good. No wahalla, it was a good fight. Chidi is always the best, so I don't mind too much that he beat me."

"Oh, Chrissie," she sighed, "you two, you are growin' up so fast!" She reached out and touched the side of his face where the swelling was beginning to throb. "I hope it doesn't hurt too much!"

"I'll be fine, thank you, Ma Chioma. I'd better hurry or Papa will get crazy."

Chioma nodded and smiled. "We'll see you soon at the house, I hope?"

That smile; it occurred to Chris at that moment that she was probably the most beautiful woman he had ever seen in is life. As he walked slowly to the car, he felt like an ancient king, bearing honourable battle-scars. Which was not, in fact, all that far from the truth, had his coach been there to see him, he would almost have cried with pride.

Chioma watched as the big, expensive car swung out of the yard, crunching the gravel as it went, then all was quiet. She knew Chidi would not be long. Suddenly she felt sad. *It was true*, she told herself, *they were growing up: her baby was rapidly becoming a man*. And then what would she do?

At the same moment that Chidi was facing down the older boy, Sarah was sitting on the porch outside her house and Harrison was sitting in his favourite chair, the very one he had been sitting in when he first met Chioma all those years ago. Sarah no longer wore weave in her hair and the edges were flecked with grey; she was slightly thinner than on the day Chioma walked up the path and asked for food for her child, but her handsome features were still evident as she rocked slowly in the chair that Chioma had insisted that she buy for herself. Cloth, needle and thread rested idly in her lap as she looked at her frail husband. He was dying, they all knew, but now it was different. She thanked God daily for sending her Chioma and the extra years she had had with her husband. Harrison had at least been able to say a few words to her; it had been hard for him to speak and he had tired quickly, but little by little the words had come and the last few years of his life had not been so different to those of any other frail old man tended upon by two doting women.

Harrison had never forgotten the vision he had been granted. He understood that his suffering had been necessary, a scourging of his sin preparing him for the kingdom. He was also an educated man, and it had become clear to him that what he had seen held great import for the future. When he was younger he had travelled widely in Nigeria and, on the banks of the Niger, he met the Iddao Ishaak. A man who had recently found God, he was fascinated by these people. They fiercely claimed their Jewish origins, though now they practised Islam, seeing themselves as descendants from the patriarch through Issak. They were the Jews as God had intended and they were, to the best of his knowledge, the only Muslims who traced themselves through Sarah. He had marvelled at his country whilst the world focused on a tiny region of scorched desert thousands of miles away; the real conflict was here in the heart of Africa; it was here that Eden would be regained.

It had seemed so obvious to him then: why would a strip of barren sand be the promised land? Surely that must be the legacy of sin; the land God gave to Cain. The true inheritors of paradise would be the sons of Abel.

On returning to Port Harcourt he had approached his old pastor with his ideas, and had been sharply rebuked and even warned that he was on the path of heresy. He then had other things to occupy his mind. Decades later, though, during his long, silent convalescence, he had had time to muse and revise, and as he watched the young Chidi grow he remained convinced that he was in the presence of the patriarch. But for whom had he come? The battle lines were being drawn; were Haga and Ismael walking the earth to redress the wrong done to them, the stealing of the inheritance of the first born? Or were they agents of the other place, condemned to march forever across time? He knew he was witness to a special moment in history; it would soon be time to stand up and be counted. Even the Old Testament bore witness: the ancients had practiced the arts of deceit with impunity, Esau had been robbed, Joseph had been left in a hole to die, words and histories had been changed, rewritten in favour of the victor. But there could be only one truth, and Harrison had begun to think that it lay not in the Torah, the Bible or the Koran, but in the empty spaces between and behind the mysterious eyes of Chioma.

The mid-afternoon sun was strong. Sarah fanned herself lazily as she watched the most wonderful man she had ever known snooze lightly beside her. She was ready; they both were.

A tear formed in the corner of her eye, but now there was no bitterness, just memories.

Harrison seemed to mutter in his sleep.

A well-dressed man in middle age was walking towards the house. He was wearing sunglasses and looked strong and healthy. As he approached, his shadow stroked the edge of the porch. Sarah felt the hair on the back of her neck stand up. She swallowed hard. Even though she had thought she was ready, now that the moment was upon her it was going to be too much.

The man stopped and looked straight at the house. He looked from her to the old man and then back at her, the sunglasses hiding his expression. He paused, appearing to be about to speak; he had the air of one who was about to ask directions. He stepped forwards and then, as if thinking better of it, stopped.

With relief Sarah watched, as Death turned on his heel and walked back up the street, returning whence he had come. She crossed herself and asked God for forgiveness.

Behind his expensive sunglasses, Azzi's eyes were full of tears. He knew he had just looked on the face of his mother.

As relief seeped through Sarah's body, it was gently followed by a drowsiness, like soothing waves tumbling over the pebbled shore of her soul. Her head sank onto her breast and she slept, deeply and at peace.

Harrison had not been asleep: appearances can be deceptive, as well he knew. He had seen the young man walk towards them and, with that gift of perception that is granted to so few, he had known. He had always known that eventually this day would come, and for forty years he had waited. He had watched as the son stood before the mother he had never known, and had smiled to himself. It had all been worth it, the story was complete.

A lifetime ago, a young pastor learnt that the pretty chorister with the powerful voice was pregnant. He was a young idealist and had taken a vow that he would save her. No one was without sin, and everyone had a right to salvation. Christ came into Harrison's life whilst he lay face down in a pool of his own blood and vomit. The two brothers of the girl who had died at the hands of a backstreet abortionist had left him for dead in a roadside sewer. He was seventeen at the time and it changed his life. When he had come to hear of Sarah's plight he had seen it as a second chance, an olive branch from God, and he had grasped it with both hands and held it to his breast for forty years.

Azzi arrived at the corner. He looked back along the near-empty street. The pothole-ridden yellow earthen road shimmered slightly in the heat. The air was still and there was an occasional movement, barely discernible, behind the windows of the rude homes. He took one last look, lowered his head, and turned the corner.

Beside Sarah, Harrison's soft breathing slowly faded as she slept and the sun began to slip from the sky into the western sea. His head crept forward and, ever so quietly, he breathed out for the last time.

Azzi walked back towards the house where his life now was: to Amanda, and their unborn child, a new future, a new beginning, new roots. He held in his mind the face of the handsome old lady sitting on the porch next to the sleeping old man. He had not needed to ask; he saw her features every time he looked in the mirror. When he set out he had wanted answers, explanations, almost an apology. He had been a man on a mission. But he had looked at the simple house, smaller than the one in which he had grown up, and much simpler than the one in which he now lived. What would it do to the old man and his wife if he walked up and introduced himself? How many decades had they lived together in peace? What was he really expecting?

Chapter Nineteen

Ron Forrester sat in his office behind a desk whose size told people how important he was. He was also backlit by two windows. He had arranged his office so that his desk was as far from the door as was physically possible, given the dimensions of the room. He had had deliberately kept the passage from door to desk clear of all obstructions, so that when visitors entered his office it was, he thought, as if entering a throne room: the summoned nonentities had to embark upon the long walk across his tiled floor, whilst Ron sat majestically in his raised chair, the sun streaming in through the floor-to-ceiling windows, shrouding him in light over both shoulders. On the far side of the room, arranged neatly by the wall, stood three small, uncomfortable chairs reserved for visitors. On Ron's command to sit, they could drag the rickety contraptions through the pools of light before his desk and into his illuminating presence. The chairs were of course significantly lower than his, so those granted audience must not only look up at Ron but also into the sun. It was rumoured amongst Niger Marine employees that Ron had come into the office one night and filed down one leg of each of his visitors' chairs, so that they wobbled when people sat on them: he liked to see people quake in his presence.

Now, however, Ron cast his squat shadow on an empty room; there was no one to impress or intimidate, and for once he was glad of it. He needed to think, to plan, to scheme, to do what he did best: profit from others' misfortunes.

His Faustian gods were being kind to him today, and the blessings were coming so fast and thick that he was worried that even he might not manage them correctly, and fail to gain all possible advantage. Yet again, the bounty had come from the hated diving department; they were being fed into his hands and it was an opportunity not to be missed.

Ron was anally retentive by nature (though the French expression of that much maligned and generally misunderstood personality type *anal sadique* would probably have been more literally appropriate), but the years spent at the marine academy had refined the compulsive obsessive tendencies and, followed by years at sea in cramped quarters, had created nothing less than a monster.

His opposite number in the diving department was a totally different story. Mike Parry was a gangling, charismatic, heavily tattooed, long haired, scruffy ex-saturation diver with a lifestyle that Keith Richards would have considered a bit rough. He was, however, popular: brilliant at his job and a fully qualified engineer. His very existence irked Ron, who knew that neither verbally nor mentally nor in the popularity stakes was he a match for Mike. Everyone else at Niger Marine and in the industry at large knew it as well.

To Ron, Mike epitomised everything that was despicable about commercial divers: they were arrogant, ill disciplined and overpaid. On top of which, they all seemed to have appalling personal habits and yet, somehow, these sub-sea monkeys seemed to enjoy a prestige that came to them almost overnight, which an honest, hard-working seaman like himself would have had to work for years to achieve. Today, though, was a bad day for the diving department, which meant that it was a good day for Ron.

When Dricus and the others were taken from the barge, Mike had been prospecting for contracts in Equatorial Guinea, visiting the major contractors and oil companies exploiting the rich fields around Malabo. On hearing the news, he had revisited all his contacts in Guinea as an exercise in damage limitation and then hurried back to Nigeria. He had been back for two days – five days into the hostages' captivity – when, on leaving his compound for the office, his Toyota Highlux was cut off by an ageing and recently stolen Ford Transit van. A second vehicle slewed across the road behind him, making it impossible for him to reverse. Four men spilled from the back of the van and a large number of shots were fired into the tyres and the sides of the Toyota. He and his driver were dragged from the cab. Mike found himself bound and gagged in the back of the Transit; the driver was executed at the roadside.

Ron was now in total control of both departments until Mike's release. He had, however, some immediate issues to deal with, and knew he had to think carefully. He was no fool; he understood that sooner or later questions would start to be asked; he had been in Port Harcourt longer than anyone else on the Niger Marine staff and he alone had never been attacked, mugged or kidnapped. It was he who maintained unofficial contact with the communities and militant groups, and he who invariably negotiated when Niger Marine personnel were kidnapped. He was not naive enough to believe that the coincidences would go unnoticed; that there was a long-standing feud between him and Mike was well known, and the fact that he would stand to gain by Mike's absence needed little publicising. It was just a matter of time before people began to put two and two together and start coming up with five. His next move was critical.

In fact, *five*, he reflected, was not that far from the truth; perhaps it was more of a four and a half. As negotiator for Niger Marine, he was of course in regular contact with MEND, and in conversation he had managed to drop the details of Mike's return to Nigeria and the guy's position in the company piecemeal into various conversations. Technically, he had nothing to do with it, and he knew that no investigation could possibly do anything but exonerate him; morally, though, he had at least been complicit. Not that morality was something that particularly concerned Ron, but he knew that other people set great store by it, for which he was glad in the final analysis because it prevented others from treating people the way he treated them himself, and in his book that was a good thing. He was aware, though, that it was a double-edged sword: it created a standard by which, if he wasn't careful, he could be measured, and he knew that, under close examination from the eyes of people who might have power over him, he would be found wanting.

The present incident had taken a lot of nasty twists, all of which, with careful thought, could be turned to his advantage in some way. The multiple deaths on the barge had changed the rules: whilst it was true that the death of Captain Lee would be written off as 'natural causes' and the black engineer's family could be paid off by the oil company, there was still the issue of a dead American leader-man with a body full of bullets. So far the news had been suppressed. It was clear to everyone on board at the time that this had not been an intentional killing. The bullet holes in the door told the whole story. Those with the hostages' best interests at heart wanted the information kept quite, lest MEND summarily execute all the hostages, then deny ever having had them and blame the whole fiasco on pirates.

The hawkish elements in the Nigerian government saw this as a final excuse to get tough with the Delta. A more pragmatic school of thought suggested that military action should be taken, otherwise the Americans might decide that the murder of one of their citizens and detention of several more justified their military presence. That was the last thing the government wanted, Nigeria becoming another Iraq. The gravy train would dry up, Halliburton contracts would be imposed, expatriate personnel would reappear but would fly around the place protected by heavily armed private security – who would of course be immune from prosecution and therefore unlikely to be making 'voluntary' donations to the Nigerian judiciary. There were, of course, people in opposition who thought, for exactly the same reasons, that this might be a good thing.

Ron considered himself, with some justification, to be reasonably well connected in government and security circles: ten years of hard networking well spent. And yet, whilst he was right in that he was well known and had, on occasion, rendered service to the 'right people', he had slightly over estimated the esteem in which he was held.

From Ron's perspective, a military solution was appealing. He did not rate the abilities of the Nigeria military in hostage rescue situations; on the only occasion that, to his knowledge, they had attempted it, the hostages had been killed in the crossfire. This was definitely an attractive proposition. A botched rescue attempt would not only remove particular thorns from his side, but it would certainly also cause an increase in international pressure to clean up the security situation. Worst-case scenario was an all-out American presence, and for people like Ron that was a gold mine. He had a friend (the term was a loose one when used by Ron, readily interchangeable with 'acquaintance' and indeed 'enemy', as circumstances dictated) who had made millions in two years in Iraq as a subcontractor. The scam was this: the contract was awarded to a major American company who would price the job in the normal manner, they would then skim off their normal profit margin and re-subcontract to an expat outfit on the ground. The expat subcontractor (such as Ron's acquaintance) would then repeat the process and subcontract out to a local contractor who probably, as a result of the fighting and heavy bombing, had neither the equipment or facilities to do the job. On realising that the task was basically impossible with the remaining funds, he would in turn remove his 'overheads' and then contract some local backstreet outfit who had no intention of even trying. Thus, everybody ate and nothing got done, and when accountability was required in the boardrooms of Washington, the security situation on the ground and local corruption would be blamed. The shareholders would be satisfied, the lobbyists would push the senators for greater military investment – which further pleased those investors who had been astute enough to spread their portfolio between oil and arms and everyone was happy.

Ron ripped himself away from his reverie and forced himself to focus on the situation as it was; he had work to do, but if he played his cards right he could come out on top of the pile. He was a major shareholder in Niger Marine and a lot was at stake.

He paused, sucked his lips for a moment, and came to a decision. Decide on a course of action, and then *commit; commitment*, that was the secret. He leant forwards across his desk, picked up a phone and dialled a Member of Parliament who owed him a few favours.

Chapter Twenty

"Did you meet with her oh?"

"Yes."

"Well?"

"We didn't speak."

For all her force and bluster, Amanda could be a much more perceptive woman than many people credited. She looked at her man, put her hand on her hip in a pose that those who knew her well would probably have described as characteristic, sucked her teeth and looked hard at him. Azzi stood still by the wooden fence that marked the edge of the bush bar, dangling like a lost child. Amanda sucked her teeth again, walked to the gap in the fence, and round to Azzi. As she came up to him, she could feel the pain and confusion radiating from him.

"Come inside, honey," she said quietly, then she put her arms around him and hugged him. There was a muffled cheer from the men drinking inside the bar. Amanda looked around at them, and her glance was as effective as a burst of machine gun fire: the drinkers cowered over their bottles and glasses. Not a word or jeer was to be heard.

"Come inside, honey, come home."

She loosened her arms from around him, took him by the elbow and walked him through the bar to their home behind. A quick glance to left and right – let every man in the bar know that it would be a brave or foolish man indeed that passed comment or showed too much interest in what was going on.

Terry sat behind the bar. As she watched her mamma and Azzi walk through the crowded space, she felt that this must have been what it was like when a Pharaoh (Terry was fond of the history channel on TV) passed amongst his subjects: bowed heads hoping, praying, to go unnoticed lest the wrath of the god-king should smite them. She smiled to herself as the image faded; she loved her mamma dearly, but she, along with most of the regular customers, knew well enough the consequences of getting on the wrong side of Amanda.

The couple walked through the bar and into the little kitchen that served as a threshold between bar and home. Amanda pulled out a chair and sat herself down, setting her legs slightly apart to support her distended womb. She placed her linked fingers on the top of her belly, feeling the little life stretching inside her. She looked at Azzi as he lent against the battered sink: his face was tired and charged with emotion.

Amanda knew him well. Wait, it would all come out; it might take some coaxing, but out it would come. And she was carrying his baby – she could afford to wait. Azzi was not the kind of man to disappear.

Chapter Twenty-one

Mo found himself walking on the side of a hill lined with olive groves. In the distance he could see the sea, a perfect, languorous turquoise shimmering beneath the haze. He turned his feet in that direction and wandered down the gentle slope, picking his way between the lines of ripe olives. *They needed to be gathered soon or they would spoil*, he thought to himself. But there was no one about. A gentle breeze picked its way from the sea and meandered up through the groves, caressing his face as he made his way down the hill.

He bent down and picked up a handful of dirt from the foot of one of the plants. *It's good*, he thought as he crumbled it between his fingers, letting it fall back to earth. Part of him wondered how he knew; he had never been a farmer.

He carried on his descent and stepped from the last line of olives planted across the hill. *That was good too*, he thought: they were trying to stop the soil eroding. And again he wondered how he knew.

Before him was a short stretch of land ending in a cliff that jutted over the soothing blue sea. Sheep roamed unattended by any herder, wandering right to the edge of the jagged cliff. Mo felt a wonderful sense of ease wafting over him.

He decided to lie down and rest. The land felt good beneath his back. He gazed up into the clear blue sky and an angry sun beat down.

He felt a nuzzling in his ear. One of the sheep had wandered over to him and was nosing gently against the side of his head. Mo gently pushed it away, then turned to look at the animal.

To his horror the sheep's eyes were hollow sockets dribbling blood.

Mo leapt to his feet in disgust then he forced himself to take a closer look at the animal. Its wool was hanging off in clumps and it was covered in festering sores. But it showed no sign of distress. Mo backed away in terror and almost fell over another animal grazing peaceably behind him. As he picked himself off the ground he realised that half this animal's face was missing, rotted away, and he was looking straight into teeth that were masticating casually on human flesh. How he knew he could not explain, but he had no doubt that that was what it was.

He started to run, to run back to the sanity of the olive groves. But the slope seemed to have got steeper than it had been and the dirt had churned itself into cloying mud. Gasping for breath, he threw himself into the first line of olive trees, grasping at the first stem he came to, gripping it with both hands and hauling his body into the safety of the tree line. Sucking the air into his lungs with a desperation that his exertion barely justified, he rolled onto his back to try and compose himself.

He looked up at the blue sky and blood dripped off the leaves onto his face, landing in his mouth. Again he struggled to his feet; what choice did he have? Up the endless hill through the bleeding trees, or back to the festering, deformed sheep? But beyond the sheep lay the clear blue sea.

He ran.

A pile of stones appeared on the edge of the cliff; they seemed strangely familiar. The trees were reaching out grabbing at him, tearing at his flesh and clothes as he ran through them; human hands appeared on the ends of branches.

He ran.

Then atop the small pile of stones, he saw a young girl. It was Houda, his little girl; she was surrounded by the sheep and she was screaming like he had never heard anyone scream before. A heavy machine gun opened up behind him.

He ran harder.

He could see the impact of the bullets as they ploughed the fertile land where the sheep grazed, and the shots were moving ever closer to his little girl. He threw himself forwards and as he passed the advancing line of rounds that were tearing up the earth, his momentum took him over the mound of rubble. His body connected with the little girl's whilst he was still in mid-air; he wrapped his arms about her and held the little body close to him. He hit the ground hard, back first, protecting her from the impact. Together they rolled down the pile of rubble into the sea.

The impact with the cool water separated them. Mo found himself sinking alone into blackness and then hands were guiding him through the darkness. He no longer seemed to need to breathe. The darkness welcomed him, enfolding him in tranquillity.

Drowning really was this easy.

He was guided gently into a cave which he guessed must lie beneath the sheep-infested cliff top. The cave was not large and the darkness was absolute. A faint white light began to glow in the distance; it shimmered and was sometimes briefly dimmed, but on the whole it grew stronger. Mo found himself still floating in mid-water, unable to touch the sides or floor. The light approached him; gradually it revealed itself as having human form, a human figure shrouded in a soft white light. It dawned on Mo that the form was female and suddenly he realised it was Sally. She also appeared to be suspended mid-water; her hair, which he noticed was much longer than usual, floated around her and she was hanging with her arms out in the posture that Christ was supposed to adopt when appearing in visions. She floated closer to him and he could see the familiar contours of her body through the thin white gown that wrapped itself about her. She was close now and he could make out every familiar detail. She spoke. Her mouth did not move but he heard the words form themselves inside his head.

Read, she commanded.

Mo knew the next line and spoke it.

"But I cannot read."

Read!

"But what shall I read?"

Sally wrapped her arms about him in an embrace that was anything but angelic. Her legs wrapped themselves about his and her tongue searched for his mouth. Words started to form inside his head, words that should not have been there in this context.

Read. 'In the name of the Lord thy God.'

Mo was beginning to panic; this was wrong, it had to stop.

Who created man from a single drop of blood...

Mo was beginning to feel sick; he had never been a religious man, but he knew that this was definitely wrong.

Who teaches with the pen,

Teaches man that which he knows not.

He felt a sharp pain in his arm; his hand, too, seemed to burn. He pushed hard against Sally's chest, and as she separated from him she appeared suddenly reptilian, her long black tongue reaching out for his face as she fell backwards into oblivion. At long last his lungs found air and he screamed.

Dricus looked over the prostrate body from which the piercing cry had just come. His hand still held the hypodermic with which he had injected Mo. He said a silent thank you to the field medic instructor from the military academy, a man he had known and who was later killed by a land mine whilst working for UNHCR in Angola. Dricus' face, which had been taut and drenched in sweat, relaxed slightly as he caught the eye of The Secretary who was squatting quietly opposite him.

"The fever is breaking. Thank you, bru, we have probably saved his life."

"We did not bring you here to die. Just to make that

government listen to us. We wish you no ill, we are not killers, we just want what is rightfully ours."

Mo lay on a raised platform under a makeshift roof just to the side of one of the huts. A plastic drip hung from one of the wooden posts that supported the roof. Mike, Dricus and The Secretary tended him. A little way off stood Jackson, quietly smoking as he watched the scene unfold.

When the funny looking white man had first fallen ill with the fever, Labo had been convinced that the gods were answering his prayers and were going to remove him to the spirit world. On that first day, Labo had slipped off on his own. Not far from the camp, but far enough not to be stumbled on by accident, he had built a small shrine to the Owuampu water spirits, the *Mammi Water*.

Labo had been brought up with the traditional beliefs lightly garnished with Christianity, but he held firm to the belief that water spirits were like humans in that they had diverse personalities with various personal strengths and shortcomings, and that humans dwelt amongst the water spirits before being born and it was there that their characters were formed. Now Labo prayed to the water spirits amongst whom he himself had dwelt before being born into this world. He prayed for their support, protection and intervention. When Mo had fallen sick he had thanked them, even shedding his own blood on the ground in gratitude.

Now he did not know what to do. Had the spirits of the water deserted him? Or, more frighteningly, was the strange white man attended by stronger spirits than he? Was he confronting a man whose ancestors had been great warriors? He had heard commander Jackson telling some of the other soldiers that at least two of the men worked underneath the water and could disappear beneath the surface for long periods; they must be greatly loved by the spirits. Labo had grown up on and around the water, but he had never once put his face beneath the surface, for fear of what he might see.

He had watched the fever unfold, and he had heard the man talking and shouting in some strange language. He had obviously been to the spirit world. Labo, too, had heard the horrifying scream that had come from the man when he started to come back. Evidently he had not wanted to return, but the white men with him had had strong magic and had dragged him back against his will. The spirit war was obviously about to begin.

The Secretary stood up and stretched his legs slowly to get the blood flowing back in to them. He stepped out from under the shelter and back into the sunlight. *It was as well that they had built the shelter*, he thought, looking at the sky: despite the clear blue above him, he knew rain was coming. He walked slowly over to his friend Jackson.

"How is he?" Jackson enquired as he stubbed out his cigarette.

"He will live. They are well trained, these people. I learnt something to day. You know the South African one?"

"Dricus, yes?"

"You know he even offered to teach the men how to dress bullet wounds and other basic first aid. Why aren't our people doing such things? Sometimes I wonder about all this: all the white people we have had here have been like this, helpful. You know when you were away he removed an abscessed tooth from one of the guys?"

"I know what you are thinking, my friend, but what other way is there? Anyway, it might all have been in vain: I have had some bad news. Come, walk with me, I do not want anyone to hear us."

The two men walked a little way into the bush. As The Secretary had predicted, clouds began to roll overhead. Jackson pulled out a packet of cigarettes, offered one to his friend, and then, using his mouth, pulled one from the packet for himself.

He lit both cigarettes using a Zippo lighter that had come from a previous hostage. Jackson inhaled deeply, tilted his head back and let out a long plume of smoke that rose up into the jungle canopy above them.

He sucked his teeth, then he spoke. "There were casualties."

"What?"

"On the raid. There were casualties. The companies and the government are keeping it under wraps, but it has filtered back. At least three, possibly more, and one badly wounded British captain."

"Jesus, that's the last thing we need. So what happens now? Are we to kill these guys? Then deny all knowledge of the raid? It's a bit late for that – we've already asked for a ransom and Youth Shall Prosper has identified himself. He's in the shit with central command I guess?"

"You are right, it's messy. If it was just one, we could deal with it, but three! For Christ's sake, what were the guys doing?"

"I don't have exact details yet, but there are at least two dead white guys, though – and I don't understand this – apparently one of them might not be a major problem now. I guess that might mean he fell down the stairs running away or something, but apparently the other one is full of bullets, and, even worse, he's American. If he was British, less of a problem, but the Americans get quite excitable about this sort of thing."

"So you've spoken to central? What have they got to say?"

"Well, as you can imagine, they are not happy. But first thing is they want the general up there next week with a fucking good explanation."

"And?"

"Well, my old friend –" here Jackson smiled "– I am sure you will be pleased to hear, I have come up with an idea."

"And my friend I am sure by the look on your face that you know already that I am not going to like it! But what choice do we have? Come on, let's hear it."

For the second time that day, The Secretary's prediction proved accurate. He didn't like it one bit.

Mo's body was drenched in sweat. Dricus was sitting cross-legged near his head when he began to regain coherence.

"Hey, it's lakker to have you back, bru? You scared us for a bit, then! How you feeling?"

"Weak."

"Yeah, well, that's pretty normal after what your body's just been through."

Mo lay under his improvised canopy for another two days. From somewhere mosquito nets had been found and draped around him. Mark and Dricus spent most of the day alternating between sitting beside him and walking circuits of the small parade ground. The plastic top of an old food tub had been turned into a frisbee, which marked the slow passage of the minutes as it arced from hand to hand across the parade area.

Mo's illness had distracted the whole camp from all other concerns. The effort that had been put into acquiring medical treatment for him had given the hostages hope. Their value was intrinsically linked to their staying alive and well. The militants' panic over Mo's bout of malaria implied that they expected to produce their hostages in public in the near future.

The crisis had also broken down barriers between the hostages and their captors. Mark, in spite of his inherent reservations, had detected genuine concern for Mo, from the lower ranks of militants, that transcended the need to preserve the merchandise.

It was on the third day after Mo's fever broke that Jackson implemented his plan. The Secretary had made what he acknowledged to be a futile argument against it. In the battle between ideology against pragmatism, they were not affluent enough to choose the former.

195

Chapter Twenty-two

Junior Minister Chief Akintola received Ron Forrester's phone call reluctantly. He knew there were many favours owed and that it was all one way. Ron had never called him; it had always been he who had called upon Ron, to request small favours. Ron had never collected.

The simple solution would have been to have Ron killed, but Akintola was no fool. He was aware that the wily white man would have made provisions against his sudden demise; indeed, Ron had once hinted at it. At the time, it was true, the reference had been in connection with another politician, whom they apparently both disliked, but Ron had carefully explained how he regularly updated files with names, addresses and details of transactions and favours. These files were held by British and Swiss lawyers and were to be handed to the international press and the Nigerian government in the event of the politician's unexpected demise. Akintola had had no doubt at the time that he was being told politely that the same arrangements would be made in relation to Ron Forrester.

Of course he did not know exactly what those files contained on him, but he could make an educated guess. And even if it was only half of what he feared, it would be enough to have him executed in Nigeria. Or if he managed to flee Nigeria, the contents of the files would ensure that his funds abroad would be seized. Except for international law enforcement officers, 9/11 had done no one any favours. His access to government funds had allowed him to launch a small, but relatively successful, arms and cocaine business amongst the gangs of Port Harcourt. Whilst his clandestine business was more on the level of protection, racketeering and organised prostitution than the international arms trade, he was nonetheless gently filling a variety of international accounts and paving the way for his early and luxurious retirement. Unfortunately, Mr Bin Laden and his associates had put all that in jeopardy, now such cash movements, which had once largely been ignored by the CIA, or indeed in many cases actively facilitated, were becoming more and more subject to close scrutiny and punitive court orders.

Akintola reached over his desk and pressed a button on his intercom. He would take the call.

He took a deep breath. Then, with a voice that proved his worth as a politician, as it in no way reflected the way he felt, he took the phone and said, "Ah, Mr Ron, it is such a pleasure to hear from you, after so long, what can I do for you?"

Forrester's reply came as a pleasant surprise to Akintola who, despite his relief, was not naive enough to take it at face value.

"I think, Minister, we should be discussing something I can do for you."

Akintola wondered what this was going to cost him. In the time he had known him, Ron had never volunteered anything and never asked for any favours, nor had he required payment for those he had rendered. Akintola knew instinctively that the bill would soon be coming in and he doubted that it would be cheap.

Ron, however, was not that straightforward; he did not see things in simple terms of debt and payment. He saw things simply in terms of what was good for Ron Forrester and, if payment was not required now, that was fine, as long as it did not in any way affect him. There was of course the fact that he liked causing pain, but that was just a luxury, and it could wait; he tried not to let it interfere with business. Fortunately, pain for others was frequently a by-product of his success. He was, all in all, he felt, an extraordinarily lucky man, or maybe it was just pure talent.

Chapter Twenty-three

During their frantic dash across Port Harcourt to the rivers where their boats were waiting they had been spotted by the MOPOL (the black-uniformed mobile police, synonymous with the Nigerian federal government). Shots were fired, though in an uncharacteristic moment of professionalism the police realised that there was probably a hostage aboard and curbed their fire. The kidnappers had taken fire and two of them sported light wounds, one from a MOPOL round, the other a badly grazed arm sustained when he had fallen from the back of the truck as the driver took a corner badly. It had been a precarious moment as he scrambled back in the MOPOL that had been gaining on them when he fell. It was only the fact that the MOPOL commander was mindful of the risk to the hostage, whom they had now established was definitely onboard, that had allowed the militants to make their escape. The contact had raised their already soaring adrenalin levels and their handling of Mike had been less than tender in consequence.

When they had reached the riverbank, Mike had been thrown into the boat and the helmsmen had used every one of the 115 horsepower available to him to get the little craft away from Port Harcourt. There was, they well knew, no way that the police would fire on them with a hostage aboard; but there were far more dangerous people out there in the swamps than MOPOL.

As requested, The Secretary had kept the morning's dancing going for twice as long as usual. Jackson wanted the men tired and dehydrated. The extra chanting, he hoped, would cue their malleable minds into the right spiritual groove and make them more receptive to his rousing. He had no illusions about what he was doing, contrary to The Secretary's fears.

Dricus and Mark were sitting with Mo on the makeshift trestle that had served as his bed during the worst of his illness; it had come to be seen by everyone as the hostages' seating area. Mo was up and alert and, apart from quite considerable weight loss, was looking relatively healthy. The extra length of the morning ceremony surprised them; they wondered what might be was leading up to.

Suddenly the chanting stopped and The Secretary let loose a howl that seemed to shake his whole body to the point of convulsion. The effect on the cavorting militants was almost diametrically opposite. They all went rigid, while the drums took up a frenzy that the hostages had never heard before.

"Asawanna?" came the shout from The Secretary, followed by the invariable reply, "Wannaa!"

The exchange was repeated again and again, its speed seeming to attempt to catch up with that of the crazed drumming. The three hostages sat transfixed. Tommy's bloated form was the other side of the clearing, separated from them by the chanting mass.

"Something's up," said Mark, just loud enough to make himself heard over the drumming.

"I know, bru, this is orchestrated, he is whipping them up into a state of hysteria. But you watch him. He knows exactly what he's up to."

Just as the clouds rolled over the top of the clearing, The Secretary raised both arms above his head and let out a huge cry that brought all the soldiers to a halt. Dricus sat up straight: whilst he admired the theatre of The Secretary's action and could see what was being done, it also appeared so out of keeping with what he had perceived to be the man's character that he sensed that something was wrong.

Dricus continued to watch with interest. The Secretary climbed onto the little bench that served the drummers and stood with both arms out stretched, looking for all the world like a crucified, black Che Guevara. To Dricus's surprise, much of what followed was in English, interspersed with what he assumed must be Ijaw. It occurred to Dricus that this was either for the benefit of the hostages or, more likely, because not all the Niger Deltans spoke the same tribal language. Even in Ijaw, he guessed, there were probably dialects that would be almost incomprehensible to others.

By now The Secretary was shaking; his face was drawn, his eyes huge white orbs in his shining face. His whole body was drenched in sweat. Mo moved up close to Dricus.

"He's got to be on some sort of drugs to be in that state? And I thought he was the sanest one of the lot of them."

"Listen, bru, don't take this the wrong way, but I grew up with the black man. Never underestimate him and never overestimate him. Jesus, bru, I've seen educated African surgeons collapse in a gibbering heap because some juju man pointed a stick at them, and I've seen uneducated kaffirs from the townships perform acts of selfless heroism that you would not believe. Never try to understand them, T.I.A, bru! T.I.A!"

"T.I.A?"

"It means 'This Is Africa'. Don't try and understand – it is what it is."

As if coordinated by some divine stage manager, thunder rolled overhead and the first drops of rain began to fall. The militants remained motionless. The Secretary was shouting, his voice rising almost to a scream then plummeting to depths that were hard to credit from the look of his thin, wiry body. His arms became mobile, his body swayed; one by one the drums began to beat, a solid, flat beat lacking the complex syncopation that

200

normally characterised their playing; just one grinding beat, like the stroke being counted on a Roman slave ship.

The hostages made out from the English being spoken that there had been deaths on the barge. The Secretary was telling the soldiers that treachery had been committed: people had been unlawfully slain, the gods and spirits of the water were displeased, they were sending back the murdered spirits to identify their assassins.

"He's a clever motherfucker in't 'e?" hissed Mark under his breath. "You know, I don't believe that sly bastard believes any of this, he's just doing it to scare 'em!"

"You're probably right, bru, but like I said don't over estimate them."

A knife appeared in The Secretary's right hand and, with a theatrical flourish that would have done credit to any mountebank or strolling player, he plunged it deep into his camouflaged combat jacket. Blood gushed forth. The soldiers stepped back as a unit. Some of them fell to the floor, others beat their chests and wailed horribly. Dricus was a good enough field medic to recognise the stunt for what it was: to produce blood like that he would have had to rupture an artery. Nonetheless, he was impressed.

The rains were coming in torrents now. Suddenly, a new figure appeared amongst the militants. The wiry black body was naked but covered in white paint, and hundreds of strips of rags, red, white and black, had been tied to the limbs and around the body. The figure wore a large and grotesquely painted wooden mask that completely obscured his face. Smoke appeared to billow from the mask's nostrils.

The soldiers were clearly terrified. They all stared intently at the apparition as it gyrated and swirled to the drums. Only The Secretary and the drummers seemed able to look at the vision without quaking.

Jackson held a skull in one hand and a short stick in the other;

he beat on the skull with the stick and then pointed at the terrified militants that encircled him. As he pointed at each in turn, the man selected would become bolt upright and shake, until the masked Jackson approached him and touched him with the stick. At that point the man would collapse in a lifeless heap on the floor.

"I've read about this, guys," said Dricus carefully. "It's called *Igbadai*, and they are asking the murdered soul to identify its killer."

In spite of himself, Dricus discreetly made the sign of the cross. He hoped Mo had not noticed. *He was*, he thought to himself, *sometimes far more African than he cared to admit, even to himself.*

Labo was terrified. The spirit master had not yet looked at him but he knew that the truth would out, that the white devil-spirits would expose him. The man standing three places away from him was touched by the spirit master and fell to the ground. It was close! His life, he knew, was drawing to a close. He urinated, and felt it running down his leg, mingling with the cool rain.

The hostages were transfixed. The rain was falling harder and the circle of militants lay partially scattered on the ground as Jackson whirled amongst them like a demented demon. His painted wooden mask snarled in every direction as his painfully thin body jerked and flailed, as if every beat of the drums sent a spasm through it. Thunder rolled overhead.

An automatic weapon opened up, a long burst that was quickly joined by another weapon of a different calibre and thus with a different sound, creating a chorus of munitions that synchronised with the endless driving rhythm of the drums. The roar of an outboard motor at full throttle burst through the storm as if a maniacal composer had suddenly been inspired by a new and discordant theme but hadn't seen fit to bring the original movement to a suitable conclusion – the passion of a post-industrial Beethoven at his most irate.

Mark grabbed Mo by the shoulder; the intensity in his face flashed over into his voice.

"Get ready to run, we're under attack!"

Dricus, his deeply ingrained training instincts taking over, was already in a crouch, his body taut with anticipation. Some of the prone militants were starting to move, dragging themselves bemused from the mud and scattering across the camp in search of sanctuary. The Secretary, his fluid movements betraying no sign of any injury, now held a Kalashnikov that he had grabbed from a prostrate soldier. Dricus noted that The Secretary had cocked the weapon. Jackson and the drummers seemed oblivious.

A flash of lightning sliced through the clearing, and the white paint on Jackson's body seemed to soak up the bolt and spit it back. Still he danced, and the intensity of the drums seemed to increase, as though defying the weather. In any other circumstances the contest would have been ridiculous, but the drummers played on, their whole bodies driving the rhythm into the tightly stretched animal skins. Their bare feet sank into the mud, like powerful roots sucking the power of the sacred land so that it would rise up through their bodies like sap, fuelling the incessant beat, proclaiming to anyone who would listen, be it man or god, that they were as one with their homeland and neither weather nor weapon would displace them.

A small boat of a similar design to those that had attacked the barge slewed around the bend in the river, and a great spray of water flew up in defiance of the driving rain. The light hull was raised above the surface of the water that was being churned and pitted by the torrents of rain, penetrating the sacred river, disturbing the spirits and *Mammi Water* in their own dominion. The boat was full of militants in black, white and red rags and white body paint. A European sat cowering in the centre of the boat, his hands bound and eyes blindfolded.

The Secretary appeared to relax slightly, though Dricus noticed that his weapon was still conspicuously at the ready. It occurred to Dricus that it was the first time he had seen The Secretary with a firearm, and that in itself did not augur well. The small boat came alongside the small jetty and, within seconds, two militants with the European between them were on the rickety structure. They walked straight up to the circle. The man to the left of the European fired a shotgun into the air. "Sawanaa?"

Labo knew now that this was definitely the end. The spirits had brought back the dead white man to identify him; things could not get worse. He threw himself on the floor, grabbing at the feet of the spirit master.

Mike Parry was in a trance, somewhere beyond the known realms of fear. Time had lost all meaning to him; minutes seemed to stretch into hours as his senses were bombarded with confusing stimuli of pain and fear augmented by the sensory deprivation of blindness. The discomfort of the twisting boat ride, the constant firing of weapons, the shouting in strange and unfamiliar voices had screamed through his nervous system, wreaking havoc with his consciousness. The cumulative effect had led him to a level of disorientation that was beyond terror: his mind had begun to shut down.

The walk from the jetty, if terror can be quantified, was, however, the worst moment of the whole experience so far. The knowledge that he might really be at his journey's end, the overwhelming thought that at any moment he could be shot, proved almost too much for him, and his will began to fade as the light drains from the eyes of an exsanguinated corpse. With or without the bullet, he was moments from death.

The Secretary was furious. He strode into the centre of the circle and ripped the blindfold from Parry's eyes. This was exactly the sort of thing they were trying to avoid.

The Secretary's apparently miraculous recovery was to prove too much for many of the soldiers. They had seen him thrust a knife into his side, had witnessed with their own eyes the blood spurt from him – he was truly protected by the gods. Most of the assembled soldiers believed, as did Labo, that the white man who had suddenly materialised in their midst was truly the spirit of the expatriate oil worker who had been killed on the barge and had retuned to identify his murderer. The fact that he was blindfolded only served to heighten the impact of his presence. Fear fed upon fear; it was as if a vortex of base emotion had been unleashed amongst them, twisting and turning into a maelstrom of hysteria.

Jackson now pointed to two of the drummers. The men scuttled forwards, grabbed the prostrate Labo by the arms and dragged him across the muddy parade ground. The fever that was burning up the atmosphere found a home in Labo's body: hands and feet began to assail his writhing form as he was dragged through the mud.

The Secretary looked on helplessly. He was revolted by what was happening, but he knew he was powerless to prevent it. Labo's colleagues began to grab sticks and ropes with which to flay him. He had only been wearing a pair of jeans when he had thrown himself at the feet of the spirit master and they had become caked in mud as he was dragged across the parade ground. Now, as blood began to stream from his back, the brown mud was turning black.

The psychology of crowds was something that had fascinated and horrified The Secretary equally throughout his adult life. It was a fascination that had led him to read a great deal of extra-syllabus texts before his university career had abruptly ended. Nevertheless, what he was witnessing now was far more disturbing than anything he had read in the safety of the university library. He had long ago lost any illusions about the quality of the men who served under him – romantic neo-Marxist notions of the noble peasant had long been dashed on the jagged rocks of daily existence. It had been a painful process, but he had come to the conclusion that an uneducated man, irrespective of his racial or cultural origins, was little more than an animal. He wryly remembered reading *The Lord of the Flies* at school and presenting his teacher with an essay, full of adolescent rage, about how the book was a racist postcolonial novel showing white children behaving in a parody of a 'stereotypical European ethnocentric view of African tribalism' (he had been particularly proud of that phrase). Now he watched in despair as the people for whom he was fighting set about one of their own, like a pack of savage dogs. *Golding's imagination*, he thought, *had fallen far short of capturing the real human capacity for cruelty*. As a student he had been enamoured of the cliché 'man's inhumanity to man', of late, he had revised his opinion of humanity to such a point that he now felt that its true nature was evil, and that the qualities to be sought might better be described as 'inhumanity'. He stood transfixed as Labo's shuddering body was forced up against a tree by the salivating mob. Labo's jeans had been torn from his body, and one leg of the jeans had been used to lash his right arm to one of the trees whilst his friends drove nails through his hands.

At last he could stomach no more. He turned and started to walk away from the clearing, then remembered the hostages. He looked across the clearing; they were still sitting on the small platform that had served as Mo's sickbed. The horror was written across their faces. The new white man was with them, so too were three of the new arrivals, who were now looking decidedly uncomfortable, their painted faces streaked by the rain.

The Secretary started to walk towards them, the shame of what was taking place seeming to suck his feet into the mud. He knew that he had to say something, had to explain, reassure – but how could he justify the unjustifiable, defend the indefensible? He was, he realised, thinking in convenient clichés that might help him avoid the appalling reality that was playing out before him. What message were they sending out? Were they not just reinforcing the image of the savage African? There was no point, he knew, trying to explain that this was not an African 'thing', that the same scenario was played out the world over, by black and white alike – one only needed to look at Kosovo, Bosnia, Afghanistan, Iraq but that did not justify what was happening here under his command, on his watch. He had always liked the quotation: 'For evil to triumph all it takes is for a few good men to remain silent.' In fact, in his self-righteous student days, he had frequently trumpeted it as a taunt against the silence of the academic establishment in the face of government censorship. These days the mere memory of his idealism made him wince, but now that he had remained silent in the face of the butchery of Labo, what did that make him? A man, nominally under his command, and by extension under his protection, was being crucified by other men under his command, and there was nothing he could do to stop it, or was there? Had it been fear that had stopped him, that had closed his mouth and rendered him complicit? He was no Pilot: he could not, he knew, wash his hands of Labo's blood.

As the first wave of violence had broken over Labo, Mike Parry's escort had reacted quickly: they grabbed their prisoner and dragged him out of the path of the onslaught. As soon as he was clear, they helped him, more gently, walk to where the other hostages were still seated. His hands were unbound and he now squatted beside the platform, retching endlessly, even while his stomach complained that there was nothing left to regurgitate. One of the other new arrivals squatted beside him, his arm about his shoulder.

As The Secretary approached the small group, he recognised a man in war paint standing in front of them. An AK47 hung loosely in one of the newcomer's hands as he watched in horror the suffering of Labo, the baying pack flaying his suspended naked body with any implement to hand. The Secretary recognised the observer: he had been a few years above him at university, a youth who, even when he graduated, had already been a marked man due to his involvement in certain underground pro-independence student newspapers. He had, The Secretary knew, eventually fled into the swamps.

"Is this how you run things here?" The contempt rang out in his voice. "Is this how you plan to build a nation?"

The Secretary had nothing to say. No amount of scorn could equal the contempt that, at that moment, he felt for himself.

Chapter Twenty-four

Chioma made her way to Uchende's store. Harrison's death, whilst not unexpected, had still been a shock to her. It was also Chidi's first close encounter with mortality and his mother had watched with concern as his adolescent mind dealt with the sudden absence of the man about whom the whole house had revolved – who had been, no less, at the centre of their existence. Despite Harrison's weakened state, the underlying strength of his personality had always been present in the house. And despite their rocky start, the two women had become close over the years. There was no question of Sarah asking Chioma to leave and in fact Sarah was more grateful than ever for her and Chidi's presence, but Chioma knew that she had to start looking to move on in her life. Chidi was growing into a man, what was next for her? With this in mind, she made her way to the place that had been her sanctuary over the years, the man that had taught her her people's history and had helped her teach and guide Chidi.

She entered the little back room as usual and was surprised to see that, for once, Uchende was not alone. A very tall man, who appeared to be slightly older than she, was seated in what was normally her chair. As she entered, he rose to his feet. He wore a simple blue suit that, judging by the way it hung, had probably cost more money than she had ever seen in her life. What struck her most about him were the large, soft eyes that looked at her enquiringly.

"Welcome, my daughter, I would like you to meet my nephew Joseph," said the old man, his voice filled with pride.

Chioma shook the man's hand. When he spoke his English was deep, clear and well enunciated.

It was an introduction Uchende had long been waiting to make. Joseph had for years been his favourite nephew; indeed he was closer to Joseph than any of his own children. Even though they did not see each other that often, they had for years maintained a regular and exhaustive written correspondence with each other.

To Joseph, the old man had been an articulate and enthusiastic touchstone with his past, a benchmark of who he really was. Often, lying in a hotel room in Monte Carlo, Joseph had turned to Uchende's letters as a lifeline to reality; his old uncle's often funny stories of gossip and corruption from the villages would allow him to turn off the lights and know that he had not completely sold his soul. Uchende, on the other hand, was made to feel involved in the exciting world in which his nephew now moved.

Joseph had always admired the old man's knowledge, integrity and business acumen. As a young child, Joseph had been taken to Cameroon at the outbreak of the Biafran crises, and it was there that he had grown up. His parents had both died back in Nigeria, but the eldest brother of Uchende, keeping a promise he had made to his most junior brother, had funded Joseph's education. Joseph later made a fortune rebuilding an immigrant township after a pogrom visited on his fellow displaced Biafrans by the indigenous Francophones. In the wake of the devastation, he had seen the material need. He had had the necessary business sense and administrative skills, and had provided his fellow Biafrans with the materials to rebuild their shattered township. Joseph had been astute enough to provide his displaced compatriots with what they needed at reasonable prices and with affordable credit. He had thus ensured himself a captive market and, credibility for not having obviously exploited the suffering of his own people. So he became a moneylender: reasonable rates, lots of customers, a steady income and no enemies. As his business grew, other people began to notice him. He had natural organisational abilities, he was articulate, well educated and had charm and charisma by the bucketful. He was approached, by a local construction company, to help facilitate the building of an overland pipeline. The American contractors were becoming bogged down with the corruption and inefficiency of the local administration and they had no idea of how to deal with it. One of their local agents, a fellow Biafran, had suggested Joseph.

To the Americans, Joseph had been a revelation. He spoke English in a way that even they envied, he had presence and authority that commanded respect from African officials and he knew how to get things done. Unlike many people who have risen rapidly in such positions, Joseph had the intelligence not to kill the goose that was laying golden eggs on a daily basis and never took more than was reasonable. Soon, different companies were vying for his services. Joseph and his assistant, a Métis (mixed race) boy who was somewhat younger than him, travelled widely, Paris, New York, Houston, and back to Africa; together they had a talent. They made Africa comprehensible to outsiders and, they appeared to all who met them to be on the gravy train for life.

They worked hard for anyone who paid and that, in the end, had been their downfall: *anyone who would pay*. With the increasing introduction of ethical legislation, consultants such as Joseph began to have their portfolios scrutinised more closely by prospective clients. It wasn't that the oil companies had suddenly developed a conscience, but the legislature stateside had, and suddenly consultants who had been closely involved with arms deals (whether or not funded by the CIA) were being sidelined. Too many interests in the newly classified 'rogue states' could also prove a black mark against a consultant.

Joseph and his partner sensed the change in the wind and decided to retreat back into Africa. They divested themselves of any properties that risked being seized in the wave of the ethical self-righteousness that was sweeping the United States, but retained their interests in the more pragmatic regions of old Europe. Now Joseph was back and, for the first time in his life he had time on his hands, so he had come to see his favourite uncle, whom he knew wanted to see him settle down and was also a great believer in the Igbo nation.

Joseph waited for Chioma to be seated, then he in turn returned to his seat.

Chioma was no fool. She knew she was being set up by the old man and a little part of her was angry with him, but a much bigger part of her felt a surge of love for him such as she had not felt since her own father's death.

Africa and the Middle East are full of Mercedes cars and trucks. It has long been said that the Mercedes is the taxi of Africa and the Arabs: elderly Mercedes diesels chug their way diligently across the deserts of Arabia and along the arteries of Africa. Frequently, vehicles that have been condemned in Europe live another twenty years in Africa before finally giving up the ghost. The carcass will then be scavenged, parts will be taken to extend the lives of their aging sisters, seats will find their way into shanty-town living rooms and hairdressing salons – nothing will go to waste until eventually all that is left of a Mercedes corpse serves out the rest of time as a chicken coup.

The example that stood idling before Chioma did not belong in that scheme of things. It was as if a messiah had arrived from Germany to save the lost souls of the vehicles that had served out their purgatorial sentence and to take them back to chauffeur-driven luxury on the streets of Nuremberg, Paris and Geneva. Even in the desiccation of Port Harcourt, Joseph managed to look the perfect gentleman: his body hardly seemed to bend as he opened the door for her, though Chioma knew well that with his imposing height it must have done. She sank into the front seats – she had never been inside a house that contained so much luxury, let alone a car – and made a mental note to give the old man a huge hug when she next saw him – after she had given him a good telling off for being a meddling old matchmaker.

The afternoon had been a pleasant if slightly uncomfortable one. Chioma had been desperately hoping to snatch a moment alone with Uchende, to interrogate him about this charming stranger and find out what he thought he was playing at. Uchende, however, was old and wise and knew enough about women to avoid the situation. Every time she thought she had him cornered, she found herself confronted with the tall, well-suited stranger. He was exciting, and she liked it when he spoke to her. His voice was rich and captivating and on the few occasions she spoke to him (usually when Uchende had manipulated the conversation so that she had no choice) he gave her his undivided attention: for a few brief seconds he made her feel as if she were the most important woman in the world. Then, as his gaze swung away and she was once again simply Chioma, an Igbo woman from Onitcha, she would chide herself: Joseph was a star out of her sphere. Was the old man taunting her? She did not think so; she had known him for long enough and was confident of his genuine affection for her. *But, perhaps it was his age, perhaps he had become so out of touch with the modern world that he thought a man like that could be interested in a woman like her!*

Chioma had sorely underestimated Uchende. During his correspondence with his nephew, he had come to understand Joseph's predicament. The dynamic of his existence was starting to slow and he was beginning to want a more sedate life. His wealth, charm and good looks would have enabled him to find a wife in Europe or America, but there was always a catch. Beneath his education and finery, Joseph was an *African* African; as such, he was a threat to black America, and wealthy liberal white America had proved somewhat *less* liberal up close than he had expected. Europe had been different, but the complex nuances of the old class system irritated him and interfered with normal relationships. Women who were suitable and available to him he always suspected of having ulterior motives; others would shy away because of his links with the arms trade.

The pseudo-diplomatic community in which he had lived and worked had proved to hold its own social and ethnic surprises. He had moved in the yacht-hopping circles of the international fix-it men, but he had come to notice that their marriages were rigidly on ethnic or interest lines: it was always about power. The Lebanese married their daughters to other Lebanese – or, in an attempt to buy respectability, to foreigners far from their shady world. Impoverished European aristocracy seemed to be preferred, or the sons of wealthy clients in the Arab world. Whilst that was true, Joseph had observed that amongst the Arabs blood was no guarantee of loyalty: when dynasties started to topple, the right marriage might mean that the patriarch had to look over his shoulder slightly less often.

A wealthy Arab of uncertain antecedents (the man was officially Lebanese, though was frequently referred to as 'The Palestinian') had tried to bring Joseph into his family. The man's daughter was extremely beautiful and well educated, but Joseph recognised the move for what it was: the man's influence in the Gulf was fading and he was looking for a way into the rich markets of Africa fuelled by civil war and inter-tribal strife, and paid for in oil, gold, coffee and diamonds. Joseph was a clever man who had worked hard for his wealth and the freedom that came with it. After such a struggle, he had no desire to live with a spy in the bedroom. It had all too quickly become apparent that his position in the family would be a fairly lowly one. As a result of his natural intelligence and the world in which he had come to move, Joseph had learnt to speak fairly proficient Arabic, but had he gone through with the marriage he was fairly sure he would have remained an outsider. A man, he decided, may change his country, his lifestyle, and even his way of thinking, but he will never change the colour of his skin.

He later learned he had had a lucky escape. As Joseph sat in the domestic comfort of Uchendu's parlour, the young lady's eventual husband was languishing in a UN jail on charges relating to the provision of the weapons used during a massacre in Darfur, whilst his wife perfected her tan and her indifference on the deck of her father's Sunseeker Yacht at an exclusive marina in Corsica.

So Joseph had stayed single. True, there had been liaisons, but his main companion had been his assistant, the Métis who had travelled with him from Cameroon when it all began.

The Mercedes pulled out of Uchende's compound. There was barely a sound as the motor purred beneath the bonnet. The journey to the house was short and not much was said, though Joseph made some polite conversation. When the car finally arrived outside the house and Joseph stopped the car, got out, walked round and opened her door for her, Chioma felt like a queen.

She knew Sarah would have something to say.

Sarah did indeed have a lot to say to Chioma, although that was not in itself unusual. She had never been the silent type and she had found the confidence in herself to become far more expressive with Chioma than she had been with her husband. Chioma was her junior and over the years she had developed a proprietary, almost maternal affection for the younger woman. She had not been intimidated by Chioma's education, even though Chioma was considerably wider read than Harrison had been (albeit as a result of the restrictions that Sarah herself had imposed, with the best of intentions).

She was happy for the younger woman – though, as she shamefully admitted to herself, she was also scared that if Chioma were to move on she would be left alone, a thought that terrified her. But the years had mellowed her somewhat and she knew that she owed Chioma a lot, so she attempted to ignore her own needs and advise her young friend accordingly. This too, however, proved conflicting, for there were things that the woman she once was wanted to say to Chioma that she knew would sound ill from a pastor's widow. Like many women in old age, Sarah had become a mirror of her late mother; it was the mantle of religion that shrouded her innate pragmatic femininity from public sight. She thought to herself, now that she was in full maternal flow, that Chioma, whilst still beautiful, was not getting any younger, and this elegant man from whose car she had so recently alighted was definitely a once-in-a-lifetime catch. Sarah had been lucky and had found her gift from God in the form of her late husband; he had given her a happy life in, she felt, much better conditions than she really deserved. Now she hoped that Chioma would have the same blessing: a good man to take care of her. There was, she knew from years ago in the early bush bars of Port Harcourt, one sure way to catch a man, but out of respect for her late husband she dared not say it.

Chioma had again started to take on a supernatural mystique; she had, Sarah reflected, appeared miraculously in her life exactly when she was needed and, now that Pastor Harrison was no more, it seemed that some further miraculous event might take her away. Sarah cast her mind back across the years to a hot afternoon when she had been accompanied by her late husband's lifelong friend the doctor; she had come rushing back into the very same house where she now sat gently rocking on the chair Harrison had brought her so many lifetimes ago. She remembered entering the house and seeing her husband lying immobile, as she had left him and as he would remain for many years, on the old battered sofa that still stood alongside the wall of her parlour. The strange, silent Igbo girl who was to become such a part of their lives had been sitting by her husband's head, the quiet Chidi asleep in her arms. Her headdress she had loosened and allowed to fall about her shoulders; the room had an air of peace about it. From the shuttered window just behind Chioma's left shoulder, the occasional ray of sunlight crept through, casting a gentle pall of light about her. Sarah remembered vividly the jolt she had suffered as the black Madonna had been revealed to her, seated at the head of her dying husband. The vision came back to her now as if a timely sign or a heavenly rebuke for her first selfish instinct of not wanting Chioma to move on. Chioma had been a gift from heaven, and now she was needed elsewhere; or perhaps she was a fallen angel serving her time in purgatory by ministering to the sick. Sarah's mind was running wild, her imagination conjuring up all sorts of ideas: that the tall man in the car was in fact an angel come to move Chioma to her next task.

With a jolt, her head fell forwards. She had been dreaming, she realised, as she sat in her chair. "Curse this old age," she said. She kept dozing off at the most surprising moments.

She looked up. Chioma was sitting opposite her in Harrison's old chair, smiling gently. "You did sleep, Oga, you are too much tired!"

Sarah stirred in her chair, making herself comfortable. She smoothed the front of her dress, a compulsive action she performed whenever she prepared to speak, especially if it was upon a matter that she considered weighty.

"So. Tell me bout dis man den, waitin' he be like? If he be good man or no?"

What *was* he like? It was a question that Chioma herself was struggling with. That he was charming and good looking was inescapable, but that in itself made her feel slightly ill at ease. It was too much: his fine manners and impeccable grooming seemed out of place amidst the squalor and poverty of Port Harcourt. He had, as her mother would have said, 'the charm of Satan'. He was just too perfect, and she thought there had to be some sordid secret. She had no evidence of such a thing though, and felt that the notion was uncharitable: it was merely her own cynicism, or perhaps a deep-seated jealousy of his apparent good fortune.

Chioma tried as best she could to explain her feelings to the older woman, but Sarah was no fool. "Bikin you do like 'im very well, I savy." She arched her eyebrows, folded her hands across her ample stomach, and regarded the younger woman as Chioma, quite uncharacteristically, played with her hands. "You is fidgitin' like a young virgin dat want ask her papa for bring a boy in de house for meet him de first time! You t'ink I no shine my eye? Jus' 'cause I old no make me blind, my girl."

Chapter Twenty-five

Joseph had been acquainted with Chief Akintola for many years and whilst he did not actively dislike him (active dislike was not part of Joseph's nature), he had little positive feeling for him. But people like Chief Akintola were as necessary to Joseph's peculiar line of business as Joseph was to people like Chief Akintola. The main difference between the two men's feelings towards each other was that the vanity that had propelled Akintola into the political arena required that he believe that the people he needed actually liked him. Joseph, though, had been blessed with a much greater clarity of vision where such things were concerned.

When Joseph's cell phone rang, it flagged up Akintola's number. He had already anticipated the trivial niceties that would be showered upon him before he, the politician, came to the point. The point would invariably be that he required Joseph's particular brand of service. Joseph knew his business and never allowed his irritation at the politician's hypocrisy to show in his voice or demeanour. Given the choice, though, he far preferred to deal with the likes of Ron Forrester, who did not insult his intelligence with this charade friendship, but got straight to the point.

Joseph took the call with his usual patient good grace. He was a smart man and he realised immediately the importance of what he was being told, and the even greater importance of what he was not. Unfortunately, even he was not astute enough to detect the hand of Ron Forrester in the mix. It was, though, immediately clear to him that behind Akintola's effusive burbling was a much sharper mind and that indirectly he, Joseph, was being used to do someone else's dirty work – but then that was his line of work. He had had his eye off the ball in the game of Nigerian politics a little too long however, and he assumed that the mind behind the fluster would be an ambitious politician making a power play for the big job. Not for one moment did he think of the stocky little man from Hull.

Joseph naturally, and correctly, assumed that this was a far-reaching chess move, that the player behind Akintola was not thinking of the immediate consequences of the move but was looking further ahead. The player would have calculated his opponent's reaction, his own next move and the anticipated reaction to that. It appeared to Joseph that whoever was manipulating Akintola wanted the Americans to put pressure on someone very highly placed in Lagos, possibly the president, to act. Joseph doubted that the president himself was the actual target of the present move; it was far more likely that whoever had instigated the play wanted the president in turn to pressurise an underling and it was the reaction of the underling that was desired. Such was the nature of Nigerian politics.

Normally alarm bells would have rung in Joseph's brain: Akintola should not have known that he had direct access to the CIA man in Lagos. True, it was an open secret in certain circles, and Joseph had acted on several occasions as a conduit in both directions when official contact would have been politically unseemly for both parties. But Akintola did not move in those circles. Joseph would normally have expected to have been primed in some way, either directly or indirectly, that such a contact was coming. He was getting tired of these games. They did not hold the excitement that they once had and he was losing interest. He was aware that he had not given Akintola the meticulous attention he would normally have afforded such an important conversation as a new scenario had begun to unfold; he found it slightly disturbing, but his mind seemed strangely occupied by the woman with the haunting eyes whom he had met at his uncle's house the night before.

Akinetola put down the phone. He had opened the game, the die was cast. He loved that expression; he had been a good student at school and the private English school that his colonially educated father had insisted his children attend had given him a cursory introduction to the classics. The idea that he was a Roman god casting dice to decide on the fate of mere mortals was a fantasy into which, years later, he still found pleasure in retreating. The rest of the fantasy, where he lay draped in a toga on a sumptuous couch, his every whim tended by equally sumptuous and muscular young men, was one that he now had the money to, on occasions, render reality.

A little detail of which he suspected Ron Forrester was aware.

This was a thought that afforded the chief little comfort and he tried to put it out of his mind. Instead he concentrated on Joseph; he had, he thought, delivered the little bombshell rather well. Enola Gay was about to taxi down the runway, her deadly load primed and ready to drop. The idea amused him – Joseph as Enola Gay. Joseph was a beautiful man and he had aroused a special type of desire in Akintola on the rare occasions that they had met. The boys that Akintola frequented serviced his needs and his fantasies, and he admired beauty. They had to be beautiful, little African copies of ancient Greek statues. Akintola considered himself a connoisseur of the beauties of the male form – not that he himself considered it necessary to indulge in exercise, but he knew the requirements of the body-building gymnasiums: he had a fantastic understanding of the necessary requirements of all the individual muscle groups, he was an authority on high-protein diets, and frequently provided hormones and steroids to the gyms that most adequately fulfilled his desires. Like a collector at Christie's or Sotheby's, he would carefully examine each exhibit, the ends of his fingers finely trained tools of examination, tracing the sculpted contours of his intended purchase.

But Joseph was a different matter. Akintola envied and desired Joseph; it was his long-lashed eyes that appeared to hold so much sorrow and so much compassion, and his tall, slender but (Akintola was sure) muscular physique called out to Akintola as an undiscovered masterpiece calls out to a trader jaded by reproductions and second-quality antiquities of dubious provenance. There was something else as well: Joseph displayed no sign of homosexuality, but Akintola was sure that if he slept with women it was simply the fulfilment of base physical needs, much as he, Akintola, relieved the frustrations of his life with muscle-bound young men. With Joseph he would find some deeper pleasure; he could imagine that low, creamy voice, the perfectly enunciated words flowing without a trace of the barbarisms of his native tongue; Joseph was truly the work of a Renaissance master and Akintola wanted him. Akintola wanted him and what Akintola wanted he was used to getting.

He pressed the intercom on his desk and called through to his personal assistant. "Bring me a bottle of Bordeaux and hold all calls." About five minutes later, a young man in a grey suit and pale pink shirt entered the room. He removed a glass from the large cabinet that took up most off the office wall, carefully opened the bottle and poured the chief a small glass. He handed it to his master, who, with great show, sniffed it and then tasted it. He nodded his approval and the young man poured a full glass. Akintola took a long slow draught and placed the glass on the desk. "Fetch yourself a glass, James, then take off your clothes."

Chapter Twenty-six

Not many miles away, Ron Forrester was walking through the chaotic yard of Niger Marine. The yard was muddy and he was careful about where he placed his feet. A collection of overall-clad workers turned to face their various projects, real or imagined as he passed. It flashed through Ron's mind that it would be a nice gesture of respect if one of them would come and lie down in the mud and form a human bridge so that he would not need to sully his expensive shoes. In an uncharacteristic moment of self-knowledge, Ron smiled at the ridiculous nature of the vision. Still, he thought as he picked his way around a particularly large puddle, *the gesture would not go unappreciated*.

Ron was happy, or as close to that state as his personality would allow (it would perhaps be truer to say that he was in a state of excitement that alleviated the anger towards the rest of the world that for so much of his waking hours attempted to engulf his entire being). The reason for this elevated state was that he had started the game. It was beyond the point of no return – total commitment from here on in, a rush of blood to the head. Like the Scottish thane, he was already so steeped in blood that returning would have been as wearying as going o'er; but unlike the thane, and even though the killing had yet to commence, Ron had no thought of stopping it.

He was so wrapped up in his train of thought that he totally failed to notice a large pool of oily water that sat alongside one of the containers filling the yard. The water seeped over the top of his shoe, soaking his white socks. He swore.

Across the yard, an elderly African worker smiled to himself. *God was just in small ways*, he thought.

Joseph made a few discreet phone calls. He needed to confirm as far as possible the information he had received from Akintola. His preliminary enquires tended to confirm – or at least not refute – that information. There had definitely been Americans on the barge that had been attacked and there were probably some unaccounted for.

Joseph called up his faithful assistant and despatched him, armed with a suitable amount of tongue-loosening dollars, to the port areas, to see what he could uncover. A few hours later he gave his report. His research had led him to a number of Philippino seamen and two Egyptian pipe-welders who had been aboard. Several of them had definitely seen the fat American barge foreman in the hands of the militants, his face covered in blood. What followed was a little more confusing: all agreed that they had not seen Captain Lee after the attack. Some thought he had been taken; others were sure he had been killed. There was apparently another American aboard, whose function nobody seemed sure of. Again, opinion was divided: some thought he had been taken and one was adamant that he had seen the body riddled with bullets; all agreed, however, that, like Captain Lee, he had not been seen since the attack.

Joseph noted the inconsistencies and decided that, on balance, there was enough to go on; the general impression was that Akintola's information had been correct. Joseph was also aware that Akintola's abilities did not extend to the orchestration of a sophisticated cover-up. Had the cover-up been orchestrated by Akintola, the men would have all told identical stories; the discrepancies tended to imply that the seamen were at least telling the truth and had not been primed. The cover-up was at a higher level and Akintola was probably telling Joseph what he believed to be the truth.

Joseph poured himself a scotch and watched as three ice cubes began to melt into the golden liquid. When they had all but disappeared, he downed the liquid in a single motion. Then he picked up the phone and dialled the number for his contact at the American consulate.

Chapter Twenty-seven

The Secretary had no answers for his former student colleague or himself. He knew in his heart that Labo's suspended body symbolised their defeat; they were fighting for a free and just nation, fighting for an end to corruption and the establishment of the rule of law, and here he was allowing a lynch mob to execute what may well have been an injustice. It was true that Labo had admitted killing the foreigners, but it had never been established how or why. Mob rule was not the vision that he and Jackson had harboured for a free independent Niger Delta.

The older man looked at him for a moment and then: "If you are not prepared to put a stop to this, then I will." He cocked his weapon and walked towards the mob, then let fly a burst very close above the heads of the salivating pack. There was immediate silence as they all stopped and turned, startled, towards him. He strode into their midst; he seemed so hedged about with natural authority that none would dare confront him. Eyes were cast down as he passed and heads were bowed, in shame, humility or fear, it was far from clear, but no one moved. Like a medieval king moving amongst his terrified subjects, he walked through the aisle created by their obeisance.

Arriving at Labo's feet, he raised one hand to the suspended knees. At his touch he noticed movement in Labo's eyes: they slowly reached out to him, the eyes of a confused and desperate animal that no longer had the will to fight, whose pain had transcended all understanding. He held Labo's eyes with his own and in a strong low voice said: "Be strong, comrade, it is almost over."

He stepped backwards, and in a much louder voice he uttered words that came, even as he spoke them, as a surprise even to himself: "Forgive them, my brother, they are but ignorant animals and they know not what they do."

He raised up his gun and added under his breath: "And forgive me, Lord, for what *I* am about to do."

With which he fired a single round that entered the skull between Labo's eyes and ended the misery of his existence once and for all.

Chapter Twenty-eight

Whilst Chief Akintola indulged himself in the pleasures of Bacchus, and was for a time oblivious to the squalor and chaos of the world beyond his Romanesque fantasia, the airwaves were full of the news he had leaked. Joseph's phone call to Linus, the CIA operative, had unleashed a frenzy of international and intergovernmental communications, all at a decidedly unofficial level, and all had agreed that, whilst this stayed out of the press it could stay there. Oil money buys a lot of silence; none of the major players wanted an international incident and foreign troops would look like an invasion. In the wake of the Iraq fiasco, no one wanted another oil-related conflict with an indeterminate presence and an endless stream of body bags being sent home in front of the waiting news cameras.

The incumbent but struggling Whitehouse Republican PR machine was also acutely aware of its poor showing amongst the black community, and thus, combined with the fact that they would soon be facing a challenge from a charismatic, articulate black democrat, they had no doubt that scores of African civilian casualties in a corporate oil war would drive them out of the Whitehouse and far into the wilderness for decades to come. Oilmen were dragged from the Miami golf courses, senators of both parties overheated their cell phones in desperate attempts to find out for themselves and play down to others the truth of the situation. Nobody wanted a public outcry; everybody wanted it to go away.

Across the globe, other men like Joseph – men that governments, oil companies and multinationals employed to get things done – started to call each other, to carry messages on behalf of their various employers. A natural filtering process occurred: suggestions were made, hints were dropped, until, eventually, certain things were becoming clear to all concerned. First, the oil companies and the Americans wanted the situation tidied up; secondly, the Americans (and to a slightly lesser extent the British) did not want to be seen to be involved. It was generally agreed that, whilst some pressure on the Nigerian government was necessary, too much was a short road to disaster. Any massacre that was carried out by the Nigerian military would inevitably be blamed on Western pressure or lack of Western restraint; either way, it did not bode well for the Republican oil interests.

Few options remained. The two front-runners had to be the British or the French. Both had a long history of involvement in the region and their contacts and influence were well embedded; both had major financial interests, Total and BP; both the British and the French – especially the latter – had sizable expatriate communities along the west coast of Africa; and more importantly, both managed to maintain a diplomatic and strategic world that was far from public scrutiny. On the other hand, the amorphous diplomatic community that was making these decisions needed time and information. Publicly at least, procedures and protocols needed to be followed, so the Nigerian government was leant on and a clear message was sent: *negotiate with these people on our behalf and your indiscretions shall remain secret*. The quiet men behind the Nigerian power structure breathed a collective sigh of relief; their Swiss bank accounts were safe.

MEND had opened negotiations and the interested parties wished for that to proceed as long as it was under their direction; a suitable negotiator of their choosing should be appointed – and so one duly was. After a few hints were dropped in the right ears, the candidate was obvious: Joseph.

After the attack, Azzi had returned home a hero. The company pin-up boy had saved the life of his captain and mentor, and had by his actions justified the company's investment: he was, they were sure, a blessing from the god of PR.

On his return to the house, Amanda noticed that he seemed changed in a way that went beyond the expected fatigue and shock that would be normal after such an incident. He seemed somehow consolidated; it was as if he had been loosely assembled before and then, when at last all the pieces were aligned they had been pushed into place and securely welded down. Amanda was unutterably proud of her man. He did not speak much about the incident; but where the old Azzi would have bottled it up and then would have let it out in sudden bursts of emotional release, the new-model Azzi seemed able to talk calmly about the experience. It was as if he had absorbed the force of the trauma and internalised the energy of the attack, and it was that energy that had served in the final fusion of his personality into an ordered structured whole.

Together they visited Captain Evans in hospital. It had been Azzi's prompt and decisive action that had saved the old man's life, but he had lost a lot of blood nonetheless. He was still weak, but he would live though his seagoing days were over. The publicity surrounding the attack had ensured that the company would pay him a disability pension and he would live out his days in relative comfort.

Amanda sat beside her husband next to the bed of his old friend, brimming with pride; it was, she realised, the first time they had actually been out together in public as a couple, and the pride that she felt at being presented as Madame Azzi was almost more than she could bear. As she sat and watched the two friends talking quietly about things she barely understood – parts of ships and ports – she looked at the old man who had given her back her childhood sweetheart and made him whole again, and felt a deep love for him. That much of Azzi's current happiness and stability was actually due to her was a fact to which she was totally oblivious.

Chapter Twenty-nine

It was a crisp but sunny morning in London; faint wisps of condensation appeared at the mouths of the well-heeled joggers who sported their brand-named tracksuits round St James' Park. Less than a mile away the traffic fumes were beginning to build up on the main artery that bypassed London's other great lung, Hyde Park, as the morning surge into the city gained momentum.

At 4 St James' Square, in a building that was formerly the residence of Nancy Astor, Britain's first female Member of Parliament, is one of those peculiarly British institutions from which the country and its overseas interests are discreetly run whilst elected politicians divert public attention elsewhere. Its single entrance is bizarrely labelled 'In and Out', a uniquely British idiosyncrasy that pays homage to the institution's heritage. In truth it is a gentleman's club, the Naval and Military. The club was originally situated in a large, squat, white building set back from Piccadilly and overlooking Green Park; entry was through a small courtyard which was protected by a solid white wall, punctuated by two gates labelled 'In' and 'Out'. As there were no other obvious external identifying features, the building became known to its patrons as simply the 'In and Out'. In 1999, the In and Out's lease expired and it moved down the road. Whilst its location had changed, its character remained essentially the same.

Inside the In and Out, a small table had been set. A tall man with a long, thin face and grey hair that fell in a fringe over his forehead sat in a well-tailored, double-breasted blue suit. In front of him there was a pot of coffee, a plate with two croissants, and a copy of *The Times*. He was draped in the chair in the manner that only a well-bred Englishman can be. He was joined by a slightly shorter man who was equally well dressed but appeared somehow harder and more muscular, his movements were slightly more dynamic and lacked the studied languor that the British upper class had refined though centuries of in-breeding.

A waiter who was quite clearly ex-military appeared and a second breakfast was ordered.

"I take it, Charles, that you have been fully briefed?"

"Not really, sir, just a general outline, but I think I get the basic picture."

"Well, what we have is a problem with our friends over the pond. That barge that was attacked the other day in Nigeria, actually it was one of theirs, bit of a rogue company but one of theirs nonetheless. Also a British-flagged tugboat got a bit shot up. You know, there was a time when we would have considered that an act of war! Anyway, times are changing. Well, it seems that there are a couple of dead Americans, and they want things tidied up with out that hillbilly president of theirs finding out. If he finds the darkies have been knocking off good God-fearing white folk, he'll be all for sending in the cavalry and we will have another Iraq on our hands. With me so far?"

"Pretty much, sir – what about our chap, does he know?"

"Yes and no, just asked for it to be delegated, so pretty much a green light. Usual story. No knowledge, no responsibility. I must say, for a lefty he's pretty good, this boy, knows to keep his nose out of where it's not wanted, but I digress. We need this wrapped up fast, no obvious British involvement, get our American friends their chaps back and let the MEND chappies know that just because we let them have their country back does not give them *carte blanche* to go round executing expats."

"With respect, sir, I have dealt with some of the Delta brigades before and that does not sound like them at all, they're usually pretty well disciplined for African irregulars and very

231

careful about not killing foreigners – that's part of the deal. Didn't we arm and train some of them ourselves after that Charles Taylor debacle?"

"Yes, but they need a gentle slap across the wrist every now and then, just remind them who pays the bills and all that, not too hard, just enough to keep the Americans quiet and restore the status quo."

"How many of our chaps have they got?"

"All in all? About twelve, scattered about the place, that's the usual number at any one time. On this raid it seems that they got two, and injured one old sea captain. Some old boy who had lost his ticket over here a good few years back, run off to Africa and gone native."

"Have we got any one on the ground? Influence? Assets?"

"Yes, the usual Nigerian ministers with some rather dubious bank accounts in British dependent territories, that sort of thing, you know, good for manipulating and massaging. Also we have a gopher, good chap, darkie, well-educated, very well spoken, charismatic sort of chappy. Arabs loved him when we used him with the Libyans, good language skills, and very, very discrete. No real muck on him, just what he does, which could get him shot in quite a few countries. Always been a few rumours about him batting for both sides, but there are heartbroken ambassadors' wives across the globe who will testify that he plays straight as well. Good chap, we would rather you tried not to damage him, but obviously," he paused, "priorities."

"Is he activated?"

"Yes, though not directly by us. We have a low-grade asset in Abuja, bit into the old Greek homoerotic thing, you know, muscular young chaps and the like – well, we have photographs and access to his bank account. He was actually roped in by a local Brit and he initially got our friend involved, basically as a way of creating a leak to the Americans, but his personal secretary is also on our payroll so we found out pretty quick. We'll give him a hard time later for not telling us himself, but we don't want to blow his secretary for a while, or so the embassy boys in Lagos tell me. Anyway, to cut a long story short he can be used as a conduit to our man if it becomes necessary, if not we'll just get secretary boy to listen in, keeps our hands clean. The Americans know our gopher chappy, it was him that passed on the information and they quite like him. They have already pushed him forwards as a negotiator for their own ends, but we're pretty sure that if they are running him it's completely unofficial. But as you know, you can never tell with the Yanks, so many different agencies and interest groups, but we're ninety percent sure it is not official. You see, he got too close to the Palestinians a long time ago and their political boys blackballed him, but Langley throws him the odd job every now and then, when they need a black face."

"What's his provenance?"

"Interesting chap, Biafran refugee, made a lot of money after the anti-Igbo pogroms, then started facilitating for the oil companies in Equatorial Guinea and Cameroon. How we picked him up is quite a story. Do you remember the Yvonne Fletcher affair? Bit before your time probably, guess you were probably still square-bashing at Sandhurst or something."

"WPC; shot outside Libyan Peoples' Bureau in Berkley Square. PM then had no choice but to let the Americans use UK air bases to strike Libya. Police Federation been banging on about it ever since, reckon we or the Yanks shot her to force Thatcher's hand, that's the one isn't?"

"That's right, pretty young thing too, damned shame. Apparently they had hopes she would be the first serving WPC to go to the Olympics or something – good swimmer, if I remember. Anyway, it wasn't us, it was the Yanks. The old girl at number ten put up a fight, but public opinion was too much even for her, so she gave in. Well, from our point of view it was an absolute disaster, the last thing we wanted was the Yanks getting rid of Gaddafi, he was holding the place together and keeping their hands off his oil. Trouble with him was he would only talk to Africans, so we used and burnt one of our best black gophers. To cut a long story short he made sure that old *Mad Dog Ghadafi* was well away when the Americans hit. Obviously we couldn't use him after that, but he pointed us in the way of this chap, rising star, he said, a sort of 'thank you' for the hotel in the Bahamas that the taxpayer bought him as a retirement present."

"And this new chap, does he know he's been working for us or not?"

"He's supposed to be pretty smart so he has probably figured it out; but officially? No. Met him once in Geneva, charming fellow."

"What's his name?"

"Joseph Eseweh, or at least that's what he calls himself in public. Anyway, old chap, I suggest you trot off to the 'other place' and get things moving, I'll be off to the country for the weekend. Wife's dragging me to some awful wedding thing for one her chums' intellectually stunted offspring. 'Spect you'll have it sorted by the time I get back. Good luck, Charles."

On another continent, Joseph had long been thinking that it was due time he retired. He was getting tired, his interest was waning and he yearned for a normal life. And he knew his good luck could not hold forever. He had thought about going back to Cameroon; there was a large Anglophone community in Limbe, and he could afford an extremely luxurious residence by the sea – or perhaps the more touristic resort of Kribi, where he could still maintain much of the lifestyle he had enjoyed for years but in a sedate African setting. He had long harboured a vague desire to write a history of the Igbo people; it was not as if he was short of money or potential projects, but he feared boredom. This job, this project, had to be the last. He knew he was losing his edge.

It was time to get out. His ever-changing world had evolved around him; there were new alliances, new rules, new priorities. It was time to move on.

In a most uncharacteristically rash move, he picked up his cell phone and invited Chioma to dinner.

Chapter Thirty

Azzi stood by the roadside, in exactly the same position he had stood sixteen years before. He could still identify the spot where his beautiful young wife Chioma had stood beside him for the last time, with Chidi, who had then been only two years old, perched on her hip, a wide-eyed spectator of a scene he could not possibly have comprehended. Now, as then, Azzi remained upright, once again the tired old soldier, but now his dignity had substance, a history. He had lived a hard life; he had come under fire and not been found wanting. To many people, especially those who really mattered in his life, he was a hero.

He looked around where his house had once stood. The road had only cut through the front half of their land, but later a petrol station had been built over the rest of the site. Nothing remained of his old existence, no sign, no trace that a house had once stood here, a house that had been home to his family and which Chioma had swept every day. For the first time in sixteen years he desperately wanted a drink.

He had begun to feel that his life was at last complete. He had everything he could want. He had built a career that had given him position and wealth, by dint of a little luck and a lot of hard work and talent, he had a home, a financially independent wife who clearly loved him far more than Chioma ever had, and they had a child on the way. He had finally learnt the truth about his own ancestry, seen his birth mother and laid the ghosts to rest. Last night should have been fantastic. After the fiasco in the oilfield, he had come back a hero. He had finally had the confidence to take Amanda to meet his mentor, Captain Evans.

Standing in front of the captain with his woman at his side, they had finally met as equals, and it had been a very special moment in Azzi's life, almost a rite of passage. Captain Evans had assumed the role of a surrogate father in Azzi's affections, and now he knew in his heart that the old man was proud of him. On leaving the hospital Azzi had felt like a king; in the foyer they had met one of the company executives from Aberdeen, who had also been on his way to visit Evans. The man had immediately recognised Azzi from the numerous publicity photographs in which he had appeared, and was well aware of Azzi's role in the recent drama. On seeing the couple and Amanda's obvious pregnancy, the enthusiastic executive immediately ordered the couple a table at the hotel restaurant where he was staying and ordered his car to drive them. Full of excitement, the couple made their way to the Borgon Villa, one of Port Harcourt's better hotels.

Azzi had once or twice set foot in such places, but only as an errand runner delivering messages to visiting executives. To Amanda the place was a revelation. They made their way, a little nervously at first, into the crowded restaurant. As soon as they had identified themselves, hardly believing their luck, they were ushered to a table by a waiter who had been well briefed prior to their arrival. They took their seats, Azzi feeling proud but still a little nervous that he might commit some *faux pas* and show himself up; Amanda was simply brimming with pride at the importance of her man.

Whilst Azzi diligently perused the menu, Amanda gazed around herself at the glittering splendour, the fantastic array of people black, white and Asiatic and all at ease in their surroundings. This was a different world, which till now, had existed for Amanda only on television screens. Opposite them, a table was set with a reserved sign on it. It occurred to Amanda that someone must be exceptionally important to have such sign placed on a table; she had been too distracted by her surroundings to notice the little triangular sign that the waiter had deftly removed from their table as he had shown them to their seats. Whilst they were enjoying their entrees, a couple were shown to the reserved table. The man was tall and impeccably dressed, but it was the woman who made Azzi almost choke on his prawn cocktail.

Despite the long passage of time, Chioma was almost completely unchanged.

Chioma had been seated with her back to him and had not noticed him. He was probably fitter and healthier than the last time she saw him, and he was no longer dressed in old jeans and a T-shirt, but time had changed him. He was now a middle-aged man; *it was not surprising*, he thought, *that she had not recognised him*. He excused himself and made his way as rapidly as dignity would allow to the men's room, where he locked himself into a cubicle and was violently sick. It was just shock, he told himself, the culmination of the effects of being attacked – and then this. This had proved to be the last drop of water that spilt the glass.

He wiped his face with toilet tissue, flushed the cistern, then sat on the toilet, head in hands. He must get back to Amanda, he did not want her to worry. It was so long since he had seen her this happy, he could not bear to spoil it for her. This was, he knew, a very special evening for her. She had never before eaten in a restaurant like this, and she was with a man who was now a local hero and was probably going to be on television.

He left the cubicle, washed his face and tried to make himself look normal. When he returned to the table he discreetly rearranged his seat so that he would have his back to his past. He tried to give Amanda his undivided attention, tried to convince himself that his ears were not straining to catch just a note of Chioma's voice. Every time he looked at his wine glass he caught sight of her profile, her gleaming white smile reflected against the blood red wine.

Chapter Thirty-one

Now, as the morning sun struggled to find its way through the heavy cloud and industrial smog that conspired to shield Port Harcourt from its life-giving rays, Azzi paced the ground where his life had changed. Where the fat man from the federal government had stood, there was a pile of rubbish, a collection of domestic and commercial waste festering by the road. Azzi glimpsed the flick of a rat's tale as it darted back inside the rank pyramid of human debris. The path of the bulldozer was now the entrance to the filling station. Azzi looked back down the road and for a moment he saw a smiling Chioma walking towards him, waving to him, little Chidi riding as ever on her hip. She was pointing him out to their son, whose huge round eyes were gazing out towards him from the folds of his mamma's lace, his face cracked into a smile of recognition. Then the vision was gone and Azzi was once again staring down the road built to feed the oil industry, to service the insatiable desire for black gold that had destroyed his home, had made young men of his own tribe shoot at him and had ultimately made him a rich man.

The skies could no longer support the combined weight of cloud and smog and the filthy rain began to fall, rank upon rank of poisoned soldiers hurling themselves towards certain death in the muddy streets of Port Harcourt.

The cardboard boxes crowning the pile of rubbish that served as a memorial to where the fat man from the federal government once stood began to crumble with the weight of the rain. The rat that Azzi had seen scramble inside emerged from the pile and sat a metre away, watching helplessly as his home disintegrated and started to drift into the open sewage system that lined the road. The rodent turned his head as if to look at Azzi.

The warm rainwater was running down his back and his clothes were sticking to his body. The street was rapidly emptying as the few remaining street traders picked up their goods and ran for shelter from the deluge. The station forecourt was soon deserted except for Azzi and the rat, which, despite the fact that his fur was saturated and hung in clumps, seemed unable to leave the crumbling cardboard pile that was rapidly turning to sludge.

Azzi watched with fascination. "I know exactly how you feel," he said out loud.

At the sound of his voice, the animal finally turned and ran. Despite the rain and the despair he had felt weighing down on his soul, Azzi suddenly laughed. There was something he too needed to do. He turned on his heel and left the site forever.

Chioma was totally oblivious to the fact that she had been just metres from Chidi's father. Like Amanda, she had been entranced by her surroundings and company, Joseph had been an excellent companion. He had comported himself as the perfect gentleman and delivered her to Sarah's door, his car attracting a fair amount of attention in the street despite the lateness of the hour. Now she and Sarah sat together in the front room where for so many years they had tended Harrison, both cradling hot cups of Lipton's whilst the rain hammered on the iron roof. Inevitably, they were discussing the previous evening. Sarah had insisted that Chioma skip no detail, even down to the colour of the tablecloths – she wanted to hear everything.

It was whilst they were happily engrossed in this that they heard a knock on the door. Chioma pulled herself up; she was astonished that any one would be out in such weather. Chidi had told her that he was studying at a friend's house, a story which she only partially believed, and she knew that Joseph would never arrive unannounced, even though she found her heart racing as she approached the door. As she opened the door, the sound of the rain rushed in and water ricocheted up off the floor. The rain was so intense that the houses opposite, not ten metres distant, were barely visible. Water was pooling in the road before her – *no sane person would be out in weather like this,* she thought as she opened the door.

The man standing before her was soaked. It was as if he had been pulled from the very puddles in the road. His clothes clung to him like sodden tissues. But this time she recognised him immediately.

Chapter Thirty-two

The hostages sat together, immobile, watching as Labo's body gave one final spasm and at last went limp. Mike Parry became suddenly aware again of the rain; it was as if the sound of the downpour had been suspended by Labo's suffering and with his death had reasserted itself. There was hardly any movement; the militants stood round the body as if awaiting some sign or instruction. Only the executioner moved; he was taller than most of his colleagues and seemed to have held the assault rifle in position for a long time after he had fired the shot. At last he slowly lowered it. He straightened himself up and slowly turned and started to walk back through the corridor the militants had left him. He was fine featured with intensely black skin and as he walked back towards them, the weapon hung limp in his hand. To Mike he seemed to be the only person in focus, whilst the rest of camp faded into a sepia haze somewhere behind the rain.

The executioner arrived before them. He stood absolutely still but his eyes betrayed him: he needed to speak, to say something that would undo what could not be undone, that would heal the wounds of the last few minutes, that would purge the shame he felt. Suddenly the war paint and the robes he had worn so often felt stupid and childish. He felt his shame rising like poisoned sap through his veins, taking succour from the bloodstained land. He looked at the white men that they had dragged here by force to convince the world that Niger Deltans were ready to have their own country. He needed to tell them that his country would not be like this, that he had graduated in philosophy, that he dreamed of a just, civilised republic built on a constitution based on the fundamental inalienable rights of man, of which his people had so long been deprived. But one look at their faces told him that they would never believe him.

He turned towards his former colleague in academia, The Secretary. He could feel the sense of what he needed to say hurtling up through his body, but he could not turn the sensation into words. His mind, mouth and body seemed to be locked in a conflict in which each was evenly matched and none would give quarter. The pressure was overwhelming. He was about to erupt; he grasped his rifle by the barrel and swung the butt towards the head of his friend. His anger at the betrayal of their dreams was too much for him; it was as if, by imploding The Secretary's skull, he could smash Labo's pitiful death from his own conscience.

Despite the pain, there was something still human deep down inside him fighting for air, desperately swimming upwards through his turbulent emotions. And it was the same humanity that was hurting so badly that made him pull back sharply on the rifle so that the butt missed The Secretary's head. He continued the swing until he finally released it and it flew out over the sacred river to splash down and sink into the realm of the *Mammi Water*. As the gun left his hands he let out a howl: it was a howl that contained all the years of oppression, all the frustration of his own thwarted dreams and desires and the agonising pain of Labo's final moments. It contained the brutality of the jungle and the pain of his own birth. It was a scream so primal it made the jungle seem young. From deep down in the roots of the earth, the scream picked up on the dull echoing harmonics of the cry of Cain that had reverberated across time, that first scream of despair as self-knowledge had broken over him. Aaron's anguished howl mingled with them, infused them with a new lease of life, and in one almighty heave unleashed a symphony of discord that threatened to bare the very soul of man.

The Secretary had not moved. The rifle butt missed him by centimetres, but as it swept past him it took with it all sense and all mobility. The two men seemed to exist with only one another in a space that transcended time. There was nothing else, just the cry and the despair, the broken dreams, the shattered faith, its splintering shards suspended in the turbid air between them.

Mike wanted to turn towards Dricus, but such was the intensity of the charge passing between the two Niger Deltans, he found he could not draw himself away. He needed to breath, he forced the air back into his lungs and slowly the spell began to break. As he managed to bring his eyes to bear on his fellow captives, he found that they too were as if cast in stone, rigid, breathless observers of a drama that transcended writing, undermined language and went straight to the heart of the paradox of being.

Chapter Thirty-three

It is but a short walk for a healthy man from the In and Out to the Reform Club in St James', and Charles was a very healthy man. He could never quite pinpoint when he had stopped being a soldier and become a politicians' errand boy. It had been a gradual process, but it appeared to have been a one-way transition; to attempt to return would be like a butterfly attempting to turn back into a caterpillar. *That was what he was*, he thought as he walked rapidly past The Ritz, his breath barely visible in the crisp air – *a butterfly*. All he did was flit from military top brass to politician, or any other undesirable, carrying messages and dropping hints that would not be fitting to be seen done by direct contact. Charles had been educated at what was euphemistically termed a 'solid' public school. It was a good school, but it was not one of the elite; his military career had been a successful one, but he had soldier written all over him. That was why he did what he did. He was not and could never be of the inner circle, but his military bearing made the non-military feel reassured and his minor public school background and slightly rough edges meant that he was unlikely to harbour secret ambitions to a world whose doors were permanently closed to him, but was educated enough to know it. The man he was going to meet, however, was of the inner circle, and Charles found him sitting alone on the first floor of the Reform Club, his back to the balustrade that overlooked the great hall.

"Ah, good morning, Charles. How is the admiral today? I trust he is well? Please, take a seat. Breakfast?"

Charles took the seat but declined the offered breakfast. He noted that both men had the same breakfast, the same newspaper, and the same apparently indifferent languor about them. Whilst he had great respect for the admiral, the man who now sat opposite him made Charles feel decidedly uncomfortable; he was quite sure he was a sadist and he seemed to move all too comfortably in a world in which other people's morals were their weakness, where human life could be dismissed over a glass of sherry. Charles had the usual soldier's distrust of the intelligence services, but this man was not even a legitimate part of the intelligence service, he was, Charles felt, something far more murky.

In fact he was no different from Joseph: he was a fixer, a negotiator, a doer of unpleasant deeds, but Charles was blinded by the man's education and his own cultural heritage. He would quite happily deal with the Josephs of this peculiar world into which he seemed to have drifted, but when the man was an Englishman it was distasteful. Charles certainly did not consider himself a racist, but when it came to the crunch he did not expect too much in the way of ethics from 'Johnny foreigner'. When it was one of his own kind, on the other hand, this sort of skulduggery wasn't quite cricket.

And it was precisely that mindset that made Charles so useful to such men.

"So I guess the admiral wants the Americans bailed out in the Delta, does he? And I suspect he wants no direct contact with our ambiguous friend Joseph? Am I correct?"

Charles nodded. Sometimes he wondered why they used him at all: the messages invariably seemed to arrive before he did.

"Well, there's no need to disturb the old chap whilst he's away, but on Monday let him know, Joseph is doing the face-to-face negotiations. More to keep the game going than anything else, but also so we have some proof of life. He will think he's working for the Nigerians or the oil companies. As for muscle power, I thought about Sandline, but after the Equatorial Guinea disaster they're far too political in that part of Africa and the whole thing could backfire on us horribly. Then there's 'Executive Outcomes', we've got a couple of good chaps from the Sierra Leone business on board as admin, but they're too political again and basically too *white South African*. So what I need is for you to pull some strings in the army pay corps."

It was one of the rare occasions that Charles was caught completely off guard. Following the references to two organisations that, depending on one's perspective, were either the best-known private security organisations in the world or a miscreant bunch of mercenaries, he had at least expected to be talking about front-line infantry units, not people whom he had always considered to be a bunch of overweight pen pushers. The surprise must have register on his face.

"Don't worry, Charles, I am not asking you to lead them on a hostage rescue mission, though the idea is, now that I come to think of it, highly amusing. But no! Let me explain what I need." He proceeded to detail the information that he required. "Once you have that, I want it subdivided by ethnicity, and then I want outstanding leave entitlements, marital status and any known financial debts."

Suspicions began to form in the back of Charles's mind, about what might actually be going on. But he decided not to think about it.

"Our chap Joseph will be going into the bush later today to meet with these MEND chappies face-to-face. We have sent one of the Scotland Yard hostage negotiation boys over to give him a brief – not that I think he really needs it – and he will be told that the man is an oil company security specialist with a police background. I am here for the weekend. I'll need that information by this evening, so you had better get your skates on, old boy."

Chapter Thirty-four

By the time Joseph arrived in the camp, order had been restored. Labo's body had been buried at a distance from the camp; those identified as being the most involved in his scourging were quickly and quietly transferred to other camps. Aaron, the man who had finally ended Labo's life, had stayed in the camp to attempt to restore order: Jackson was clearly unfit to command. The MEND leadership in Yenagoa had been aware of his drug habit for some time, but the extent of the problem had not been recognised. It was decided not to remove him immediately, but to marginalise him slowly. They were aware that he was usually a charismatic and effective leader, and that many of his men were profoundly loyal to him; hence pragmatism again took precedence over ideology: his power base was gradually to be dismantled and the transition made as smooth as possible. As it was, Jackson was still nominally in command of the camp on Joseph's arrival, though under strict surveillance from Aaron.

Joseph's journey had been a long and tortuous one; he had frequently changed boats, each time being searched, and he had travelled deep into the swamps of Bayelssa. He was a tall man who had become accustomed to luxury, and by the time he arrived his back and legs were aching from several hours of squatting in the small damp boats.

Mike Parry and Dricus were sitting together when Joseph arrived. Other than by Aaron and the camp boss who served them their meals, they had been largely ignored since the Labo incident. Joseph's arrival was discreet; Youth Shall Prosper was again in the camp, though he had only been seen by the hostages minutes prior to Joseph's setting foot on the jetty. Joseph spent a few minutes with Youth Shall Prosper prior to being taken to see the hostages. Both Mike and Dricus noticed that Youth Shall Prosper was particularly fawning towards them, over-anxious to demonstrate to Joseph that the hostages were not being abused. Mike and Dricus automatically assumed he was terrified that they would mention the events that had recently transpired in the camp. They were right in recognising his discomfort, but for Youth Shall Prosper things were really falling apart: his men had killed foreign workers on a raid and upset the delicate balance of power between Abuja and Bayalssa; he had almost lost a hostage to malaria; his commander, who he himself had appointed, had proven to be a drug addict and dangerously out of control; and now there had been what was tantamount to a mutiny in his camp, which had required the commander from a different camp to draw arms on his men. So he needed a result, a rapid end to the situation. Youth Shall Prosper had, however, a certain credibility in the movement. His grandfather had been in the boat outside Okrika when Addaka Borro had been assassinated; indeed, the great leader had died with his head cradled in Youth Shall Prosper's grandfather's arms.

From his childhood in the Biafran era, through the pogroms and afterwards, throughout his life, upon the strange paths that fate had led him down, Joseph had seen many people in captivity, some deserving of it, others not. He had seen hostages, refugees and war criminals, and he had come to have a fairly sound instinct as to their condition when he was introduced to them. These men in front of him now appeared to be as well as could be expected physically, but there was something about their demeanour that spoke of something worse than the defeat of captivity. This surprised him: from what he knew of MEND, they treated their hostages as well as anyone; human rights abuses were not in their interest, nor particularly in the organisational culture. These men, though, sat a little too close together, their shoulders a little to hunched. Youth Shall Prosper had briefed Joseph that one of the men had had malaria quite badly, and had gone to great lengths to point out the effort and expense that had been put into the man's care.

Joseph was allowed, only briefly, to speak with the hostages, and this was heavily supervised. He confirmed their identities, asked about any medical requirements, explaining that General Youth Shall Prosper had agreed that he could bring in medication if required. He mouthed the usual platitudes – that the companies and government organisations were doing all they could to bring the situation to a satisfactory conclusion, and that he was sure they would all be home with their loved ones in the not too distant future.

Giving his familiar speech this time brought Joseph to wonder who his own loved ones were. Who would be waiting for him if their situations were reversed? It was not something that had ever disturbed him before, but standing here in the jungle looking at the hollow-eyed hostages, he envied them. They had homes, they had somebody sitting anxiously by the phone waiting desperately for news. Joseph had money and freedom, but he had nothing that could not be taken from him.

He looked around him. The militants, too, they had little, but they had an identity and a cause and a homeland, something to believe in.

He noticed that Youth Shall Prosper was beginning to talk to him. He dragged himself back to the situation – this was another sign that it was time to change: he could no longer focus like before.

"As a gesture of goodwill, we shall allow each of the hostages a phone call to their families. I will ask you to supervise them. This also is a sign of our trust in you. I hope you understand, we want this to finish well and safely. I want to send these people to their families."

One of Youth Shall Prosper's smartly dressed entourage produced a satellite phone, which was handed to the hostages. One by one, each man called home, each exhibiting his own unique body language as he briefly connected with a familiar voice in a world that seemed impossibly far away. Joseph watched, and as the range of emotions was paraded in front of him, he felt ashamed of his voyeurism.

Chapter Thirty-five

This was not how it was supposed to be. This was not how he had imagined it, not here, not now. Azzi had always known that one day he would find himself face to face with Chioma again. It was a moment he had both longed for and feared. He had hoped that he would meet her in a position of power and dignity, to show her that, in spite of everything, he had survived. He had wanted her to see that he had made good and moved on, that he now had a woman that would not leave him in the middle of the night without a word. He was a changed man: he no longer drank and, since he had been with Amanda he had never touched another woman. He wanted her to regret what she had lost, wanted her to question herself. He knew he had not been an ideal husband, but he wanted her to feel doubt – maybe she had made him like that. He wanted her to demand of herself what Amanda had that she did not, in that Amanda had made him into a good husband. When he saw her walk into the restaurant his heart fell: this new man of hers was clearly wealthier than he would ever be. He could not compete on that front, but he had hoped that that in itself would give him the moral high ground: he had worked hard to gain his new life, while she had sold herself to a rich husband.

On leaving the garage that had been built on the site of their old home, he had decided this was the moment that he should complete his trip through the past. Seeing Chioma like that had been a sign. He had revisited their home and now, with nothing but the wet clothes he stood in, he would confront the woman who had given birth to him, then given him away. Then it would be finished forever, he would at last have closure and be able to move on with his life with Amanda in peace. On his way to the house he had been planning what he would say: the questions he needed to ask, the things he had to get out of himself. He had not been angry, there were just things he needed to say; the woman who had raised him had been a good mother to him and he had had a relatively happy childhood. The man he had called father had died when Azzi was still quite young – a combination of cigarettes and smoky, grimy engine-rooms had taken their toll – but he too had been as kind and generous a father as his means and education would allow. All in all, Azzi bore no bitterness towards the woman he was going to visit; he just needed to speak to her, to know her, to be known to her. It was important, but it was not supposed to have been like this, standing bedraggled, not in front of his mother, but Chioma.

His mouth began to move. He had to say something before she did. But it was as if all the hurts of his life that had crawled away and hidden in the darkest recesses of his psyche were suddenly infused with life and were emerging from deep hibernation, preparing themselves to once again wreak havoc with his conscious mind. He was forcing himself to speak, trying to hammer his mind into accepting what he was being confronted with.

Chioma too was speechless; her mind had been so full of Joseph and was now like a Sunday afternoon promenader that had suddenly been swept over the railings of a pier. Her mind struggled desperately to accept that the bedraggled creature standing before her was Chidi's father. There they stood, subsumed in a silent duel as to who might first overcome their shock at this sudden reappearance of the other.

A voice called out from inside the house, accompanied by the sound of approaching footsteps. "Who is it, dear?"

The rain pounded the ground, clattering off the tin roofs, but the words cut through the rain, cut through the tension, stressed the air between them, and hammered like bolts of thunder into Azzi's stupefied brain, as he realised that, for the first time in his conscious life, he was hearing his mother's voice.

Chapter Thirty-six

Charles found that it did not take long to garner the necessary information. He was used to the admiral's name opening doors for him, but there were times when he suspected that the path had been facilitated well in advance and he was merely going through the motions, to serve some higher design to whose purpose he was not privy. Again he was forced to wonder why they played out these charades. If the information had already been requested, why did they not communicate it directly? Charles, though, was well trained and, even though these thoughts did occur to him, he never followed them through. Consequences were not his concern. These decisions were made by his superiors. They knew better than him. Which is why they held the positions that they did.

When Charles returned to the Reform Club later that day, his contact was seated in the same place, in the same suit, with the same languorous attitude. The only thing that had changed was that the coffee had been replaced by a glass of sherry. Charles had always been slightly suspicious of men who drank sherry. He considered the long-stemmed glasses slightly effete. In keeping with his social and educational background, he harboured the suspicion that many of these gangly upper-class men (excepting of course the admiral) were closet homosexuals or worse. Charles was not one for radical thinking; accordingly, he considered homosexuality to be absolutely disgusting, though there were times when he found it strangely fascinating – something better not thought about too deeply.

He handed the manila folder to the dubiously effete man

across the table. The recipient produced what was quite clearly a gold pen from the inside of his double-breasted jacket. With barely a glance at the pages, he proceeded to place marks by certain names. The procedure was so quick that Charles was sure the decisions had already been made: there was no way his contact could possibly have read all his carefully prepared profiles at that speed.

"These are the chaps. Brize Norton, oh nine hundred hours tomorrow morning. This is the kit they'll need; you'll find it's already been arranged. Just sign it out tomorrow morning at the airport. Oh, and by the way, you'll be going with them, good experience for you."

"Thank you, sir, it's a long time since I've done any real soldiering."

"Oh, no. Don't misunderstand me, you're not going to play with the boys, you're going to babysit Joseph – debriefing and all that. Do you good to get to know him, very clever chap. I am sure you two will hit it off splendidly."

The man opposite him then gave Charles a look that, had they been in a bar, would probably have made Charles punch him.

Chapter Thirty-seven

"Bekin, who be dis mon out dere in de rain like a drowned rat?"

Sarah had arrived in the doorway behind Chioma and was looking over her shoulder, her glasses perched on the end of her nose as she peered over their rims.

Chioma began to speak, slowly forcing herself back into real time. "Ma Sarah, he be de –"

Before she could finish Azzi cut across her. "I am your son."

The rain continued to fall, hitting the wooden floor planks and splashing upwards on to the legs of the two women. Nobody moved. Azzi's words seemed to hang in the air between them, an invisible chain that bound them all.

Sarah felt frozen to the spot. It was a lifetime ago that she had hidden her shameful secret beneath some baggy clothing and tight bandages prior to the flight to Lagos. In Lagos her own mother had wrested the little bundle of life away from her before she had had the chance to bond with it. That much of her life had been based on a lie was a fact of which she had been painfully aware, but she had done her best to atone and be a good wife and a good Christian. She had often wondered what had become of her firstborn; but slowly, as the years progressed, she had become more and more desensitised. Still, though, in her nightly prayers she would ask the Lord for forgiveness for her first transgression and pray for the safety of her lost child. And now here he stood before her, water running down him like a drowned rat, confronting her with her past.

"And he is Chidi's father," Chioma added quietly.

Sarah felt her world shake. She put her hand on Chioma's shoulder for support. "Dis ting be too much, all dees years ah been livin' wid my own grandchild an' I no know it."

Chioma saw the old lady's knees start to give. She turned and put her arms around her old friend, and helped her back into the house. Tears were streaming down Sarah's face as wave upon wave of long-forgotten emotions broke over her with a force for which she was in no way prepared. Chioma helped her to he sofa, the same sofa where for so many years Harrison had lain. When she had seated her, Chioma, with her arm still around Sarah's shoulders, turned to the doorway to speak to Azzi.

But the doorway was empty. Azzi was gone.

Chapter Thirty-eight

Mo was sitting with his back to a tree, vainly trying to clean his fingernails with a twig. It was a minor obsession: he felt that if he could keep his fingernails clean he was still in control of his mind, it was the details that counted. Not far away, The Secretary was seated on the small bench that served the drummers during the morning ceremony and where Jackson had danced with his grotesque mask. Opposite The Secretary, Scarface squatted. Both were smoking quietly. Not far off, Jackson paced backwards and forwards; he appeared to be talking to himself.

A slight movement caught Mo's eye. He looked up, and at first could not locate what had attracted his attention. Then he noticed that there was a tiny dot of red light flickering on the back of The Secretary's head. It took Mo a couple of seconds to register what it was he was seeing and he only just managed to restrain himself from reacting. Seconds later, The Secretary's head exploded, spraying blood and brains over Scarface, who was simultaneously suffering an identical fate.

Mo threw himself to the ground as hell broke loose. Rounds seemed to be flying from all directions, militants were dropping across the parade ground, very few of whom had had arms to hand.

The massacre was over in minutes. Mo was still lying face down in the mud when a man in what he recognised as a Nigerian military uniform rolled him over. Another black man similarly attired covered him with an assault rifle. Both men had radio mikes in front of their mouths and were wearing Kevlar helmets.

It was not long before Mo found himself seated in one of the militant's boats alongside Tommy and Mike. In another craft not far off were Mark and Dricus. All the boats were filled with heavily armed men in Nigerian military uniforms. The flotilla sat bobbing at the small jetty as two more members of the assault team walked through the carnage, checking the bodies for signs of life. Now and then a single shot rang out.

The two soldiers started walking back towards the boat. One of the men signalled to another of his colleagues in the boat; Dricus noticed that the man who climbed down from the boat was not wearing a radio mike. The new man walked into the camp. Then, to the horror of the hostages, the first soldier who had signalled to him emptied an entire magazine into the man's body. The soldier then returned to the boat and, without a word of command, the engines were fired up and the boats began to lift clear of the water as they sped back through the mangroves.

The soldiers maintained defensive positions as the boats flew past the run-down villages that lined the creeks. As the creeks started to widen out and the villages became fewer, the soldiers seemed to relax. Dricus had been watching carefully; he spoke to the man nearest to him, a large black man built like an American football player.

"I guess we should thank you, bru."

"You're welcome, mate."

"That's not a very Nigerian accent," ventured Mark.

"Na, Hackney born and bred, mate. First time in Africa. Shithole innit!"

"You're British?"

"Too fuckin' right mate. 2 Para at your service."

"I thought the kit was a bit smart for the Nigerian military."

"So what was the score with that bloke you shot, then, at the end?"

"Oh, he was Nigerian military. We had to leave at least one behind or no one would believe it was them. International incident, an' all that. I think they pulled him out of military prison, told him it was his chance to redeem himself."

Long after the sound of the boats' engines had faded into the distance, Aaron swam to the shore. He walked, a forlorn figure, through the field of corpses that were already engulfed by swarms of flies. This was not what he had been fighting for. He made a silent vow to himself that, someday, someone would pay.

Chapter Thirty-nine

Ron Forrester sat in his office, looking across the vast expanse of desk. He was a little, though not unduly, concerned that he had heard nothing from the jungle yet. That Akintola would somehow get the information through to the right Americans he had little doubt; pressure would be brought to bear on the Nigerian government, there would be a spectacular but ultimately botched rescue attempt by the Nigerian armed forces, then the Americans would wade in and he, Ron Forrester, would clean up. Akintola would achieve a more powerful position under the new regime, and as a 'friend of America' he would channel more contracts Ron's way, to both their advantage.

Across the city, Akintola heard voices in his outer office. He arranged himself in his seat and waited for the intercom that would surely sound as James buzzed them through. It was a little ritual he enjoyed. The large double doors swung open to reveal a tall man in a suit, followed by three MOPOL officers.

"Minister Akintola, I am arresting you on suspicion of treason," said the tall man. Two of the MOPOL officers stepped forwards and pulled Akintola none too gently to his feet.

He was speechless. He would normally have tried to bluster his way out of the situation, intimidate this man with his rank, but there was something about the tall man's demeanour that told him the effort would be wasted. As they led him through the outer office, he noticed to his dismay that James was nowhere to be seen.

A few minutes after Akintola's arrest, Ron Forrester decided that he needed information. He picked up his cell phone and dialled Akintola's number. There was no response. Against his better judgement, he dialled the landline to the office.

In the outer office, the phone rang while two grey-suited agents from the state security service were going through the filing cabinets under James's direction. One of the agents looked at the other and then answered the phone.

"No, I am sorry, you cannot speak to the minister, he is late."

"When do you expect him in?" asked Ron, assuming that Akintola's taste in young men had distracted him from the job in hand.

"No, sir, you do not understand me. The minister is *late*, he is now the *late* Chief Akintola. He was involved in an accident. He will not be here, thank you. Will you please tell me who is calling?"

Ron hung up. He started to clear his desk. It was time to leave. He picked up the phone again and reserved a ticket to South Africa – Cape Town was nice at this time of year.

The two boats carrying the freed hostages sped through the Delta, this time heading inland instead of back out to sea. After about two hours' passing through spectacular countryside again, the boats pulled alongside a jetty. The soldiers disembarked and were replaced by others; these men, however, were not wearing radio mikes, carrying weapons with laser sights, or wearing Kevlar vests, nor did they have British accents. The boats carried on inland for another two hours.

It was dark by the time the hostages disembarked. There had been little conversation during any part of the journey and the later part – at night, with the wind chill and the onset of shock at the fire fight setting in – they had huddled down and each man had retreated into his own private world.

They eventually arrived at another wooden jetty that led to a long series of concrete steps. They made their way wearily up the steep incline to be greeted at the top by a cavalcade of buses, police vehicles with flashing lights, and several huge black Humvees with blacked-out windows. Smartly uniformed military and MOPOL were everywhere, brandishing clean, new-looking weaponry. They were clearly 'on show'. Mark suspected that the hostages would quite soon be exposed to the press.

Chapter Forty

"Your men are free, and the local military have taken over, as we discussed. They are on their way to the residence of the governor of Bayalsa state, where there will be a reception and a small press conference; I have tried to keep it minimal."

While Joseph spoke to Charles, he kept a careful eye on the British military man to observe his reaction.

"The main event will be in PH tomorrow. The local press have been told that they cannot ask about the rescue: that will be dealt with tomorrow."

Joseph saw that Charles was about to speak, and pre-empted him.

"This is Nigeria, Charles! I have chosen the pressmen carefully and they know the consequences of disobedience. Anyway, they are all from very pro-government newspapers. We will have to make sure that the hostages are debriefed with great care before we let the real press get their hands on them."

Charles was again feeling out of his depth; he had the feeling that he was nominally in charge, but everything seemed to be happening around him without the slightest involvement on his behalf.

Chapter Forty-one

When Azzi awoke, he wished he hadn't. He was curled up on a hard floor, the same ragged splash of concrete on which so many years ago Amanda had found him, in front of the bush bar that had become home to them both. He lay still, trying to get his numbed mind around the events of the previous day. He dared not move: ancient memories warned him of the pain that would start to grind away at the base of his skull and then start to hammer through his cranium until his whole head felt as it were compressed in a vice, whilst some manic blacksmith vented his fury on an anvil a few metres away. His mouth was dry, but he could still taste last night's beer. He had not touched alcohol for nearly twenty years. His clothes were still damp and he wanted to vomit.

To her credit, when she found him, Amanda was more concerned than angry. She knew Azzi as well as it was possible to know someone and she genuinely loved him. On top of that, the years she had spent running a bar had taught her a lot about human nature. She knew that such outbursts of uncharacteristic behaviour were usually symptomatic of a deeper malaise. Now she knelt as low as her eight-month pregnant belly would allow and gently brushed his head.

"Come back to me, Azzi, what happen? Did you go see your mamma?"

Her intuition pierced Azzi to the core. With some difficulty he raised his head to look at her. As he met her eyes, he knew that the big face looking down at him would never fail him.

"Azzi, I been vexin' 'bout you all night, I no savy where you be!"

Azzi pulled himself up on one elbow, and his whole body screamed out at him in pain. He inched towards her, placed his head in her lap, and, hugging her leg, burst uncontrollably into tears.

They sat like that for a few minutes. When Azzi's sobbing began to diminish, Amanda pulled her own bulk to her feet and helped her man into the house. Slowly he began to regain his composure; Amanda quietly went about making him coffee. When it was ready, she placed the cup on the table in front of him and sat herself down opposite him.

"You know it is nearly twenty years go by since last time I do dis wid you. I know you a good man an' you a good 'usban' to me, so you sup that coffee and you tell me what is vexin you so bad. I knows you not be a drinking man."

Azzi picked up the coffee and clasped it in both hands, as if the heat coming through the mug would somehow infuse him with energy. He tried vainly to smile, and almost cried again. That was enough and he managed a laugh. "I love you, you know."

"I know dat you stupid man! Now drink some coffee, wipe your nose an' tell me what is wrong!"

Azzi did as he was told; he had learnt over the years with Amanda that this was generally an advisable course of action. As he put his cup down and prepared to speak, Amanda raised her hand.

"Somet'ing I no did have time to tell you. Dat man from your company he did come here yesterday looking for you, we 'ave to go to dat big hotel again for de television, an' you is goin' to get an award for bein' a hero. So you had better get yourself cleaned up an' into a suit pretty damn quick."

Several cups of coffee and a lot of bustling later, they were both dressed and looking smart. Azzi did not feel particularly well but Amanda assured him repeatedly that he was more than presentable. Much to Amanda's joy, the car that the man from the company sent to pick them up was a Mercedes. She truly felt like a queen.

Joseph left Charles for a few moments. He had already made most of the arrangements for the press conference that evening, and briefed those that needed to be briefed, and he was fed up. This was definitely the end.

He went off through the hotel; he wanted a quiet moment on his own with a cup of coffee and no one to disturb him. He found a quiet table, and after the coffee had arrived and he could feel the first wave of caffeine starting to soothe his nerves, he made a decision. He called the waitress over, ordered himself a brandy, flipped open his mobile, and called Chioma.

"I would like you to come to this press conference tonight. It's work, but you can see a bit of what I have been doing, and then I would like to take you somewhere really nice to eat. And bring Chidi. I think it's time I got to know him better."

On the other end of the phone he could hear Chioma flustering slightly. Joseph smiled to himself.

"I will send Joshua with the car round for both of you. Joshua, he is my assistant and my oldest friend, he will take Chidi out and get him a suit for the occasion. Don't worry; Josh can arrange water in the desert. I will see you both later."

The oil company had already contacted Sally, and she and Houda were about to take their first helicopter ride from Lagos to Port Harcourt.

They had briefly been able to speak to Mo by phone. They had all been together a long time, but it was when she heard his voice that Sally really knew just how much he meant to her.

The hostages, who were now officially 'free', were brought to the hotel under heavily armed police and military escort, where they were reunited with their baggage from the barge and had their first chance to shave. Joseph had wanted them to appear as rough as possible for the first press exposure in Bayalsa state – this would help justify the military action – but now that they were in Port Harcourt they had to appear well cared for. It was this attention to detail that made Joseph so valuable to his diverse employers.

When Charles had introduced himself, Joseph had had no doubt as to his real profession, even though he had described himself as a 'security consultant' working for the oil company on contract. Joseph was well enough known in the upper echelons of Sandline and Executive Outcomes that a message would have been sent to him in some way, to let him know that this person was legitimate or otherwise. Charles was not enough of an actor, he had government stamped all over him, which did not particularly bother Joseph, as he knew from past experience that Her Britannic Majesty paid her bills on time. Joseph knew that if he planned to enter at least semi-retirement, then well-placed friends and a good reputation in a friendly foreign government were a worthwhile investment. This might be the end of the road, but it was worth leaving on a high.

He had made his decision. He just had to get through this evening, and then he was going to devote his time to getting to know his newfound interest. He had a lot of faith in his old Uncle Uchende and, if the old man thought Chioma was a good thing, she probably was. Joseph was aware that Uchende and Chioma had been friends for many years, and had never doubted the old man's affection for him.

He himself found her intriguing, after the over-sophistication of the society he had been moving in. There was something about her that he could not identify – it was as if she cast a shadow on his mind; but above all there were the eyes, he could not shake them from his mind. And she was a good listener, and seemed to be able to think for herself. That she was devoutly committed to her Igbo identity also appealed to him. It was his Igbo blood that had uprooted him as a child and sent him to a foreign land. It was an identity that was dear to him, but sometimes seemed an exotic mirage shimmering on the horizon, always threatening if he drew his eyes away once too often to disappear forever.

Chidi and Chioma arrived at the hotel in the car driven by Joshua. Joseph had met Chidi before, and had been struck by the boy's resemblance to his mother. But seeing him away from the student uniform of T-shirt and jeans was a revelation: the boy – or rather, young man – had a quick intelligent face and in spite of his recent decision to retire, Joseph immediately found himself thinking in terms of a successor. He had no acknowledged children, though there was at least one illegitimate daughter in the town where he grew up. He had kept a watchful eye from a distance throughout her early years, and then, after a row with her own family, she had vanished and he had lost touch with her.

Much of the hotel had been taken over by the oil company for the event. The guests were gathered in a large open area that contained the swimming pool and several bars; the steps up to the main hotel formed a natural stage. The president of the oil company introduced the hostages to the media; there was a token army officer present and much praise was heaped upon the Nigerian Special Forces for their assistance in the resolution of the situation, and the avoidance of casualties.

Chidi was enjoying the surroundings; being surrounded by such people made him feel very important and he definitely approved of this man who was taking an interest in his mother. He looked around and, as his courage and confidence increased, he started to walk about. At first he was terrified that someone would speak to him, but all that happened was that every now and then someone would nod in acknowledgement to him. Not far away was a girl about his own age, and Chidi could not resist glancing at her. She was, he decided, the most beautiful woman he had ever seen in his life (with the possible exception of his mother). She had long, brown, almost black hair, and he suspected that she was Arab or Italian. She was standing with a handsome-looking woman, a little too stocky to be beautiful, whom he guessed must be her mother.

Chidi started to work his way across the plaza. He knew that he had no way of introducing himself, or indeed anything to say to her, but he was being led by his hormones – he was drawn to her.

Cameras clicked as the president of the oil company and the state governor presented the freed hostages one by one and asked them to say a few words to the press. In turn, the freshly shaved men stepped up to the microphone and said a few meaningless and clearly prepared platitudes of thanks to the governor and the military, and expressed their wishes that the problems in the Niger Delta would soon be brought to a peaceful conclusion.

Chidi was getting closer to the girl who, for a brief moment, had become extremely animated. He guessed it must be something to do with what was happening on stage. The state governor was now presenting the representative of the shipping company whose vessel had been attacked.

The man who took the microphone was the man who had arranged Azzi's night out with Amanda. He was tall, thin, and middle-aged, with fresh but intense features; he gave the impression that he was the sort of person who ritualistically punished himself with a ten-mile run every morning. He spoke, expressed his thanks to the governor and then: "I would like to make a special announcement and an award. One of our crewmen acted extremely courageously and his actions saved the life of one of our longest serving captains. I would like to present the first mate of the MV *Aberystwyth*, who is incidentally the company's first Nigerian-born first mate, with a cheque for 2000 dollars, and announce that we are promoting him to captain. Please give a round of appreciation for *Captain* Azzi Alison."

At his side, Amanda almost fainted with pride. Azzi, who was no natural exhibitionist, started to walk towards the stage. He could feel the heat rising in his cheeks. His head was slightly bowed in embarrassment and he bumped into a young man. Azzi looked up and almost froze: the face into which he looked was unmistakable. He stopped and stared.

Chidi was on the verge of panic. He thought that this important man was going to be angry with him for getting in his way.

At that moment, Chioma appeared at his shoulder, and smiled. "Congratulations, Azzi, it's been along time, I am proud of you."

Chidi looked from one to another in bewilderment. Chioma continued. "Chidi, this is your father. He's a hero, and he always was."

Azzi was almost in tears. He hugged Chidi briefly.

"Go on, Azzi, go up there and enjoy your moment, and be proud your son is here to watch, it must have been God's will."

Azzi could barely contain himself as his emotions cascaded in his skull. He smiled but could not speak. He squeezed Chidi's shoulder and turned towards the stage.

Chioma looked at Chidi. "Wait here, I am sure your father will want to speak to you when he comes back. I will talk to him later."

With that, she vanished.

Chidi found himself alone in a crowd. The pretty girl, he suddenly realised, was standing next to him. Chidi was awash with emotion, he had just met his father, who appeared to be some kind of hero, and he was standing next to a beautiful girl. If he could just pluck up the courage to talk to her, his world would be complete.

The engines of the bulldozers that had destroyed both their homes had long since fallen silent, but now, for a brief moment, two children whose lives had been derailed as the walls that would have surrounded and protected them had crumbled in the path of mechanised steel stood side by side, cheering and applauding fathers who had been called upon to perform acts of heroism in defence of the greed that had destroyed so much hope and potential. As they stood applauding, filled with happiness and pride, and totally unaware of the similarities of their histories, across the world the sleepless, unquenchable thirst for oil was felling new Jerichos, uprooting forests and creating new orphans. Even as the applause for Azzi died down, a young girl, who had recently graduated from university, walked into a police station in Baghdad and blew herself up, Israeli bombs rained down on Gaza and the price of crude reached 100 dollars a barrel.

Epilogue

A doctor walked into the canteen area holding a tray of food. The canteen was crowded, the chatter and hubbub created a pillow of noise into which one could quietly sink unnoticed, or raise up one's voice and float a conversation across the top, adding another stratum to the weave of human discourse. The doctor looked around, spotted one of the few empty tables and headed for it. There were still a few old coffee cups waiting to be cleared away, but the table was in the corner and appeared to have gone unnoticed for a while. To his left was a large window. Rain beat heavily on the panes, allowing only the blurred lights of Paris at night to make it through the window.

A copy of *Le Monde* had been left on the table in front of him. The front page showed an all too familiar scene: the bloody, shattered bodies of children being carried in the arms of weeping parents. The headlines proclaimed that Gaza's hospitals were overflowing, that the Israeli onslaught had killed over 700 civilians in the preceding twelve days. Dr Said slowly turned the pages, allowing his eyes to dwell on the images of horror. One picture in particular caught his eye. It showed a large open space, roughly the shape of a square, surrounded by damaged buildings and rubble. The dismembered body of a child was discernible in the foreground amongst the debris.

Said knew that square well. His hand went to his throat, where a spent cartridge case was attached to a fine silver chain. It was in that square that he had killed, and then taken an oath never to kill again. He had been true to his word and had devoted himself to the saving of life.

As he continued to dwell on the images before him, he knew it was time to go home.

Palestine was calling.